PENGUIN BOOKS

1821

THE SHORN LAMB

JOHN STROUD

JOHN STROUD

The Shorn Lamb

PENGUIN BOOKS

Penguin Books Ltd, Harmondsworth, Middlesex
AUSTRALIA: Penguin Books Pty Ltd, 762 Whitehorse Road,
Mitcham, Victoria

—

First published by Longmans 1960
Published in Penguin Books 1962

—

Copyright © John Stroud, 1960

—

Made and printed in Great Britain
by C. Nicholls & Company Ltd
Set in Linotype Pilgrim

TO THE MEMORY
OF MY FATHER AND
MY MOTHER

I

'OVER 80,000 children in this country are in the care of local authorities because for one reason or another they cannot be looked after adequately by their parents.'

The light of the June sun poured down on the red-brick building, came optimistically streaming through the window, and arrived, dusty and dispirited, on the desk of the Reader in Social Administration.

'The Children Act, which will become operative in July 1948, sets out to provide for the care and welfare of boys and girls up to the age of eighteen, when they are without parents, or have been lost or abandoned by their parents, or when their parents are unfit or unable to take care of them.'

This was the last lecture of the last term of the last year of our Social Science course. By now, we knew everything – physiology, psychology, psychiatry, genetics, statistics – you name it, we knew it. Human behaviour, studied from every angle, had been reduced to essentials and immortalized in enormous black folders containing three years' notes. Egg-sucking? Yes, granny, here's what you do . . .

'The Act defines the powers and duties of the local authority regarding these unfortunate children.'

Well, boarding-out in foster-homes, of course, that was the answer, I mean, this I *knew*. The Children Act was an open book to me; as a matter of fact I was going to work in the new service: after Degree Giving I was going to join one of the newly-hatched Children's Departments as a Child Care Officer.

'Child Care Officers will be appointed to ensure that plans for the welfare of these children are made and carried out. Decisions of great importance to these children, and their families, will be made by this entirely new species of local government officer.'

Oh, well, I can easily do that, just wait till I start, I thought. There was a tremendous crusading atmosphere about the new service. Our impression at the University was that the country outside was dotted with castle-like institutions in which hundreds of children dressed in blue serge were drilled to the sound of whistles. We were going to tear down the mouldering bastions. We were going to replace or re-educate the squat and brutal custodians. I had a dream of myself letting up a blind so that sunshine flooded into a darkened room as I turned, with a frank and friendly smile, to the little upturned faces within.

'The Child Care Officers' duties should turn out to be varied and full of human interest, and it is to be hoped that the work will attract persons of high ideals, professional skills, and sensitive humanity.'

Well, that's me, of course, and I modestly massaged the lobe of my ear. Ideals? Yes. Skill? Yes: perhaps leaning a shade towards Adler rather than Freud, but – Humanity? A vague concept, my good fellow, I said in my head to the lecturer, but I think I know what you're trying to get at, and I can only reply that in two months' time I shall be running my Department in quite the most sensitive way imaginable. . . .

Nobody seemed to have heard of me when I arrived at County Hall. Asked to wait, I sat for an hour in a corridor, watching people giving pieces of paper to each other. Then I was invited in to see the Chief Welfare Officer. She was the tiredest-looking woman I had ever seen: she looked as though she had spent the last two months on some maniac task, such as trying to get a swarm of flies into a tea-chest. Yet she could still spring up and greet me radiantly.

'So sorry to keep you waiting,' she said. 'We're jolly glad to have you, we're up to our eyes here.'

I made a small deprecatory gesture.

'I'm allocating you to Area 2, Westburn,' she said. 'Miss Dashforth. 48 Seed Villas.'

Westburn was ten miles away. I opened my mouth to speak, but two telephones began ringing on her desk. I was dismissed with a cheery wave of the hand, and went moodily down to the bus-station.

Seed Villas was the devil to find, and that summer morning I tacked round Westburn for an hour or more looking for it, all among the waste paper blowing down the sunlit streets. I had a cup of tea in a trolley-bus drivers' shelter, and then I bought a street guide. Eventually I found my way to a row of paunchy red-brick houses, steps up to the front doors, glum-looking shrubs in the front patch. Outside No. 48 was a notice-board which said 'Relieving Officer'. Hanging by one drawing-pin from this board was a piece of cardboard which said 'Area Children's Officer'. I went in. In the hall were a lot of bulky women and a notice saying 'Children's Office Up Corridor End Door.' I went up the corridor, tapped on the door, and walked into a lavatory. I backed out into a fat typist who had come up behind me.

'The Children's Officer is up the *other* corridor,' she said through tight lips, barging past me.

I went back, edged past the bulky women in the hall, and found the right corridor and the right room. As I went in, a small woman crouched over a telephone gave me a kind of Roman salute with her arm, but continued talking into the phone. It was a small room, which contained a cupboard, two trestle tables and one chair. Both tables were covered with sprawling mountains of paper and files, and so was much of the floor; more paper, tied up in bundles with string, was spilling out of the cupboard. The small woman's salute appeared to be an invitation, so I picked my way farther into the room, hitched myself on to the edge of a table and surveyed her.

This must be Miss Dashforth. She was thirty-fivish, thin, dressed in a brown skirt and a red-and-violet striped jumper. At first glance I thought she had some pitiful facial disfigurement, until I realized that she had a cigarette jammed in a corner of her mouth and was allowing the smoke to pour into one eye. She had short prematurely grey hair, like steel wool, through which she frequently, excitedly, but quite unconsciously, drove her fingers. She was speaking on the telephone in a rapid, beautiful voice, to which, after a moment, I found I could not help listening.

'... no, she's only thirteen, you see, not fourteen till February, and if she's got her dates right her baby should be due next month, though I must say it doesn't show at *all*. ... Oh, yes, the doctor confirms it. ..., Well, the girl says it was her uncle who lodges in the same house – he denies it, of course, and says it must have been the stepfather, and I must say stepfather *does* look a bit queer, he's an Eighth Day Pentecostal and if he eats too much marmalade his head steams, so I suppose he *might*. ... Right-ho, dear – you'll ring me ? Right ... bye-bye.'

Miss Dashforth put down the telephone, lit a new cigarette from the old stub, shook me warmly by the hand and said: 'Maule, isn't it – they rang from County Hall you were coming – I say, could you find a chair from next door and amuse yourself with these files for a minute ? I must go and see these women waiting – they're all confinements, short stays you know.'

She disappeared. I couldn't understand this: had I got into the wrong office after all, and was this really some depot of the new National Health Service, where you collected wigs, teeth and short stays ? I looked worriedly at the files on the table beside me. They were all rather dusty and dog-eared, though the handwriting on the covers was a beautiful flowing copperplate. One near me said on the outside: 'PAC/71917/C/412.' I opened it: inside were two foolscap forms. The first was headed in the beautiful copperplate: 'Rosetta Valentino (Miss).' In the columns underneath, in a much more impatient hand, was scribbled: 'Woman applies for assistance. Pregnant. Destitute. Admitted Stark House.' Of course, yes, these were the old records of the Public Assistance Committee; as that Committee had now been entirely superseded by among others) our own glittering new Children's Service, these files would have been put out, I presumed for burning. Casually interested, I read on :

12.1.33 : Male child born.
27.1.33 : Woman absconded.
29.1.33 : Child, John, transferred to Slag Dell Nursery.
4.2.33 : Warrant issued for mother.

And that was all about her. I turned the page. The next form was headed, in copperplate : 'John Douglas Valentino, b. 12.1.33.' The impatient hand underneath had written :

12.1.33 : Stark House.
29.1.33 : Slag Dell.
16.8.33 : Resolution under Sec. 52.

and then, underlined in red ink :

1.9.33 Boarded out with Mrs E. Champion, 19 Binns Close.

Underneath this entry was a long line of rubber stampings, each saying : 'Reported to Committee,' followed by a date. Fifteen years of rubber stampings, I thought, presumably this little fellow was still in his foster-home and must now be – fifteen and a half – he must be in employment now. Well, well : and I'd thought that boarding-out had only just been invented, that my mission was, by introducing this startling new idea to Westburn, to overcome the hidebound reactionaries and establish a New Deal for Waifs. . . .

I was still trying to readjust my ideas when Miss Dashforth came back into the room with a handful of forms; she tossed them on to her desk, ran her hands through her hair, lit another cigarette, ran her hand over her head again, and looked at me twice, sideways.

'You look a bit pensive,' she said.

'Well, yes, I don't seem to have got my bearings yet.'

'I suppose it is a bit confusing at first. Look here, it's nearly half past twelve, let's go and have lunch, we can have a natter and I can put you in the picture.'

She hoisted up her handbag, a huge affair with a shoulder-strap, pulled out a powder-puff and battered her face with it exuberantly.

'Right,' she said.

As we were leaving the room, the phone rang.

'Damn,' said Miss Dashforth in a pleased voice, and returned to answer it.

At five to one we left the room again. Half-way down the corridor we met a rather dirty Irishman who began telling Miss Dashforth that if his children were put in a Home he'd be able to land a very good job in business in Scunthorpe.

At twenty-five past one we left through the front door and were hailed from the street by the District Nurse, who wanted to talk about triplets.

At ten to two Miss Dashforth glanced at her watch.

'Hell!' she said. 'We've left it a bit late; I'm afraid the cinema café is about the only place still open. Oh, well: come on, I'll take the car.'

I was aware that if I hadn't been there she wouldn't have bothered about food at all. I was also aware that we had come up to a small, queer-looking vehicle crouched beside the kerb. It had a hood pulled down over its eyes and looked like a rather ruffianly converted perambulator. Miss Dashforth opened one door by untying a piece of string. When I got in my side the whole car sagged. However, it started promptly. I was sorry that it had, for Miss Dashforth drove very badly, operating the clutch in paroxysms and periodically soaring unexpectedly on to the crown of the road. As we went along, she pointed out interesting features of the landscape.

'See that house with the green curtains?' she would call.

'Yes.'

'One of my foster-homes.'

'Oh, yes?'

'That house on the corner, see? The big grey one – no, no, the other corner, quick, quick –'

'Oh yes, yes.'

'Woman there who looks after coloured babies.'

'Really?'

'You see up there?'

She was apparently pointing at a kind of turret stuck on to

a large apartment building. High up in the turret was a tiny round window.

'See it?'

'Yes.'

'Problem family. *The N.S.P.C.C. are going in.*'

My goodness, I thought, an absolute landmark.

'Family named Crump. Actually I may ask you to have a look in on them, there's a teenage boy there.'

We swerved violently in amongst the High Road traffic and stopped beside a cinema. It had a softly-lit but inefficient restaurant upstairs where we got a spammy sort of meal, which was all they had to offer.

Miss Dashforth did not seem to have much conversation and had not even noticed the weather. Her only remark in the first ten minutes was when she suddenly ducked her head towards me and hissed:

'See that waitress?'

'Yes?'

'Ex-Approved School!'

It wasn't until we'd got to the coffee that she began to talk more easily about her office and the work I should be doing.

'I'm afraid we're in an absolute shambles,' she said, 'and you may have to turn your hand to anything from bathing a baby to mending a chair. As you're the only man on the staff, I think it would be best if you dealt with the older boys – secondary school boys and working lads up to eighteen.'

'How do you mean, deal with them?'

'Visit them in their foster-homes, see that they're properly looked after, help them get jobs, keep them out of trouble. There's some boys in the Children's Homes who should be out in foster-homes, you might try and find some more foster-mothers, we're very short. And when the boys in the Homes get to fifteen and leave school they have to be found jobs and lodgings, you can have that duty with pleasure.'

'About how many boys do you think I'll be seeing to?'

'I dunno,' she said. 'I'm sorry, but we haven't even been through the files yet to count heads and see who's where. Never mind, we'll get straight in the end, especially now you're here as well as Harry. Harry started last week – she's a great help, but she's had to take a kid down to Broadstairs today. Another flipping short-stay case.'

'How,' I asked carefully, ignoring for the moment the improbability of a female being named Harry, 'would you define a short-stay case?'

'Why, it's a case where, as far as one can see, the children are only going to be In Care for a very short time; like, Mum's going to have a baby and she can't find anyone to look after her four other little horrors for the ten days so they come for a short stay with us.'

'Oh, I see,' I said with relief. Nothing to do with National Health after all.

'We get a terrific number of short stays. Terribly time-consuming.'

We paid the bill and returned to the car, reluctantly as far as I was concerned. Still, I thought, as we took off violently, things are beginning to make sense, I shall soon settle down, I thought, as we hurtled round a corner on two wheels . . .

A boy, wearing a man's jacket, large tweed trousers, and plimsolls, suddenly whizzed out on roller-skates from behind a van directly in front of us. I should not think we missed him by more than a quarter of an inch, and outside the glass by my shoulder his large mouth and long dusty hair burst on my senses like a bomb. I found, some time later, that I had become absolutely rigid from the top of my head, which was pressed up into the hood, to my right foot, which was rammed so hard on where the footbrake might have been that I had cracked a board.

Miss Dashforth, however, continued to soar on down the middle of the road, chatting.

'Did you see who that was?' she was saying. 'It was Egbert Crump.'

2

FLORA BELLE HARRISON was a slim girl of medium height, with jet black hair, straight jet black eyebrows, and beautiful warm gold skin. She had high, wide cheekbones, so that her face had interesting facets, as though it had been chiselled out with three quick, confident strokes. She did not talk very much, and when she did, she talked slowly. She moved slowly and walked with long strides, and when she smiled the smile dawned oh, so slowly and miraculously. She was a quiet, grave, reposeful girl. Anybody less like a Florabelle I could not possibly imagine, and from the moment I first met her I fell into the habit, universal wherever she went, of calling her Harry.

We were introduced on my second morning in the office, she having returned from Broadstairs the previous night. We were to share the second of the two rooms constituting our office suite; we had a table, I'd been round to the greengrocer on the corner to scrounge an orange-box to sit on, and from somewhere or other Harry had brought in an old piano-stool for herself. Within a very few days we had developed an easy and courteous friendship. It was a very calming thing to find, in the middle of a jangle of crises and telephone-bells and shrill cries for help; and around this friendship, or because of it, there began to creep some just-perceptible semblance of order and method in what we were doing. Miss Dashforth spent most of her time in the office, keeping records, seeing callers, presiding over the phone, and smoking like a chimney. She would sally out in the evenings to visit the Children's Homes or to see to her teenage girls who were living in lodgings. Harry saw to the babies and toddlers, and I saw to the older boys, and also I was involved in miscellaneous duties round at the Juvenile Court; and of course we all turned a hand to anything that came along anyway. Thus it might come about that occasionally I would be discovered transporting a cowed toddler through the suburbs; or Miss Dashforth find herself giving a Straight Talk About Sex to a shamefaced young coalman three times as big as she was. We used to meet together for lunch most days, but otherwise Harry and I were not often in the office together, since I would be at Court in the mornings and the office during the afternoons, while Harry wrote reports in the mornings and usually went out visiting after lunch. That was why I took her completely by surprise one morning when the Court finished early and I barged confidently into our room about eleven o'clock. I had one sensational glimpse of a long leg and a riffle of white underwear; next moment Harry had let fall the hem of her skirt and moved behind the table, blushing warmly and, of course, slowly.

'Harry, I'm awfully – excuse me,' I said incoherently, trying to back out again.

'No, no, it's all right, Charles, come in,' she said. 'I'm afraid I've Picked Something Up.'

Even now, after ten years of this sort of thing, I cannot stop myself itching when people mention vermin. And so it was now; Harry put on a rueful expression and eased her body slightly inside her clothes, and within five seconds there I was, scratching myself.

'Wherever have you been, Harry?'

'Round at the Crumps,' she said. 'Have you heard of them?'

'Yes, I've heard of them,' I said. 'As a matter of fact, we nearly killed one of them, my first day here.'

'I'm afraid that in due course they will all come to a sticky end,' said Harry sadly. 'They really are a crowd. Myrna went to school this morning with a black eye, and the Headmistress got into a flap about it, because she's convinced that Myrna needs care and protection. I couldn't find out what had happened: somebody threw something at

16

someone, but none of the Crumps seems to remember what actually happened. Or cares.'

'I can't quite see why you have to go there, Harry.'

'Miss Dashforth thinks the children ought to be in care.'

'But isn't that a job for the N.S.P.C.C. ?' I asked.

'The local Inspector can't get quite enough evidence to bring a case,' said Harry. 'I went this morning to see if the parents would agree to let their children come in under a voluntary arrangement, but they wouldn't. They were quite fierce, said they loved their children, and I was to mind my own bloody business.'

'It seems a bit rough on you, Harry. Why didn't Miss Dashforth go herself ?'

'She's had to attend a Committee meeting at County Hall. I don't mind going – the Crumps are very entertaining – it's just this biting I can't get used to. You ought to be giving a hand with them, too, Charles.'

'Oh, don't be gruesome, Harry, why ever ?'

'I'm thinking of Egbert,' she said. 'I think it's about time that lad was taken in hand. I don't think he's going to school at all now. He was at home this morning, anyhow.'

She paused; a shadow flitted across her face and she gave a little wince.

'I can't stand this,' she said. 'I'm going home to have a bath and change.'

'I have heard,' I said, 'that if you stand on a bit of news-paper when you undress, you can see them as they fall off.'

I was scratching as I said it.

I think I must have had a premonition, during that con-versation, that sooner or later I was going to get tangled up with the Crumps, but at the time I was much more absorbed in the affairs of a youth named Sidney Smee. Sidney had lived most of his life in various Children's Homes, having been removed at an early age from a malodorous tenement near the railway. He had grown up a quiet, pale, unnotice-able youth, and when the time came for him to leave school – and, *ipso facto*, to leave the Home, too – the Superin-tendent had no hesitation in recommending that Sidney be placed with a kindly foster-mother and take up normal employment. And so, a few months before I arrived in Westburn, Sidney got his new grey suit, his three sets of underwear, and his attaché-case, and went off to live with a Mrs Scatterbread out at Sprots Lea, on the Kingsgrave Estate. Meanwhile Mr Clench, the Youth Employment Man, had found Sidney a job as a general labourer with the Cheshire Cat Dental Fixative Company. Sidney's starting wage was thirty-eight shillings a week and prospects: what prospects there may be with a Dental Fixative Company I have never since discovered.

Sidney was obviously a boy who should come under my supervision, and his was in fact the first foster-home I ever visited. I found the house easily enough, knocked, and on Mrs Scatterbread's invitation stepped into the little hall. Immediately there was a pounding noise, and next moment an enormous dog had reared up, pinned my shoulders to the banisters with its front paws, and was breathing the odour of rotten meat all over my face. Mrs Scatterbread was delighted. She hopped round us like the referee in a wrestling match.

'Don't be frightened, sir, 'e won't 'urt yer, 'e's ever so sweet-natured,' she chirped encouragingly.

'Oh, yes,' I said feebly. 'Magnificent animal. There, there, good dog!' (Aside: 'Take your great slobbering chops out of my shirt, will you?' I could almost feel the hackles rising on my own neck.) The beast drew back its head, released one of my shoulders and gazed, puzzled, into my eyes.

'Oh, inny sweet!' said Mrs Scatterbread. 'He likes you, sir, I can tell; 'e doesn't take to everybody, you know, but 'e's taken to you, sir, I can tell. Now that's enough, Titty, down you get now, down, boy!'

The pressure on my shoulder relaxed as the great animal thudded down on four paws again.

'*What's* his name, Mrs Scatterbread?' I asked. I didn't think I could have heard properly.

'Titty!' she beamed.

I gaped at the great leonine mass beside me.

'Titty?' I repeated, incredulously.

The next moment my right hand, up to the wrist, had been sucked into what felt like a wet rubber shopping-bag. I snatched it back, violently, and found it was coated with slime. I couldn't ask Mrs Scatterbread if I could wash in case she thought I was accusing her dog of being leprous. However, when I was left alone for a minute in the front best room, I managed to wipe my hand surreptitiously on a velveteen curtain.

After recovering from this, I was able to have a quiet chat with Mr and Mrs Scatterbread and their Ron and their Valerie and my Sidney Smee, who was an awkward, bony lad with a pale face, not very talkative, but able to smile engagingly when conversation flagged. Yeah, he said, work was awright; his chargehand was awright; oh, yeah, Kingsgrave was a bit quiet, but it was awright, he went to the pictures of a Saturday with his mate, but most nights he stopped at home and listened to Luxemburg. (This was before the coming of telly, Luxemburg was the thing then.) Altogether, he seemed quite comfortable in his foster-home, and being properly looked after, and the family quite fond of him; and in the warm evening Mr Scatterbread, shirt-sleeved, wandered up to the front gate with me as I left, brooded for a moment over his chrysanths, and said: 'He's quite a good lad, yer know, reelly. Quiet, of course, a bit too quiet if you know what I mean, but very good-'earted and never a cross word since 'e's bin 'ere. I don't think you've got anything to worry about there.'

I didn't think so, either. That was on the Friday. On the Monday I had a letter: 'Mr Mole dear sir sorry to trouble you but could you call round at your early convenence as Sid is in the Hands of the Police your respectfuly Mrs Scatterbread.'

I was aghast. What on earth had he been up to? I fled out there at once, and found myself assisting in what appeared to be a posed scena entitled: The Stricken Household. Centre, on a sofa, sat the Criminal, looking simultaneously dejected and defiant, and proving increasingly inarticulate.

Down left was Father, chewing the stem of his pipe and (I think) pondering how he would deal with the Press. Up right was Mother, who maintained a hushed but uncertain manner, like a Women's Institute member visiting a mosque. Overhead, Our Ron was whistling in the bedroom and showing admirable indifference to the whole affair. Hanging over the back of the sofa, indeed excitedly dithering all over the background, was the fat figure of Our Val, obviously extremely thrilled by everything and already much fonder of Sid. (Though Mrs Scatterbread told me later that it was Our Val she was most worried about: '... you can't tell what this might do to the child's mind, can yer, specially with her eleven plus just coming up.')

It seemed that Sid was in the habit of going to the flicks on Saturday nights, and afterwards having a long sit-down over a cup of tea in a caff up by the Great Circular Road. Maybe a dozen boys who vaguely knew each other would congregate there, and on this particular evening Sid and a few others left together at closing time and mooched around for a bit. From then on, Sid got more and more excited and aimless until the moment when he heard midnight strike and found himself, alone, by the abattoir. (Here it is, I remember thinking at the time, here comes the inevitable touch of surrealism.) It now dawned on Sid that he was three miles from home and he'd better get a move on. On the way home he kicked against a four-pound brick, so he took that along with him, emerging, an hour later, into the square where the shops are in Kingsgrave. In the corner of this square is a shop which sells cyclists' accessories and keeps a light on all night above its display of oilskin leggings. Sid marched up to this shop window and threw his brick straight through the middle of it. Then he ran out of the square and trotted up the steps of the police station announcing that he had come to give himself up. In the face of this insistent plea the sleepy constabulary felt obliged to swoop. Statements had been laboriously written out and signed, detectives had duly inquired into antecedents, and the papers were now with the police superintendent, who would decide whether Sid was to be brought before the magistrates.

At the end of this recital I found myself gazing keenly into Sid's face, as though the whole affair was totally comprehensible to me. Actually, in my mind's eye I was frantically scanning page after page of my University psychology textbooks; but there was no help there. Why had the kid done it? He didn't know; he just shrugged his shoulders. He hadn't been drunk, he hadn't been dared to do it, he firmly reiterated that he had not wanted to steal anything; the thought occurred to me that perhaps lamplit oilskins were symbolical of fatherhood, and Sidney had either been avenging his mother or denying his own incestuous maleness – towards Mrs Scatterbread? No, no – the more I thought like that, the less I felt able to say anything.

'Well, I reckon 'e's got a kink,' said Mrs Scatterbread cheerfully. ''Aven't yer, Sid?'

Sid looked as if a knife had been inserted into his head and twisted. I devoted the rest of the visit to an emotional appeal to the foster-parents – here was this poor lad – alone in the world – no fault of his own – appalling odds – brutal police – need of kindness, patience, understanding – all will come right, thanks to you – anything to make them give the lad a bit of normal human companionship; and so I left them, two hours later.

Miss Dashforth, next morning, was brusquely sympathetic.

'I can't see what you're fussing about, it's not the end of the world,' she said, in the tones of one who will say the same thing to the end of the world itself. 'I expect the police will prosecute, but that won't do Sid any harm, and he'll only get a fine or costs or some sort of action to dock his pocket-money for a few weeks, and that's fair enough, isn't it?'

'But I wonder what made him suddenly do this,' I said.

'Deprivation,' said Miss Dashforth flatly.

'Er – ?'

'He's a deprived child, and deprived children do these things.'

'But why?' I persisted.

'Because they're deprived,' she said. 'And if you'd spent most of your life in that ghastly Rookery, wouldn't you feel like smashing things up as soon as you got away?'

The Rookery was the largest of our local Children's Homes, and I vaguely saw what she meant. Indeed, there had been occasions in my own life, I now realized, when I had thought of smashing something to get one back on the world; but I'd always been able to prevent myself from doing it, which made me think that perhaps Sidney had been in an unusual state of mind. However, for the moment it didn't seem worth probing any further into the mind of Sidney Smee until we knew what the police were going to do.

About a week later, Miss Dashforth placed on my part of the table the routine notification that a case was being brought – Form 47, which is sent to the Area Children's Officer whenever a child is being prosecuted. I glanced cursorily at this one and noted that before the magistrates next Tuesday morning, Sidney Smee, born 4.4.33, school last attended Hags Heath Secondary, would be charged with the offence of malicious damage with intent to steal.

I reserved the date and resolved to have a word beforehand with the probation officer, and then I saw that on the table lay a second Form 47. This one stated that before the magistrates on the same day there would also appear one Egbert Gary Melvyn Crump, aged 13, of The Rat Yard, Blight Street; and that Egbert would apparently be charged with (1) Larceny Bugridgar and (2) Larceny Birdseed.

3

WESTBURN Magistrates' Court is in the Hags Heath Road,
next to the trolley-bus depot. It is built in a rather top-
heavy style which I call Almshouse Gothic, and is faced
with bricks which were originally mauve but are now just
plain sooty. It has a huge pointed entrance, like a church
porch, in the front, but my way hardly ever leads through
that arch and into the hall outside the adult courts; I go
round the corner and down an alley which brings me to the
building's side door, marked 'Juvenile Court' and unexpectedly opening outwards. If I go in, I am in a confusing
L-shaped passage, very narrow; one arm of it acts as a
cramped waiting-room, and the other leads to the Magistrates' Room, and the doors from it lead into the Court-
Room. If, however, I continue down the alley and round the
back of the Court House, all in among the coke stores and
overflow pipes, and then up an iron fire-escape, I come to a
door with faded, peeling paint and a cracked frost-glass
window. On it is painted: 'Probation Officers'. That was
where I went first on the morning of November 3rd, 1948.

There were at that time two probation officers for Westburn – Mr Bland, who had been a bomber pilot, was a large,
fair, meticulously tidy man, whose sports jacket always
looked new, whose dark twill trousers were creased to a
knife-edge, and whose hair and moustache were brushed
till they shone. His colleague, Miss Perrett, was tall but
round-shouldered, and very dark and hairy. They treated us
in a kind but slightly condescending way, as though they
were stagehands at the London Palladium unexpectedly
having to deal with the winners of the Rutland Amateur
Drama Festival.

They were at their desks when I went in.

'Ah; morning, Maule,' said Mr Bland. 'I see one of your laddies is on the list this morning.'

'Yes, Sidney Smee; have you seen him?'

'Oh, yes, old boy, I've been up to his home.'

'Did you like it?' I was always a bit worried when somebody else visited one of my foster-homes, in case what I thought was good they thought was ghastly.

'Very nice,' said Mr Bland. 'He'll be quite comfortable there, I should think, if he looks after himself.'

'Why do you think he chucked the brick?' I asked.

'He wanted to pinch something from the shop,' said Mr Bland.

'He didn't say he did,' I said.

Mr Bland gave me a short but steady stare.

'I was wondering,' I said diffidently, drawing patterns on his desk with my finger, 'if you might think he did it because he was revenging himself on the fantasy-image of his father while sublimating his own incest-guilt?'

Mr Bland gave me a longer and even steadier stare.

'No,' he said, briefly. 'Look, this is the report I am submitting to the Bench.'

It was quite short – a description of the boy's circumstances and the recommendation that he pay for the damage out of his pocket money.

'What do you think will happen to him?' I asked.

'Conditional discharge, old boy, and an order for restitution,' said Mr Bland. 'They just might put him on probation for a year, especially if Councillor Trotter is on the Bench, because he's very hot on hooliganism just now. You wouldn't object if they did make an order?'

'No,' I said.

'Good. Now, look here, Maule, I'm really much more interested in another laddie on this list, and that is our friend Crump.'

Miss Perrett, in the background, said 'Ha!' It sounded like a distant anti-aircraft gun. Mr Bland stroked his moustache thoughtfully.

'You see, old boy, this is what's in my mind,' he said.

'This present affair of Egbert's is a very trivial matter, and on the face of it, he doesn't need any ferocious treatment now. But, of course, there is that background. You know it?'

I shook my head.

'Well, take it from me, old boy, it's pretty chronic,' said Mr Bland, still rubbing his moustache thoughtfully, centre to left, centre to right, left, right. 'I don't think anything we can do at present is going to make it any better, and if we leave Egbert there much longer he's going to be too old to respond to treatment anyway. I think we ought to take advantage of Egbert's appearance today and at least try and get him away out of it.'

'Plucking one brand from the burning,' I said.

'That's it, yes, you've hit it, by Jove. Yes: so I'm recommending a Fit Person Order, at least I'm asking for a remand in custody for further reports and inquiries to be made, but with a Fit Person Order in mind. How does that suit you?'

'Yes, all right, I suppose, so long as we get the remand first,' I said. 'I don't want to take the body away with me this morning, I haven't anywhere to put it.'

'Fair enough,' he said. 'Well, you'd better sit in Court this morning and hear the first run through, anyway; and by Jove, we'd better get weaving, it's just on ten already.'

Mr Bland collected a lot of papers together and stowed them in an immaculate briefcase, and we went down together. When we pulled open the side door, we found the corridor-waiting-room crammed with boys and their anxious-eyed parents.

'Good Lord!' I thought. 'This is something like a crime wave.'

When Westburn Court House was built, there were no such things as Juvenile Courts; and when this feature had eventually to be provided, the only available room was one originally designed as a retiring room. This had at one end an incongruously domestic fireplace and above that a mantelpiece and an enormous mirror. The magistrates sat at the other end of the room behind a long table, set crossways, and looked at themselves in the big mirror. On their right, parallel with the wall, was a table at which sat the Clerk of the Court and one or two senior policemen who acted as prosecuting counsel. On the magistrates' left, forming the third side of a hollow square, was another table where the probation officers sat, with any other interested official such as myself. Facing the magistrates, but about five yards away, was a single rush-bottom chair: this was, so to speak, The Dock. Behind this chair stood two others – for the parents. In a distant corner, beside the mantelpiece, were two chairs occupied by very young, very sallow, and very bored reporters from the local Press. A bald constable in uniform acted as Usher and M.C. and, in repose, stood with his back to the fireplace. All through the morning's proceedings, upon this scene and upon all the actors, a film of dust came gently, gently settling.

Mr Bland and I had only just scrambled into our chairs when we had to stand up again as the magistrates filed in. There were three this morning. The chairman was a short, white-haired man in a brown tweed suit, Colonel Plimm, head of the district's wholesale grocery firm and a County Councillor; then there was Miss Wepys, one of a very old Westburn family who kept up a tradition of public service that had begun when they were squires of the village; and finally there was Councillor Trotter, a lively man with grey hair and heavy black eyebrows, Chairman of the local Trades Council and a prominent Union man.

The first case was eight little boys who had been taking short cuts across the railway lines; they all lined up, with their fathers behind them, and were fined five shillings each. Then came seven little boys who had been playing football in the street; they got fined two shillings and sixpence apiece. This cleared the pressure in the corridor, got us down to brass tacks, and, incidentally, reduced the crime wave to reasonable proportions.

The third case was also very quickly disposed of. The juvenile involved was an immense dark youth in a dirty white pullover and black jeans who stood sneering down at the magistrates from his height of six feet four. He had been up a fortnight before for stealing a car and had been re-manded. The remand home now recommended that he be sent to a nautical approved school as soon as possible, and the magistrate saw no reason to stand in his way. So off he went, and we came next to the Trial of Sidney Smee.

Sidney, in his best grey suit, and with hair that was plastered down with oil, crouched in the rush-bottom chair, looking smaller and lonelier than ever. Behind him, in the parent's chair, sat Mrs Scatterbread, who was addressed throughout as Mrs Smee and was too confused to contradict. The police inspector described the offence very briefly, and then read out Sidney's own statement, and Sidney said it was true and he was very sorry for what he had done. Then Mr Bland gave the magistrates his report, and I added a word or two to the effect that Sidney had a very nice home where I felt sure he would flourish and be no more trouble to anyone; and the Colonel, who had been lying back in his chair looking stupefied, now roused himself and was about to address the Court when Councillor Trotter leaned across and muttered urgently to him. The Colonel nodded and muttered to Miss Wepys, who nodded, and then he said:

'Now stand up, Smee. Now, we've heard a lot of nice things about you from these gentlemen here – they seem to think you've got a lot of good in you and we want to help you make good and be a good lad and justify what these gentlemen say about you instead of doing all these silly things, you have been a silly boy, Smee, I wonder if you know how silly you have been, eh?'

Poor Sid looked as though he'd been presented with some dreadful trick question, so that no matter what he answered something would go off with a loud bang, so he swallowed twice rapidly and said in a high voice: 'Hernh!'

'Good, well, now, we're going to put you on probation. That means you must come and see Mr Bland – that's Mr Bland over there – and you must be good friends with Mr Bland and do what he tells you to do, because he'll be a good friend to you, and be a good boy and do your best and don't ever come here again.'

And Sidney said 'Hernh!' and the chairman said: 'Probation one year,' and the boy and his foster-mother filed out and the magistrates shifted slightly in their hard chairs and a loud constabular voice outside called, all on one note: 'Egbergarymelvyn CRUMP!' and in came Egbert.

He was still wearing the over-large tweed jacket and torn trousers which he'd worn when we nearly ran him down, and his hair was even longer and dirtier than it was then. He had some sort of paisley-pattern choker round his neck, but otherwise appeared to be naked under the jacket. His mother was delayed at the door by a policeman who took her lighted cigarette away; when she appeared, I saw a very short, fat woman with a flat white face and a little cherry knob of a nose. She had orange hair, clamped down close to her head with curlers, and was wearing a shiny black oilskin mack and white plimsolls. The large white stubs of her legs were covered with a magnificent fantasia of varicose veins.

The Clerk said: 'You are Egbert Gary Melvyn Crump?' and Egbert said: 'Yer.'

'And you live at No. 6, The Rat Yard, Blight Street?'

'Yer.'

'And you are thirteen years of age?'

'Yer.'

'Now you are charged with that on October 7th, 1948, at a time between 10 a.m. and 11 a.m., you feloniously did steal one – what's this, Inspector?'

'Beg pardon, your Worships, that should read "budgerigar",' said the Inspector. 'A small singing bird.'

'Ah, yes,' said the Clerk. 'Er – trum trum trum trum feloniously did steal one budgerigar, property of Simeon Wiss, contrary to Section 2 of the Larceny Act, 1916, did you do this?'

'Eh?' said Egbert, baffled.

The Clerk read through the charge again in a loud voice,

28

and at the end Egbert turned silently to his Mum, who shouted: 'No!'

'You mean, not guilty?' asked the Clerk, surprised. 'Didn't he take the bird?'

'Course 'e did,' said Mrs Crump.

'Mrs Crump,' said the Clerk, 'you must advise your son to plead either guilty or not guilty; now, did he or didn't he take this bird?'

'Well, wot I say is there was others there and why pick on Egg, as soon as that narsty sneakin' copper come around I knew –'

'Mrs Crump!' cried the outraged Clerk.

'Stand up!' cried the outraged Usher.

'You will have every opportunity of talking to us later, Mrs Crump,' said the Chairman. 'Now, just answer the one simple question: did Egbert steal this bird?'

Egbert said: 'Yer.'

There was a relaxing movement round the Court. The Usher said: 'Sit down, Mrs Crump.'

She flared up: 'You just tole me to stand up!'

He said: 'An' now I'm just tellin' you to sit down again!'

She subsided with a thump, muttering: 'British bloody justice!'

The Clerk, with a wary look on his face, now read on: 'And you are further charged with that on October 8th 1948, between 10 a.m. and 11 a.m., you feloniously did steal a quantity of birdseed, value sevenpence, also the property of Simeon Wiss, contrary to Section 2 of the Larceny Act 1916, did you do that?'

This time there was no difficulty. Egbert said: 'Yer.'

'Right,' said the Clerk thankfully. 'Now, Egbert, and you, too, Mrs Crump, you must listen very carefully to what the Inspector says and when he has finished you will be able to ask him questions about what he has said.'

Mrs Crump muttered: 'Ho, yes, very likely, I'll be bound, ho, not 'arf,' and gave an explosive sniff.

The Clerk said: 'Thank you, Inspector. Sit down, Egbert.'

The Inspector loomed up very large when he rose to his feet in all his blue and silver; he seemed to have about a fathom of belt round his middle. Egbert, hands in pockets, slumped back in his chair and gazed up at him.

'Your Worships,' began the Inspector. 'The facts in this case are as follows. The houses which comprise The Rat Yard are almost entirely let to sub-tenants, some of whom occupy only one room; and one of the rooms opening directly on to the Yard is so occupied by a Mr Simeon Wiss, who is in fact a retired person living alone, your Worships, and a former ship's cook. This Mr Wiss owns a pet budgerigar which goes by the name of Shinwell.'

I saw Councillor Trotter's eyebrows give a sudden flap at this.

'Now, your Worships, Mr Wiss is in the habit of doing his shopping each morning, and if the weather is fine he is also in the habit of hanging the birdcage up in the open window of his room, so that the bird can catch a little sunshine while its master is at the market. This is, in fact, what occurred on the morning of the 7th October, when Mr Wiss left his house to go shopping at approximately 10 a.m.'

Egbert was now concentrating on making a hole in his plimsoll by wiggling his big toe.

'It was with considerable concern and distress that Mr Wiss discovered, on his return to his room at approximately 11 a.m. that same morning, that his bird was missing from its cage. He at first formed the opinion that the bird had in some way escaped from the cage and flown off, but observing that the patent door of the cage had been refastened, he at length came to the conclusion that some person or persons had either wilfully let the bird escape or had, in fact, stolen it. He instituted inquiries himself, which proved fruitless, and subsequently notified the nearest police station.'

Glancing at Mrs Crump to see if she was still attending, I was terrified to find her gazing lecherously into my eyes, smiling and fluttering her eyelashes. I looked hastily back at the Inspector.

'Now, at 11.40 a.m. the following morning, that is October 8th, your Worships, P.C. 515 Bowman was patrolling his beat in Blight Street when he was approached by a gentleman who subsequently identified himself as Mr Wiss, and who said to him – ' (here the Inspector put on the ringing pontifical voice he always used when quoting somebody else verbatim). ' "Here, mate, them bleeding Crumps have swiped my budgie." '

'Cheeky swine !' observed Mrs Crump loudly.

'In response to the Constable's inquiries, Mr Wiss described what had happened the previous day, and added that he had just returned from his morning shopping to find that a further offence had apparently been committed. The constable's attention was then drawn to a large tin standing on Mr Wiss's window-sill, marked National Dried Milk but actually half-full of birdseed. Constable Bowman then observed that from a point just outside the window, a thin but discernible trail of birdseed led across the Yard and in at the door of No. 6.'

Mrs Crump had raised her short legs, side by side, horizontally in front of her, and was now looking at them with one eye shut.

'Now, your Worships, I must now point out to you that this budgerigar, Shinwell, had been taught by Mr Wiss to talk, and had, in fact, become very proficient in the recitation of a bawdy verse which, I understand, commences with the words : "There was an old Bishop of Brighton."

'Your Worships, the Constable, accompanied by Mr Wiss, then followed the trail of seed into a basement passage-way below No. 6, The Rat Yard, where he observed three small boys, the accused and two others, leaning against the wall, whistling. P.C. Bowman inquired what they were doing, and the eldest boy, Crump, replied to the effect that they were practising for the carol-singing season, as the Constable might have learnt had he washed his great cloth ears out. Upon P.C. Bowman making a slight gesture towards the boy, Crump recoiled in a guilty fashion, and a voice was then distinctly heard repeating: "There was an old Bishop of Brighton. ...." Constable Bowman then said: "I am inquiring into the disappearance of a budgerigar, and I have reason to believe you can assist me in my inquiries." The boy Crump then said: "Oh, all right, here it is." He was cautioned, and said: "Yes. Poor little perisher, I only meant to let him free, as his cage was too small for him, but he would not leave me then, so I had to go back and pinch the seed." Crump was told he would be reported for these offences, and he replied: "Right-ho, bighead!" '

This concluded the facts of the police case against Egbert, but there followed a rather boring interlude while P.C. 515 Bowman was led over the same story again to confirm its truth on oath. When he had finished, the Clerk said that he could be questioned on what he had said; Egbert had nothing to say, but Mrs Crump was on her feet at once.

'I saw you an' ole Wiss 'avin' a drink together down at The Dog, only yesterday,' she said.

Bowman blenched, this was true, but fortunately the Clerk diverted the question by saying: 'Mrs Crump, you must ask questions about what the witness said, you must not make statements at this stage, you know.'

This put Mrs Crump off her stroke for a moment, and she lost the thread, but recovered to say: 'There was two other boys wiv Egg when you knocked him off, why ain't they 'ere?'

The Inspector answered for Bowman by saying: 'Your Worships, the two boys mentioned have both been interviewed by the police, and it does appear that on the day when the bird was taken, they were both in school; and that on the day they were found with Crump, they could have had no idea that the bird was stolen, having expressly been misled in that respect by the accused himself.'

Mrs Crump said: 'Oh, wot's the bloody use,' and sat down.

After the justices had raised their eyebrows to each other, the Chairman said:

'Well, we find the case proved, and now, Egbert, what have you got to say to us about this affair?'

Egbert gazed blankly back at them and a long minute passed.

'Come, now, lad, you must have an explanation for this terrible behaviour ? Couldn't you even say you're sorry for what you've done ?'

Egbert said : 'No.'

Colonel Plimm said : 'You're not sorry ?'

Egbert mumbled : ' 'Course not, poor little perisher, stuck in that flippin' cage, I reckon it was only right to take 'im out.'

Colonel Plimm said : 'It was not right to do any such thing, my lad, and you must – er – get it into your head. Where would this world be if we all went about taking budgerigars out of cages, eh, eh ? You think about that.'

Egbert plainly gave up the struggle at this point, and returned moodily to big toe hole-making.

Colonel Plimm said : 'Can you help us, Mr Bland ?'

This was the moment for which Mr Bland had been waiting deferentially off-stage. He now rose and produced six copies of a typewritten report, which he distributed around, a copy to each Magistrate, a copy to the Clerk, a copy to Mrs Crump, and one copy laid on the table before him for reference. He remained standing, eyeing his report and thumbing his moustache, while a profound silence fell on the Court. Mrs Crump hardly glanced at her copy; not being able to read very well, she affected a haughty disdain.

This is what the Magistrates were reading:

PROBATION OFFICER'S REPORT

Court	Westburn Juvenile	*Date*	3.11.48
Name	Egbert G. M. CRUMP	*Age*	13 on 27.5.48
Address	6 The Rat Yard,	*Religion*	C.E.
	Blight Street.		
Offence	1. Larceny budgerigar		
	2. Larceny birdseed.		

FAMILY CIRCUMSTANCES

Barnaby Crump   (41)   Unemployed.

Mavis Nazimova Craggs (known as Crump)	(37)	Household duties.
Rudolph	(20)	(Illegitimate son of Mrs Crump.) Labourer. Gives £1.
Bebe Craggs	(19)	Daughter of previous marriage. Laundry hand. Gives 10/-.
Gloria	(16)	Usherette. Gives 5/-.
Clark	(14)	At Approved School.
Egbert	(13)	SUBJECT OF THIS REPORT.
Myrna	(12)	At school.
Cary	(10)	,,　　,,
Winston	(8)	,,　　,,
Celia	(7)	At Open Air School.
Clement	(4)	At home.
Anona	(2)	,,　　,,
Sabrina	(6 months)	,,　　,,

SCHOOL REPORT. Smirch Street Secondary Modern, Class 2 (d).

Ability and Attainment. Of average intelligence. Work poor due to bad attendance.

Conduct. Average. Resents correction.

Appearance and Attendance. Very poor. I consider that this lad is the victim of appalling home conditions, and that it would be in his best interests to be got away from them.

(*Signed*) ARTHUR JUKES
Head Teacher

The family to which this lad belongs have been a source of considerable concern to welfare authorities, not only here, where they have resided for some four years, but in other areas, up and down the country, as they appear to follow no settled mode of life. The father was discharged from the Army with psychoneurosis in 1941, and appears to believe that this excuses him from all responsibility, as he is very rarely in work, and is known to drink heavily. The parents are not married, the mother's name being properly Craggs, but they have remained together for a number of years, although the woman from time to time is believed to associate with other men and one of the children is coloured. She is at the present time again pregnant.

The family have had numerous addresses since 1937, and have lived in various huts, tenements, P.A.C. houses, caravans and even in a tent. At present they occupy two rooms in a re-quisitioned bomb-damaged house; conditions here are damp, dirty, and unsavoury, and Inspector Huggins of the N.S.P.C.C., has the family under supervision. Physical neglect or ill-treatment of the children has not been proved, and members of the family show a strong bond of loyalty, but moral standards are most lax, and it is a matter of grave concern that Egbert should be showing signs of dishonesty similar to those of his older brother, Clark.

Although this lad appears for a first offence, Your Worships may well feel that, in view of his unfortunate background, very careful consideration needs to be given to his future. Should Your Worships consider that a Fit Person Order might be in the lad's best interests, I would respectfully suggest a remand in custody for fourteen days so that the necessary reports and inquiries can be made.

WM J. F. BLAND
Probation Officer

Their Worships nodded over this document in silence: then they exchanged glances and the Chairman said absently: 'Thank you, Mr Bland. We'll retire, I think.' We all stood while the Magistrates and the Clerk filed into the little room next door for a private rumination. The reporters, in their long scarves, stretched, and talked with immense familiarity to the policemen. Mrs Crump got a stub of cigarette from behind her ear but was dissuaded from lighting it. Egbert gazed morosely at his plimsoll. The Inspector gazed morosely at me.

Then the Magistrates returned.

'Well, Egbert – ' began Colonel Plimm.

'Stand !' barked the Usher.

It was the Sentence.

'Well, Egbert,' said Colonel Plimm in kindly tones, 'we've given a lot of thought to your case and we want to help you, you know, everyone in this Court wants to help you grow up to be a decent respectable lad, but you see we want to know a little bit more about you, so we're going to send you away to a very nice remand home, you'll be very happy there and properly looked after, and a doctor will come and examine you, so off you go and be a good lad and do your best, and we'll see you here again in a fortnight's time. Remanded for fourteen days.'

There was a moment's silence and then Egbert burst into the loudest, largest, and wettest tears I have ever witnessed. His mother rushed to him, flung her arms about him, and crushed him to her oilskin bosom.

'Yercher!' cried Mrs Crump. 'Why don't you leave the pore little bugger alone?'

4

'THE trouble with you,' said Miss Dashforth, 'is that you try to see everybody's point of view, so you end up in a muddle.'

'Surely,' I said, 'we've got to make a close analytical study of every participant in a case?'

'You'll go batchy if you do,' said Miss Dashforth firmly. She shook crumbs off her skirt and I glimpsed a thin thigh clad in sensible ribbed wool.

'*Tout comprendre, c'est tout pardonner*,' I said, rather pleasedly, for this sort of remark usually occurs to me half an hour after the conversation has finished.

'That won't do, Charles, no, you can't have that,' she said, champing at an apple. 'I dare say you *comprendre* a bit better than I do, seeing that you're so highly qualified, but we just haven't got the power to understand somebody else completely, and the more you try to, the more dippy you get.'

'Well, I fancy I have rather more than a nodding acquaintance with unconscious motivation,' I said, a bit stiffly.

'Then take care the nodding doesn't turn into twitching. Anyway, suppose we did thoroughly *comprendre* everybody, what a fine thing if we, as public servants, went around pardonnaying them all! I suppose you'd pardonnay old mother Crump and leave Egbert to go to blazes?'

'No, I didn't say that –'

'Well, it won't do, Charles. We've got to take a good, sound, common-sense view and come down on the side of the kids every time; if the kids are dirty, tell the parents to scrub 'em, and if the parents won't, take the kids away and scrub 'em ourselves. After all, we can't do much with the parents, they're too set in their ways, but we can do something with the children. We're an extension of the education system, I believe.'

'Teaching what?' I inquired.

'Teaching the kids to be better parents than their own were, and better workers, and generally to have a more settled and healthier attitude to life. To be good citizens, that's the long and short of it.' Miss Dashforth took a last scrunch of her apple, threw the core into the wastepaper can, blew her nose violently, and lit a cigarette. 'I know Egbert worries you a bit, Charles, but you must surely admit that you'd never do anything with him in that glory-hole round the corner?'

'No, I don't think I could, and I suppose in a way this has been the best thing for him, but all the same there was something special that linked Egbert and his Mum.'

'Like a millstone linked to his neck.'

'No,' I protested. 'I think she did her best to stick up for him, and I know her best is nowhere near your best or my best, but I can't help thinking that Egbert doesn't know that.'

'Listen, Mum may have piped up at the first hearing, but she didn't even bother to turn up for the second, now did she?'

'No, no, that's true.'

'And the fact that her best is miles below our best surely justifies us in giving an opportunity to Egbert to gain the advantage? Put the child first, Charles, and blow the parents.'

'I am putting the child first, at least, I think I am,' I said. 'I believe there's something between Egbert and his Mum that's precious to him. Battered old hag she may be, but *he* saw her as Mum. What on earth can we set up in her place?'

'The force of our own example,' said Miss Dashforth.

'As your older girls have had,' I said. This was naughty of me, because Miss Dashforth's older girls are notoriously promiscuous.

'Well, they grew up under the old régime, and they're

institutionalized,' she said, defensively, 'and they're nearly out of care now, anyway. The younger the child, the better our chances. I think you've got the chance to do something good with Egbert; anyway, thank goodness, we've got him till he's eighteen, and by that time he'll probably have got the same idea of his mother as we have.'

I was vaguely aware that this wasn't what I wanted to happen to Egbert, but I couldn't have put my thoughts any more clearly than that, so I let the subject go. The boy had returned before the Court after his fourteen days, and reports were produced from the remand home superintendent, who said Egbert was a likeable lad in many ways but in need of firm handling, and from the teacher, who said he was retarded in arithmetic. The magistrates had then made a Fit Person Order; that is to say, they adjudged the parents to be unfit to have care of Egbert and the County Council to be fit, so they transferred the rights of parental control to the Council until Egbert attained the age of eighteen, and could (presumably) control himself. After the Court I'd taken Egbert along to The Rookery, which was the only place where we had a vacancy for him. He hadn't wept at all; he had been rather subdued and wary, and had hardly spoken on the journey. He looked cleaner, and his hair had been cut, but he still wore his old clothes and plimsolls. As I'd left him, sitting in the hall of The Rookery, he'd given me one sudden glittering glance, whose meaning I hadn't been able to decipher – panic ? Hatred ? Despair ? It had stuck in my mind like a dart.

'I think I'll drop in and see how he's getting on,' I said. 'I've got to go and see Donald and Herbert as well.'

'Which Donald is that ?'

'Donald Magoon,' I said. 'He's a school-leaver at Christmas, you know: I've got to get something worked out for him. And Herbie Slythe leaves at Easter.'

Miss Dashforth nodded.

'Oh, yes, I remember them. Quite a nice boy, Donald; I don't think I know Herbie.' She glanced out of the window. 'But for goodness' sake don't get caught in the fog and have to stay the night in The Rookery; I should think that would be absolutely horrible.'

It was one of those spells in December when fog is obviously hanging about, yellowish dark afternoons when the office lights go on early and we were afraid to go far afield in case the fog really came down and cut us off. Whether the gloomy climate had the same effect upon our clients, I don't know, but for a week or so we had a quiet time, and a welcome breather; no wild panics, no desperate descents by homeless and verminous families seventeen strong, no mad Mid-Europeans camping with their chattels in the office porch. I must add in parenthesis that this was the only December in my experience when we had such a week. Usually, the month before Christmas and the month before the school summer holidays are nightmare times for us. I have a theory that the nearly-dotty mothers – and we know a lot of these vulnerable creatures in Westburn – can chug along so long as their kids are in school and they themselves can spend their days drifting around their silent houses batting at shadows. But the colossal worry of preparing for Christmas topples them over the edge; and so, too, does the thought that for seven weeks in the summer their shrieking brood will swarm under their feet. Then they become incapacitated in droves.

However, blessed 1948 gave us a breather, and that afternoon, after we had finished our picnic lunch round the gas-fire, we spent uninterruptedly on our records and reports. Our only visitor minced up the corridor just as I was preparing to go out. He was a plump and puffy young man dressed in most delicately blended shades of plum-colour, a scheme which extended to his suède bootees and to his tie, which was unexpectedly made of corduroy. Miss Dashforth was fascinated by him and talked charmingly, but for some time none of us could make out what he was; I thought he'd come down from a Sunday newspaper, and Harry thought he was some sinister citizen who wanted to be an Uncle. His name was really Smurthwaite, but he insisted on being addressed as Anthony, and we finally found out that he was the Headmaster of a new school for maladjusted children, who had come up touting for custom. We hadn't any for him, but Miss Dashforth had been so carried away that she gaily promised that some time in the New Year she and I would very gladly come down and see Anthony in his school, which was called, I gathered, The Cottage by the Creek.

So it was none too early, after all, that I caught the bus over to The Rookery.

The Rookery is in Brewhouse Lane, next to the Alderman Scrowpe Memorial Field. Originally it had been a block of four tall, thin, three-storey houses standing on a grey and windy corner. The old Board of Guardians had bought the four and had, as it were, partially knocked them together; that is to say, inter-connecting doors and passages had been pushed through, joint fire-escapes erected, and a common hot water system installed, but at the same time the addition of extra bathrooms, cupboards, windows, and lavatories restored autonomy to each constituent house. When I first knew it, it was obviously one Children's Home, but internally sub-divided into a Boys' House, a Girls' House, a Toddlers' House, and a Nursery. In the six years that I knew it, before it was converted into a Further Education Centre, I never penetrated to some corners, and had only the haziest idea of the layout of the upper floors. This was partly because of the complicated geography, and partly because, as a field officer and therefore an outsider, I was never given the run of the place.

I touched the highly-polished brass bellpush and the door was opened by a puddingy adolescent girl who asked me to wait on the mat while she fetched Miss. Miss, a spotty house-mother, asked me to wait in the hall while she fetched Matron. Matron, who made it clear to me that she was imperially busy, said that if I cared to wait outside the office, Sir would soon be free to see me. So I settled myself outside Sir's door and regarded my shoes and inhaled air that sagged under the smell of strong furniture polish. All that had happened so far had to be patiently borne, for it was part of the protocol that governed all visits to Children's Homes by such upstarts as me. Any infringement of protocol brought forth a massive rebuke in the shape of a Memo, copy for information to THE CHILDREN'S OFFICER, copy for information to the District N.A.L.G.O. Organizer. Of course, it was a bit stickier here because of the position of Mr and Mrs Mussel, the Superintendent and Matron. They'd been in charge for twenty years and were now only a year or so from retirement; in fact they were already running by remote control their new grocery business in Haverfordwest. This meant that while in one sense they didn't really care what happened, they were, on the whole, trapped in a routine of management which they had built up and refined over the years until the Home virtually ran itself, no matter what situations presented themselves. It was theoretically possible for a child to revolt, but it would take a child of exceptional resource and doggedness to do it successfully. Flight was really the only available form of self-expression, and even that was rarely resorted to. But I have never met a child who said he was unhappy there.

Presently the office door opened, and Sir put his head out.

'Ah, good afternoon, Maule,' he said jovially. 'Come along in. I'm up to my ears in paperwork, as always.'

He bustled some papers on to a corner of his desk; they looked to me suspiciously like Trade Union stuff, for he was the secretary of the local branch of the Amalgamated Society of Workhouse Masters (shortly to be re-christened Residential Assistance Administrators). Then he settled me in a hard chair and himself in a padded swivel one behind the desk. He was a small man with a large bald head, who looked much more impressive sitting down, but wherever he was he wore an air of dignified condescension.

'Well, now,' said Mr Mussel, putting the tips of his fingers together, 'you'd like to see our Donald ?'

'Yes, I would,' I said, 'and I wondered if I could have a quick word with Egbert, too. Has he settled down ?'

'Oh, he's settling, he's settling,' said Mr Mussel. 'We're

quite used to the Egberts of this world. I would say he is –
ah – not unhappy.'

There was a tap on the door and a tiny shy child appeared
round the corner and said something to Sir, which was unin-
telligible to me and sounded merely like a pencil squeaking
over a slate. When she stopped, Sir leaned forward kindly.

'Well, you tell Miss Frogson I'm busy, will you tell her
that ?'

'Squeak.'

'And Rosaleen –'

'Squeak ?'

'Will you see if you can find Egbert and tell him I want to
see him ?'

'Squeak.'

As the door closed, Mr Mussel said : 'You see, that's what
it's like in residential work : an incessant demand on one's
time and nerves, long past the hours you fellows seem to
work, twenty-four hours a day, seven days a week. You
know, Maule, I just don't know what it is to go home and
close the door on my responsibilities.'

There was a deferential tap on the massive barrier that
lay between him and the mob, and a small clean boy came
in. I had to wrench my mind into believing that this was
Egbert. Then I realized that, of course, I was used to seeing
him in over-large tweed garments and an over-long hair
style; now, he'd been cut down to his age. He was wearing
a grey jersey and a grey shirt and red tie, and grey corduroy
shorts and grey socks with red tops, and altogether he
looked a smallish, and rather defenceless, thirteen.

'Well, Egbert,' said Sir.

'Yesser ?'

'You know this gentleman, of course ?'

Egbert gave me a sideways glance under his eyelashes.

'Yesser.'

'He's come to see how you're getting on.'

'Yesser.' Egbert obediently half-turned towards me, to
show that I was now included in his attention.

'Well, Egbert,' I said, cheerily. 'How's tricks ?'

'Awright.'

'Getting used to it, eh ?'

'Yer.'

'Er – ' Conversation was flagging already. I'd hoped to talk with Egbert on my own, but old Mussel wouldn't leave us, presiding there like some mandarin. 'Er – made friends here yet ?'

'Yer.'

'Any special friend ?'

He shrugged his shoulders. 'Oh, they're all me mates.'

'You mix in pretty well ?'

'Yer.'

'Good.' I gazed at him, what on earth else could I say to him ? My invention had exhausted itself. 'So you're all right ?' I said feebly.

'Yer,' he said, in the half-wondering tone of one who means why the hell shouldn't I be ?

'Good, well, now that's that, Egbert,' said Sir.

'Yesser.'

'But would you find Big Donald and say I want to see him here ?' said Sir.

'Yesser.'

'Cheerio, Egbert,' I said.

'Cheeroh.'

And he was gone. The whole conversation seemed to me to have been a complete and fatuous waste of time; and yet I felt there was a gulf between us and that somehow or other a bridge had to be thrown over that gulf before a significant meeting could take place between him and me. Meanwhile, Sir was much keener to talk about Donald.

'Big Donald, we call him, as there are two Donalds here at present,' he said. 'You know nothing about him, I presume ?'

'I'm afraid I don't,' I said. 'I've only just had a memo from County Hall, asking me to take responsibility for him when he leaves here at Christmas.'

Mr Mussel filled his pipe thoughtfully.

'Well, I don't think he'll prove much of a worry to you,'

he said. 'He's a nice lad, is Donald, a quiet respectful type of lad. Now, I know it's your responsibility to see him fixed up with work and lodgings, but I should like to suggest something for your further consideration. I've got a daily cleaner here, a Mrs Cole, who's been working here for years, and I know she's got a soft spot for Big Donald; and her own son's just emigrated, so she's got a spare room; and her husband, old Ted Cole, I know could get Donald in with him at the engineering works. If you care to follow that up I believe you'd very easily get the lad fixed up with a home and a job with people he knows and trusts.'

And he sat back and lit his pipe with the complacent air of one who knows that with Life two and two always come to four.

'H'm,' I said. 'That sounds very promising. Does Donald know of the idea yet?'

'Not yet. You'll have to see Mrs Cole first, of course; I'm pretty sure of what her answer will be, but naturally I cannot make an official approach myself.'

'Right. What is Donald, actually – has he got a family?'

'No, none,' said Mr Mussel. 'He's lived here all his life; or, to be exact, all but one month. He came to us when he was one month old – I can remember his coming – his mother had abandoned him in her lodgings and vanished and she's never been seen from that day to this. Oh, he was a fat little baby, he was; I can remember him as if it were yesterday.'

I suddenly liked Mr Mussel much more. This chuckling paternalism, which I didn't know he had in him, revealed to me the original devotion which had made him choose this job and no other and go on and on for twenty years. I was still grinning at him when there was a knock on the door and in came Donald Magoon.

Donald was a largish boy for fifteen, and just a shade out of focus – his head was a shade too big, his elbows were a shade to near his shoulders, his feet turned outwards a shade too noticeably. He had a round, amiable face, and a broad nose.

'Yisser?'

'Ah, Donald! This gentleman is Mr Maule, Donald, and he's a welfare officer; and he's come to see you because you'll be leaving school at Christmas, won't you?'

'Yisser.'

'So you'll be on the look-out for a job, Donald?'

'Yisser.'

'And you'll have to be leaving The Rookery at last?'

'Yisser.'

'So Mr Maule will find you a nice place to live, Donald.'

'No, sir. Me Mum's going to send for me.'

I felt that Mr Mussel and I had walked side by side slap into a thick plate-glass window.

'Now, Donald,' said Mr Mussel, when we had, metaphorically speaking, picked ourselves up off the floor, 'Donald, Donald, it's fifteen years – more than fifteen years – since your mother disappeared, isn't it?'

'Yisser.'

'And since then there's been a great world war?'

'Yisser.'

'And your mother has never written, and never come to see you, and never inquired about you?'

'No, sir.'

'So she doesn't even know what you look like?'

'She'll know, sir.'

We couldn't shift him. We went on for half an hour, Mussel growing crosser and crosser, and getting more and more hurt and bewildered, and still Donald stuck to his guns; we said ruder things about his mother than we ever would have done in calmer moments; and yet he took himself off in the end, without even waiting to be dismissed, tears in his eyes, a flush on his cheeks, but still saying: 'She'll send for me, sir, you see.'

I realized then the nature of the plate-glass we'd walked into. It was Faith.

'Well, damn me!' said Mr Mussel, reaching for his pipe again. 'Did you ever meet such a pig-headed fellow? Lots of these children have secret dreams of how wonderful their parents are, but I've never known a boy so definite and so obstinate about his dream.'

'He did seem terribly definite,' I said. 'Do you think he is secretly in touch with her?'

'Never. Never for one moment. She's gone, Maule, and he was only one month old when she went: she can't possibly have any interest in him whatever.'

'Has anyone ever tried to trace her?'

'A warrant would have been issued, at the beginning; I doubt if anybody's tried since.'

'I wonder if I ought to try?'

'Oh, for God's sake, Maule,' said Mr Mussel crossly. 'I'd have thought you had better things to do with your time.'

I knew why he was cross. He had just been publicly taught that two and two do not always make four.

I woke up next morning with Donald in my mind and the awareness that I'd slept badly. I didn't know quite what to do. On the one hand was the virtual impossibility of picking up the trail – and Mussel had been right, I had more than enough to do with my time without going on wild goose chases. The woman had disappeared in 1933, a period so remote to me that it could have been a century earlier and made no difference; a period of seven years before National Registration, ration books, and the direction of labour. She could have married three times, used a dozen names, died in any one of forty counties. And if she were alive now, in 1948, what possible meaning to her could there be in a little bundle of flesh she'd abandoned fifteen years before? But on the other hand, dare I ignore Donald's expression of faith? Dare I just stand back and let him lose his faith, probably never find another?

I decided to ask Harry.

'And besides,' I concluded, after I'd told her the whole story, 'suppose by some wild chance I do find her and she turns out to be some one-eyed horror in the Six Counties looney-bin – what do I tell Donald then? What do I do, Harry – let sleeping dogs lie? Or try and wake 'em up?'

Harry smiled – slowly, of course.

'You try and find her, Charles,' she said. 'Do your best.'

'Yes, of course, I will,' I mumbled. 'I knew it all the time, really.'

I got hold of Donald's file first. There was really nothing on it, just a line or two to say that his mother, Mrs Magoon, had walked out of her lodgings at 28 Palestrina Street, and had never come back; that the landlady could not possibly look after the child, and that no relatives had come forward to help. Nothing was known at all about Mrs Magoon, certainly her title and possibly her name being false, and in official eyes she had pulled a very successful fast one. It all looked hopeless.

I decided that Donald would need a birth certificate whatever happened, and there wasn't one on the file, so I strolled round to the Registrar of Births, Deaths and Marriages. There was a young chap on the staff there, just learning the job, with whom I had a nodding acquaintance; as the old martinet was out, this chap let me inside and we had a search through the register together.

There was damn-all for Magoon; the birth had never been registered.

And then, just as the enormous pages were flopping shut again, my eye was caught by a familiar address. On a date two days after Donald's date of birth – as we had it – at 28 Palestrina Street, a child called Donald had been born to a Beatrice Chawne; father, a blank.

'Ah - hah !'

'Is that him, do you think ?' asked Ginger.

'Could be,' I said. 'If it is, I don't know how we got it wrong in the first place; but all the same I think it's worth a trip round to Palestrina Street.'

The south-east corner of Westburn is a long flat slope covered with thousands of little houses; and, dominating this tilted landscape, the engineering works sprawls there like a great sleeping hound. By the haunch of this throbbing animal there is a small patch of streets, built over by a housing speculator who evidently enjoyed music. I have never personally come across such an unlikely combination of interests, but there indubitably was the evidence – Purcell Street, Beethoven Street, Palestrina Street, Sullivan Street, and Rossini Crescent. I found Palestrina Street, in the heart of this tiny estate, and saw that the numbers ran up one side and down the other. So I walked up the left-hand side – 3, 9, 18, 26, 27 . . .

In the place of 28 there was a large hole.

I stood there, gazing at it, my hands thrust into my rain-coat pockets, the birth certificate crammed uselessly into my wallet.

So that was that.

'It's been bombed!' said a bright voice by my elbow. It was a short woman with shiny teeth and a mauve hat.

I could have bitten her. 'Yes!' I snarled. 'Pity, isn't it?'

'Oh, well, these things are sent to try us,' she simpered.

This was an infuriating remark just when I'd come to a premature stop and would have to admit old Mussel to be right, and I was about to turn curtly on my heel and stalk off, but then I realized that giving up, in all the circum-stances, would be rotten, so I said :

'Tell me – do you happen to know who used to live here?'

'Oooh, there, now, I'm sorry, I don't,' she said. 'I only come to this part sometimes, to visit my friend. My friend might know. Is it important?'

'Yes,' I said. 'It is important.'

'Ooh, well, then, sir, if you wouldn't mind just strolling back with me we could ask, couldn't we? No harm in ask-ing, as they say, nothing venture, nothing gain.' And so, with innocent prattle, she trotted plumply back up the street, with me beside her feeling as though I was taking a Peke for a walk.

Her friend, a lonely old lady in a house full of photo-graphs, was only too willing to assist.

'Oh, sir, that was poor Mrs Whatten, a very great tragedy, sir, and why a good, kind, obliging person like that should be the only one to be took by the bombs in this street, when there's many and many a one I could mention . . .

'. . . lodgers, sir? Well, you see, Mrs Whatten took a number of gentlemen and ladies for many years. I can't say as I recollect . . .

'. . . Ooh, no, sir, I can't remember nothink like that, I'm sure. Well, I never! But then, Mrs Whatten was always a good, kind lady . . .

'. . . well, sir, I wonder if the best person to help you might be Mrs Whatten's son. He was in the Navy, do you see, sir, when the house was bombed, but except for the war, he lived at No. 28 all his life. He *might* just remember . . .

'. . . well, no sir, I'm sorry; but I'm sure he lives in one of the prefabs, down by the Gleeze, and I'm sure anyone there would know the address, sir. It's a Mr Mordecai Whatten you want, sir. . . .'

I extracted myself in the end and stalked back up the wet and clattering street with my collar turned up against the rain. It was dispiriting, when I considered the Himalayas ahead, to see what a long time it took to thread through the foothills. However, at least I was still threading them.

I went to the Public Library next and settled myself down with the Electoral Register, intending to go through the whole district street by street till I found the address of Mordecai Whatten, which would have been a long job; but then I realized that, of course, prefabs were all let by the local Council, so I took myself round to the Housing Office.

Now, Housing Officers are suspicious and cross about the whole of mankind; but of all mankind, they are most suspicious and cross about County Council Officers; and of all County Council Officers, they are most suspicious and cross about social workers; so this visit took me a long time. I had to be at once dogged and obdurate, while being charmingly apologetic, and I had to put up with a lot of arrogant obstructionism. But in the end, I got what I wanted: Mordecai Whatten lived at No. 16 Gleeze View. They could have told me that in two minutes, if they'd wanted.

5

I HAD some tea next so as to arrange that by the time I got out to Gleeze View, Mordecai would probably be home from work. The prefabs had been hastily thrown up on a barren, hilly site overlooking the River Gleeze, a trickle of muddy water heavily impregnated with chemicals. As I knocked on Mordecai's door that wet, blowy evening, I thought heavily to myself that perhaps it wasn't too bad in summer.

Mordecai had finished his tea and answered the door himself. He was a youngish, dark chap with a hairline that had receded far over the top of his head.

I said: 'I'm terribly sorry to come bothering you, Mr Whatten, but I badly need your help. I'm a welfare officer, and I'm trying to get some information about a woman who lodged with your mother in Palestrina Street.'

He said: 'Oh, yes? Well, if I can, of course, but she had quite a number of lodgers in her time, you know.'

I said: 'Well, this one was called Magoon — I think.'

'No,' he shook his head.

'Or she might have used the name of Chawne?'

'No, matey. You're off the beam this time. I've never heard them names, I'm sure.'

'Five or six years before the war?' I persisted.

'No, no, I'm sure of it. I'd remember the name if I'd ever heard it. Sorry, matey, I can't help yer. G'night.'

As the door was actually closing, I said: 'It was a girl who I think had a baby while she was lodging there.'

The door stopped its motion.

'Oh,' said Mr Whatten. 'Her.'

There was a pause that throbbed with indecision. Inky clouds were being swept across the sky. A gusty wind was bringing spatters of rain and a smell of detergent from the Gleeze.

'Come in.' He took me into the living-room and planted himself squarely in front of me.

'Now, come on, what's it all about?' he said. 'What are you after?'

I had a long look at his hot brown eyes, and then I told him the whole story.

'Pore little devil,' said Mordecai, as I finished. 'Pore little devil. And he'd be fifteen now, would he? Which takes us back to 1933 – yes, I see, but I don't know as I can help you, mister.'

His wife came out of the kitchen just then with cups of tea and we all settled down with them round the fire.

'You see, mister,' said Mordecai, '1933 was still a slump year and times was not so good in Westburn – not so good at all, and I was only a young bloke, and I couldn't get a job. So I clutters off to Bournemouth to stay with me Uncle Eddie and help him in the greengrocers till things got better. So you see I was out the way when this young woman had her baby, and in fact, I never really did realize what happened till Mum told me years later. That's why I didn't know the name – I never did know it, I only met her about twice, and then we called her Beattie.'

'That's the one,' I said. 'At least, probably – Donald's mother was called Beatrice.'

'Yeah. Well, she was a nice girl, a very nice girl, a country girl; turn her hand to anything round the house, and so she was a great help to Mum. Now, I cluttered off before anyone even knew she was in the family way, so don't take me as gospel, matey; but I think that when she had her baby, Mum had got too fond of her to turf her out, and besides I was away and me bedroom was going spare. And I think that this Beattie prob'ly saw that she was a burden to Mum but she had nowhere else to go, and was too nice and too proud to go down to the Relieving Officer. Not that I blame her, neither, ooh, he was a hard-faced bastard in them days — ole Frosty-face, we called 'im, Frost 'is name was. Yeah. I remember 'im.'

'Yes,' I nodded. 'So she bolted. Do you know where?'

'No.'

'Do you know where she came from?'

'No.'

'Oh, Lord!' It was as though I'd won the Pools and the dividend turned out to be twelve shillings and fourpence that week.

'Can you remember anything about her at all, any little thing I can tell Donald, to give him some idea?'

'No.'

He looked rather shame-faced about it, he wanted to do something for the kid, but there was no mistaking the flatness of his answer.

And then his wife said, 'Mor —'

'Yes, love?'

'I used to be in and out of your Mum's house then.'

'So you did. Soft on me even then, you was.'

'Oh, give over. I was only small then, I can't really remember Beattie 'cept she was large and got a lot of black hair, but I'm sure she came from the country not far from 'ere. Can't you remember, Mor? It was a village. Oh, dear, I'd know it if I 'eard it.'

'No, no, I don't think I ever knew where she came from.'

We all sat and stared stupidly at each other.

'Tell yer what,' said Mor suddenly. 'I gotta road map on me bike; let's have a dekko and see if anything rings a bell.'

He went outside to where he kept a motor-bike and side-car swathed in tarpaulin. He came back with the map and spread it out. We all hunched over it. We muttered the names of villages to ourselves.

'Cor, lummy,' said Mor, 'who'd have thought there was so many bleeding villages around? There's *thousands* of 'em. Oh, it's hopeless, Grete, you'll never get it, it's like lookin' for a needle in a haystack.'

'Yeah,' she said sadly. 'I dunno. It was just an idea. Something mixed up with a country pub.'

'*Pub*?' said Mor, sharply. He was standing upright, head bent, eyes shut, hand over his eyes, other hand outflung.

'Pub, I was goin' round to the pub. And she said no, she didn't care for pubs. Too much trouble came of 'em. Dad 'ud have beaten 'er if she'd even looked at the one at 'ome, what was it called, what *was* it called – cor 'blige – the Dying Swan!'

'Rudsham,' said his wife, almost in the same breath.

We were all staring at the spot on the map twenty miles north-east of Westburn.

When I got to the office next morning, there was a note from Mor stuffed under the door; he must have come past on his way to work. 'Dear mr mall,' it said. 'Hope you get on O.K. If you can't find her, or if she says she don't want donald, we will have him, yours respectfully.'

Good old Mor.

I told Miss Dashforth where I was going, and she was not a bit enthusiastic – 'Let the dead past bury its dead!' she said, haughtily – but she did not forbid me. Then I went down to the bus-station and found there was no direct route to Rudsham, and even the connecting services were pretty haphazard. It was, in fact, early afternoon before the friendly country busman set me down by Rudsham Church.

Although Rudsham Church itself is, I believe, quite renowned for something or other, the village is not at all inspiring, all brick-and-slate cottages and iron railings. I went uncertainly down the main street and presently found a little general shop with a friendly old soul drowsing among the balls of string. I asked if she had ever heard the names of Magoon or Chawne.

'Magoon, sir, no; never. Rather an unusual name for these parts, I'm sure I've never known a person of that name. But Chawne is a real old Rudsham name, sir, there are several families here of the name Chawne. Do you know the person's given name, sir?'

'Beattie,' I said.

Nothing about the old lady changed by a flicker, her glance was quiet and cool, but her curiosity suddenly shot out at me as though I had inadvertently opened a furnace door and a flame had escaped.

'I am not sure that she wishes her present address to be given to all and sundry, sir,' said the old lady.

'She still lives here?' I gaped.

'I hope I did not give that impression, sir,' said the old lady blandly.

I could see what she was up to: she was more or less holding me to ransom, and would give me Beattie's address in exchange, not for money, but for gossipable information. What I did, without really stopping to think, was to advance a step, put both fists on her counter, draw myself right up, throw out my chest, and generally try to loom over her. And then, in as deep a voice as I could manage, I boomed:

'MADAM, I AM THE LAW!'

Thank goodness, it worked, a prize fool I'd have looked if it hadn't; but the old lady became suitably flustered:

'Oh, sir, I beg your pardon, I didn't realize. Beattie lives at Quinx Green, sir, she's married now, to Mr Rodd's cowman.'

And she went on to give exact directions for the four-mile walk over the hill to the hamlet.

I am not a countryman, I am not even one who enjoys country walking, and whenever I do have to walk, I invariably start off too fast. Thus, by the time I had got three-quarters of the way up the hill from Rudsham I had a stitch and I'd twisted my ankle. It was also coming on to rain again, a steady seeping rain. If I went on up the hill, I could see that I would leave behind any semblance of cover; I would also leave behind any semblance of public transport. God knew what time I'd get back to Westburn tonight, even if I left Rudsham now; and as for getting home from Quinx Green. . . I decided to stop under the last tree for a smoke and a think. I got a cigarette in my mouth, and then I found that my matches were damp.

I cursed the matches, I cursed the rain, I cursed Rudsham,

I cursed Quinx Green, I cursed Donald, I cursed Beattie, I cursed Mr Mussel, and I cursed Harry; I cursed them with solid unimaginative Anglo-Saxon words, strung together in meaningless chunks of sound, all related to bodily functions. I hadn't known I remembered such words, I'd thought they had all been refined out of me by a Social Studies Course. I really enjoyed the fresh sound of them.

When the first wave of cursing was over, I viewed my present situation with intense depression. I had found Donald's mother; it was more by luck than judgement, but all the same, up to then the thing had been enjoyably alluring, like the appeal of a jig-saw puzzle. Now I must face the fact that if I went any further, somebody might get hurt. Beattie was probably happily married to a man who knew nothing of Donald. She might well have had two or three babies, each of whom would have swamped the memory of that little 1933 by-blow. In fifteen years she and Donald had had but twenty-eight days of common experience. They were strangers. I was about to introduce strangers to each other. By doing this I would probably wreck a marriage, drive a woman to suicide, create a country-wide scandal, smash a husband's peace of mind. I was nothing but a damn-fool maniac busybody. I expressed my searing contempt for myself and for everything that had ever happened, coming here, coming into Child Care, coming into social work, getting born, in one enormous 'God *damn*!'

And after that, things got better. The road began to go downhill. I got my breath back. The rain eased again and I found more shelter as the road went between high banks. I tried one more match and it lit. By the time I got to Quinx Green, a tiny straggling hamlet, I was whistling. I didn't have to drive Beattie to suicide; I could pretend I knew nothing about her, but as she happened to be a Chawne, I'd looked her up as a matter of routine, thinking she might be an aunt or cousin – I could give her an innocuous lead and the rest would be up to her.

As I passed the lighted windows of the village post office, a large man in gaiters came out.

'Good afternoon!' I said cheerfully.

He had a staggeringly deep voice, the voice of a huge vault: 'Good day, sir,' he said.

'I wonder if you could direct me to Rodd's Farm?' I said.

'Why, to be sure, sir. 'Tis just along the road here, I be going past there myself.'

We fell into step. He was a very large man.

'I beg your pardon, sir, but if you were thinking of visiting Mr Rodd, he's away over to Farhampton today,' he said.

'Well, no,' I said, 'as a matter of fact, I wanted his cowman.'

'I am Mr Rodd's cowman,' he said.

God save us, he was an enormous man.

'Oh,' I said nervously. 'Well, as a matter of fact – er – that is to say, as a matter of *fact* – I'm sorry, I didn't quite catch your name?'

'Portland, sir.'

'Ah, yes. Well, as a matter of fact, it was Mrs Portland I had come to see.'

'Oh, ah.' A perfectly unruffled boom.

We walked two hundred yards in dead silence.

'Very wet, sir.'

'Yes. Er – yes.'

We passed the main farm gate and turned right. Mr Portland led the way in silence up a very narrow lane and then in at the garden gate of a modern farm cottage, set in about an acre of garden.

'After you, sir,' he said in his deep voice. Even so, I thought, might Nero's guard have addressed an early Christian.

With ponderous deliberation Mr Portland walked into a large back porch and scraped his boots on a metal mat thing. Then he walked across and rubbed his boots on coconut fibre. Then he opened the back door and wiped his boots on the mat just outside. And then he said:

'Bee?'

She said: 'Yes, love?'

'There's a gentleman come to see you, Bee,' and he gave me a friendly wink as I went in.

She was standing by the dresser, a big girl with a mass of black hair and a round, amiable face. Mr Portland went over to the kitchen range and stood gazing into the glow, big and quiet and listening.

'I'm awfully sorry to bother you, Mrs Portland,' I said uncertainly. 'I should have written to make an appointment.'

'An appointment?' She was covertly laughing at me for thinking of her in such pompous terms. 'Oh, 'tis all right, sir, Mr Portland finished early and there's no rush for his tea. What was you wanting, sir?'

I took a deliberate breath and a sidelong look at the listener, and I said:

'Well, I'm afraid you may feel I'm being rather a bother, Mrs Portland, all the same; I'm a welfare officer from the Children's Department in Westburn.'

'You've come about Donald,' she said evenly.

I gave another sidelong look, which she noticed.

'That's quite all right, sir: Mr Portland knows all about Donald. Somehow I knew you'd come some time, sir, you or someone like you. How is my boy?'

'He's fine,' I said.

Mr Portland turned round, very slowly and ponderously, and looked down on me.

'Bee,' he said, 'make us a pot o' tea, lass.'

That man knew more practical psychology than I did; in the bustle of getting the tea-things ready, Bee got over the first surging blow, and when each of us had a great steaming basin-sized cup, we found we could all talk more easily.

Beattie told her story simply. Her own parents had been poor, fecund, and rigid; her childhood rather joyless. In her late teens, on a rare visit to Farhampton, she had fallen with a colossal smack for an Irishman named Magoon, who'd achieved his purpose within an hour, and disappeared within another. When she realized she was pregnant, Beattie also realized the shame and distress she would bring upon her parents, so she bolted; and, because Rudsham people are naturally drawn to Farhampton when they need urban amenities, she went the other way, to Westburn, and nobody ever thought to look for her there.

She had a great stroke of luck at first when she found work at once, for this was the depression time and jobs for women were limited anyway. She managed to pay her way, and got lodgings with the kindly Mrs Whatten, where she called herself Magoon. By the time her pregnancy could no longer be concealed, she and Mrs Whatten had struck up a true friendship, and though Beattie spoke of her circumstances in general terms, she never gave away her real name or home address. Beattie had got a little money by her, a pound or two, and somehow or other she scrambled through until the actual confinement. But after that, things did not go well; she couldn't get her old job back, she couldn't get any job; and with the countrywoman's long-memoried fear of what she called The Union, she would not bring herself to ask for poor relief. (It was not only her personal shame she dreaded, but she feared that the Relieving Officer would simply escort her back to Rudsham and hand her over to her parents to support.) But she could not go on sponging on Mrs Whatten, who was a widow whose only son was away in Bournemouth. It seemed to her that wherever she went with her baby, she would be severely handicapped in the desperate economy of the time, and the more handicapped she was, the greater the chances that in the end she would be shipped back to Rudsham. So she reckoned it all up and decided that the only course open to her which would be fair to everyone was flight. If she could get away and stay right away, really right away, so as not to complicate anything, she reckoned that Donald would 'get adopted' and then he'd be all right; so she went.

For years she'd battled on, mostly in domestic service, keeping herself respectable and swallowing down the yearning-pangs for her little son. Only once did these become irresistible, and that was when she heard that Westburn had been blitzed; she had felt an irrational panic and had rushed back to Palestrina Street, only to find the little house smashed and her old friend dead. She paused there long enough to make sure that there had only been one casualty, no small body had been brought out of the wreckage. She accepted then that her plan had worked out. Donald had not been left to be a burden upon old Mrs Whatten and no doubt had got adopted somewhere. Now she could no longer find out about him if she wanted to, but it didn't blot out her awareness of him. When she met Portland just after the war, and he had proposed to her, she had told him the whole story at once. Mr Portland was a very comforting chap, the best sort to become one's very first confidant; Beattie said it was the way he understood about Donald that made her want to marry him. And somehow, she said, somehow she always knew that one day they would make a home for Donald with them.

Throughout this story I had gladly noted that though her thought processes had been pretty feeble and implausible at times, her emotions, as she stumblingly expressed them, had been centred on the boy all the time. I couldn't see, in her artless account and facial expressions, that she was a cold, self-preserving calculator. And yet could this ever come to anything? Wouldn't a mother in these circumstances have built up a fantasy as inaccurate as the child's? How could she feel truly for a teenage stranger; how far short of the baby's promise does the teenage achievement fall?

Well, it was no good my worrying about ifs and buts and aftercare, for Beattie wanted Donald, and Mr Portland came into action like a heavy tank. Let Donald come home for Christmas, he said; it would be quiet and the countryside would be unexciting, so it would be a fair test, and if the lad didn't like it, he could come back to Westburn at once, and no hard feelings at all, it'd be understandable. But if so be as he got on all right and wanted to stay, Mr Portland 'ud be glad to have the lad in along o' him in the cowshed and he'd see Donald got a sound training and the proper wages.

And so I ended that day bouncing over to Beetfield on the pillion of Mr Portland's motor-bike, and thence catching a slow train to Westburn, where I arrived at eleven o'clock.

Miss Dashforth was not in the least impressed with what I had done.

'My dear Charles, the boy's fifteen and he can start earning money, that's the only reason she wants him. It's the oldest trick in the game.'

I said I thought Beattie was silly and muddled, but genuine. I was rewarded with a worldly-wise snort.

'Ha! It takes a woman to tell if a woman's genuine. *And* she's not so silly or muddled: dodges paying for the kid for fifteen years and then gets a fine strapping wage-earner – oh, I dunno. Well, you'll have to go ahead now, Charles, but I reckon you've been had for a mug.'

Mr Mussel wasn't encouraging, either.

'My dear Maule, you're taking a lad who's lived all his life in a town and you're dumping him down like a parcel – like a parcel, Mr Maule – in the back of beyond with a pack of strangers who'll find in no time who he is and where he's come from, and he'll be known as Beattie's Bastard for the rest of his life.'

I said I thought Mr Portland would look after that angle.

'Ha!' said Mr Mussel. 'All *he* wants is cheap labour in the cowshed, to save himself a bit of effort.'

I comforted myself with the thought that Donald could come back again after a fortnight, if he didn't like it. But in the end, I needn't have worried.

I collected Donald from The Rookery and took him to Beetfield by train. He was wearing a very new, sharply creased suit and squeaking black boots, and carried a very small attaché-case containing pyjamas. ('I haven't given him a full outfit, Maule; if he stays there, *she* can have the pleasure of buying his clothes.') In his other hand he carried a peculiar wooden object which he said was a dibber, which he'd made at school, and it was for Dad.

We got a taxi from Beetfield over to Quinx Green. It stopped by the little lane and I walked up with Donald and opened the garden gate for him. As he passed through, his mother came out into the porch, one hand at her breast as though she had been running. The boy marched steadily up the long path towards her.

'Hallo, Donald,' she said.

Donald's face was shining bright.

'Hallo, Mum,' he said.

I gave a little wave good-bye, but nobody saw me go.

6

As the weeks went by and it became obvious that Donald
was completely happy with his Mum; and as the weeks
drew into months and Sidney Smee settled down again into
laudable conformity, I found myself beetling round Westburn in a glow of self-confidence. 'This Child Care,' I would
say to myself, addressing an imaginary congregation inside
my head, 'this Child Care, while it strikes the outsider as
an unorthodox, almost surrealist, service, nevertheless deals
with its problems with acute sensitivity mingled with plain
hard work. In its best practitioners,' I would say, changing
inside my head into an eminent personage, 'notably Sir
Charles Maule, one finds that a deceptively casual approach
belies the very real amount of . . .'

I had to break off because I had come to Seed Villas.

'Put the kettle on ! I'm in !' I cried.

No answer. Nobody about.

I went up the corridor and beamed round the door.

'What-ho, what-ho !' I began, and then the words faded.
Miss Dashforth, Miss Greave – our typist – and Harry were
standing as though turned to stone; Dashforth was holding
the telephone, which cheeped out an unregarded engaged
signal.

'Why, whatever's up with you, chicks ?' I said, much too
loudly.

'Seven !' whispered Miss Dashforth. 'Seven of 'em !'

I looked involuntarily behind me and then from face to
face. Miss Greave mutely held out a piece of paper. I read:

'High Road Police telephoned. Mr and Mrs Crump have
deserted their home and abandoned their seven children.'

I turned to stone, too.

'Oh, come on, we've got to do something,' said Miss

Dashforth, breaking the spell. 'Harry, you and Charles had better go round to The Rat Yard and cope.'

'Whatever that may mean,' murmured Harry, picking up the tin of DDT she now kept on her desk.

'I'll try and get vacancies and join you later,' said Dashforth, hurling herself back to the phone.

As we hurried through the wet streets, I realized that we were up against a real problem. For months our newly-hatched department had had to care for a growing influx of children, a crowd coming into care and hardly any going out. It took a lot of ingenuity and re-shuffling at that time to find a place anywhere for one child: we were to make arrangements for seven at a blow. Well, Miss Dashforth would try and get vacancies, and meanwhile Harry and I would prepare the children for leaving their home. I realized that with children so young, we should have to be gentle and reassuring, allay their fears, avoid any shock to their perplexed minds, treat the whole affair as an interesting and pleasant experience: 'Yes, darling, you're going for a sea-side holiday, won't that be fun, and such a surprise, I bet you never guessed I was going to fix that up for you, off we go then, let's just see my big boy do his own shoelace up. . . .'

We turned into The Rat Yard. A small, square, barefooted boy rushed straight up to us and said:

' 'Ave yer come to fetch us away? Cor, you ain' 'arf been a long time.'

A smaller, squarer boy, wearing only a jersey, his bare bottom gleaming, yelled:

'I wanna be boarded out, I wanna be boarded out.'

Harry strode on in silence. I said brightly: 'Ah, well, sonny, we'll see, shan't we, we'll see, eh?'

I heard one boy say to the other, behind me: ' 'E's new, isn't 'e?'

Harry pushed in through a door which hung from one hinge, and we went into a very dark passage-way which smelt like old sour floorcloths. I couldn't see a thing, but Harry, who had memorized the route led me up wooden stairs, many of which were splintered. We went up three flights and emerged on to a very small landing littered with bits of paper and grey rag. Standing waiting for us was a girl with tight scarlet trousers, jutting breasts, and a mass of pale pink hair.

'At last!' she said, as we came toiling up. 'Cor, getta move on, I gotta getta work.'

'Hallo, Gloria,' said Harry. 'How are you, dear?'

Gloria looked surprised that anyone cared.

'Awright,' she said.

I was fascinated to see that she had so much eyeshadow on that her eyelids drooped.

A small girl wearing a short vest walked uncertainly out of the room on the landing. A dummy was jammed into her mouth and she regarded us silently, with wide eyes.

'Oh, for Gawd's sake, Anona, get inside!' said Gloria. 'You better come in,' she added to us.

We went into a dim room that seemed full of old furniture. The window had been broken and a bit of sacking hung over it, and it wasn't easy to see anything except that in the centre of the room stood a very large pram containing a very black baby. The two square boys from the Yard – Winston and Clement – came clattering in behind us and started taking headers over the back of a settee. In the middle of all this confusion Harry stood as poised and nonchalant as if she were window-shopping down Regent Street.

'Well, Gloria, tell us what's happened,' she said.

Gloria shrugged one shoulder.

'Nothink's 'appened,' she said. 'I wan in last night, but Myrna tole me Mum comes in about ten and sez cheerio, kids, she sez, I'm muckin' off out of it, tell yer dad. So Myr goes down to the yard and sees Mum goin' off wiv some feller in a van, dunno' 'oo he was, a new one to us, Myr sez.'

'Was your father here then?'

'No, 'e was 'avin' a booze-up round at the Crow, 'e come in later. 'E dint take no notice for a bit, but then after 'e sobered up a bit, 'bout four o'clock in the mornin', 'e got real worried, cos Mum's usually in by then, see. So 'bout six, cor blige 'e don't arf say a mouthful o' words about 'er, so Myr and me we sez shut up about our mum, we sez, you ain't fit to lick 'er boots, so 'e gets proper shirty and 'e sez 'e's not muckin' about wiv a lotta muckin' kids, 'e's muckin' off too, so 'e gets 'is spare teeth an' off 'e goes, wiv all the assistance money too.'

'And Rudolf and Bebe?'

'Ain seen Rude for a fortnight, 'e's got some girl up in Soil Way and 'e sleeps there. Bebe, well, puh, you know what a big fat lump she is, she's no 'elp. Gorn orf to work 'sthough nothing had 'appened, she 'as; an' I wish you'd getta move on, miss, I gotta getta work too.'

'All right, dear. D'you think your mum will came back, today or this evening?'

'I don't reckon so meself. Can't tell, can yer, but she's always been back for brekfuss before.'

'H'm. She might have got involved in an accident. I suppose, but still – Gloria, you're the only sensible one of the lot, so let me ask you this: do you agree to let me take the little ones into care, you know what that means?'

'Yes, miss. You do what's best. Can I come and see 'em if they're in a 'Ome?'

'Certainly, dear, if they're anywhere near, but I don't know where they're going yet. Now then, have you any uncles or aunts or grandparents or friends who might look after some of the children?'

'No, miss. Grandad's dead, 'e fell of the Forth Bridge, it was in the papers, Mum sez. I dunno of any Granma. We ain got no friends. We gotta aunt in Wisbech and a uncle in Kidderminster, but they don't 'ave nothing to do wiv us, well, yer can't blame 'em, can yer?'

'All right. Now, have the children had any food?'

'I give 'em a slice an' a cupper tea, and the two little uns 'ad a bottle.'

Harry blenched.

'The *two* little uns?'

'Yes, miss.' And Gloria led us into the second room, where amid a confusion of mattresses, a small and filthy baby lay peacefully sleeping in a cardboard box marked '48 × 12 Baked Beans'.

'What on earth is this?' said Harry. 'We've never known anything about another baby!'

'It's our foster-child,' said Gloria proudly. Harry and I exchanged horrified glances, but Gloria went on: 'It's Bebe's reelly. We din know she was 'avin' one – I tole you she was a big fat lump – an' then one night she 'ad it on the sofa, while we was listenin' to Donald Peers.'

'Has it been weaned?' asked Harry.

'What's that, miss?'

Harry explained.

'I reckon it's bin weaned all the time, miss.'

Harry shot a glance skywards and said:

'All right: five here and Myrna and Cary are at school. We'll take them and fix them up, now what about yourself, Gloria?'

'I'm not goin' to no bloody 'ostel.'

'I didn't say you were, dear. You're old enough to look after yourself for a bit: can you stay here with Bebe for a bit?'

'S'pose so.'

'Have you got any money?'

'I could sub off the Manager. 'E quite likes me.'

'All right; and I'll try and look in on you tomorrow and see how things are going, and then I can tell you where the little uns have been put.'

'Yes, miss. Thanks, miss. Cheeroh, then, miss.' And she picked up her handbag and took herself jauntily off to the cinema where she worked. Harry said:

'Gloria's a nice girl.'

I glanced after those wriggling scarlet-trousered hips and thought that I'd been taught either too much or not enough.

Up to now I had felt rather spare in all this, and had been standing scratching my right ankle with my left toecap. Now Harry said:

'To work, Charles. We'll scrub this lot up enough to take

them round to the Clinic, and we can get them debugged there.'

I couldn't find a sink, but I found a tap at the end of the landing with a bucket underneath it; I couldn't find flannel or towel, but I found two bits of fairly clean rag; having got all these together, I couldn't find either Winston or Clement. The latter I eventually discovered, by the gleaming of his behind, in a cupboard full of something unspeakable that looked like bulb-fibre. I hauled him out and dabbed at him incompetently with a wet rag and did something to his hair with my comb, which I burnt afterwards, and he emerged as quite a nice-looking little boy. Seeing this, Winston grew envious and emerged from under a mattress seeking similar treatment. Meanwhile Harry had fetched down some assorted clothing from a string tied across the ceiling and had made Anona look slightly more wholesome, though removal of the dummy had produced earsplitting yowls till it was replaced.

Presently there was a tootling noise down below in the yard, and Miss Dashforth called: 'Ahoy, up there?'

'Ahoy!' we shouted.

She came springily up the splintered stairs in her good plaid coat, looking like a fox terrier.

'What-ho!' she said. 'Coo, bit of a pong, isn't there! How goes it?'

Harry told her how went it, and broke the news about Bebe Craggs's baby (which was apparently unnamed and unregistered and known only as Our Baby).

'Oh, well, in for a penny, in for a pound,' said Miss Dashforth, jauntily. 'Now then: I've rung up the Clinic, they're standing by for delousing. I've got hold of a Council car, it's waiting down below, we shall need that. Myrna and Cary can both go to The Rookery to be with Egbert; Winston can go to Tots' Glade. But there's not a nursery cot to be had for twenty miles; County Hall's telephoning farther afield now. What are we going to do with Our Baby?'

'Mrs Cropper might take it,' said Harry.

'Yes, she might. Well, look, we'll take this lot round to the Clinic and while they're being done, you nip up to Mrs Cropper's. Charles can collect Myrna and Cary from school, and I'll get hold of some clothes and nappies from the office, and we'll meet up again at the Clinic.'

The Council car was a huge black limousine with a coat of arms on the door and a uniformed chauffeur in the front; it was usually used for transporting Members of Parliament, Mayors and High Sheriffs. The chauffeur gave a look of undisguised hatred and revulsion at what we were packing into his back seats and as the car moved off, even the gear-change expressed dignified umbrage.

We stopped at the Clinic, which in those days was established in an old army hut; while the children were still drawing breath for their first screams, a brisk Scotch nurse took them in hand so fast and so competently that they could find nothing to express but horrified silence. I trailed off to school, which was one of those Junior Department/Senior Department places all dark green paint and brown glazed tiles. Both head teachers said they were pleased that the Crumps were going into an Institution; the Junior headmistress personally escorted Cary from the premises, wagging her finger at him, and saying: 'I told you this would happen, didn't I? I *told* you.' Two very docile children returned with me to the Clinic.

By early afternoon the de-infestation and medical examination had been carried out by the Scotch nurse and a raven-haired lady doctor with huge spectacles. The three small ones, now clad in decent second-hand woollies, were fed by the Clinic staff; Harry and I took the other four round to the British Restaurant in the High Road, where they seemed overawed by the magnificence of the surroundings and champed away in silence.

The afternoon wore on like one of those nightmares where one is wading knee-deep through treacle in order to catch a train. Harry, for example, went first to Mrs Cropper. Mrs Cropper was out. She went on to Mrs Bulstrode, another foster-mother. Mrs Bulstrode was out. She went back and found Mrs Cropper in: yes, Mrs Cropper would be delighted to have Our Baby, but alas, she had no cot for it. Harry said she would borrow a cot from Mrs Parker; but Mrs Parker was out. Harry told Mrs Cropper she would bring the baby first and then bring the cot along later. As she turned the street corner she met Mrs Parker; ooh, dear, miss, Mrs Parker had lent the cot to Mrs Hibbert, and Monday Mrs Hibbert always went to the Basin Square Chapel Ladies' Bright Hour, which lasted from two till six. . . .

At the Clinic, County Hall had rung to say that a nursery near Rugby would take the children, but was in quarantine with measeles, had the children had measles? Miss Dashforth inadvertently said she didn't know and the nursery said, oh, well, then, better not.

At half past two County Hall said there was a nursery just being opened near Blaenau Ffestiniog, but it had no heating yet, would Miss Dashforth accept the vacancies? Miss Dashforth said yes.

At three County Hall rang to say they had discovered that the Matron of the new Blaenau nursery had already served two sentences for child neglect.

At half past three Clement broke a window and Anona was sick.

At four County Hall said a nursery near King's Lynn would take the children if they were Fifth Day Pentecostals. Miss Dashforth said they were, but she couldn't prove it to the nursery's satisfaction.

At half past four Harry got cot and baby organized at last and left Our Baby with Mrs Cropper.

At five Clement jammed up the w.c. with toilet paper and flooded the store of National Dried Milk.

At five-five we moved to 48 Seed Villas.

At half past five County Hall said it had reserved three beds in a nursery near Penzance and could we fix the children up overnight. Miss Dashforth said no. County Hall said oh, well, it was going home now, cheerio, then. Miss Dashforth said she was reporting the full facts to THE CHILDREN'S OFFICER. There was a freezing silence.

County Hall said grumpily well, it had found three nursery beds hadn't it, and surely just for one night – ? Miss Dashforth said would it put her through this minute. ... The line went dead.

At six County Hall said THE CHILDREN'S OFFICER says the children can go overnight to The Rookery.

At six-one Mr Mussel said oh no, Miss Dashforth, our establishment is seventy-seven beds and our strength is seventy-seven, we cannot take the babies, of course if the Children's Officer cares to take the matter up at National Joint Council level. ...

At six-thirty Anona was sick again, all down her decent second-hand woollies.

At six-fifty-five our neighbour Area Officer, Miss Van Tromps, rang unexpectedly and boomed that she'd heard we were stuck and she had a splendid foster-mother, a Mrs Manager, who would take anybody any time, black or white, the address was in the small village of Hansons Cross, and of course there were no buses, but ...

By seven, Miss Dashforth had ordered a taxi.

By half past eight the magnificent Mrs Manager had swept the children into lavender-scented beds and provided all of us and our taxi-driver with a supper of game-pie and cider. Mrs Manager explained that we would have to take the children to Penzance the following morning because she had three short-stays coming, and was already two over the quota.

At eleven I set my alarm clock for 5 a.m.

It had been agreed that Harry and I should take the little Crumps down to Penzance, as this would need two pairs of hands, and Miss Dashforth was already heavily engaged next day. We had to meet at six in the morning, taxi out to Hansons Cross and get the kids, taxi across to Church Deeping for the London train, and thus theoretically get to Paddington in time to catch the Cornish Riviera Express.

The first part of this journey went fairly smoothly because the children were sleepy. The second part wasn't too bad because the surroundings were novel and the children liked examining them. Our first trouble arose in the London Tube station when we were heading for the escalator. Harry was carrying Sabrina and two carrier-bags, I was carrying Anona and a suitcase, and Clement was gambolling about, barking. When he realized he had to go down the moving stairs he became rigid with terror and would not budge. Neither of us had a free hand. I had to manoeuvre behind him and fetch him a sharp biff with the end of the suitcase. He gave a sideways despairing plunge and got his foot trapped in a metal prong thing by the top of the staircase. Intending to wrench his leg free, I set down the suitcase, which soared off down the moving stairs and burst, scattering decent second-hand woollies among the feet of the throng. A man in an immaculate City suit, with a bowler, came up with a pair of those limp dangling leggings and said to me: 'Excuse me, sir, I believe these are yours.' A cross official came and released Clement, and then escorted us closely down the stairs while we collected the woollies; obviously he wanted us off the premises quick, before a major disaster took place. At the foot of the escalator we turned to thank him and the bottom fell out of one of the carrier bags.

Well, we caught the Cornish Riviera, though it was a near thing, and I had to come cantering up the platform with the tickets between my teeth and Anona bouncing about on my shoulders like an incompetent jockey. We all fell into a compartment where one thin lady was sitting; this thin lady looked very hard at the black baby and very hard at Harry and kept both under hard-faced observation until she rose to get out at the first stop, when she leant over to Harry and hissed: 'You *hussy!*'

Clement was our biggest handful all through that long day's journey; the two girls were comparatively passive. As soon as the train started to move out of Paddington I gave the boy a pile of comics. By the time we reached Royal Oak he appeared to have read them and lost interest. From then on he seemed to alternate between standing on his head on the seats, and lolling in the corner like an imbecile with one finger rammed half-way up his nose. At one point – some-where near the borders of Wiltshire – he suddenly stood up on the seat, rapped himself on the chest, yelled : 'They got me, fellers !' and died very slowly, collapsing on the seat and thence rolling on to the grimy floor. Unaccountably, this made Anona laugh and laugh and double up laughing, her face going scarlet. Clement was delighted. I have never met a child who thought that moderation was a virtue. Scream-ing 'Looka me look !' before each performance, Clement died slowly seventy-one times by my counting before we reached Devon. When at last, in the face of stony in-difference, he himself realized that the novelty had worn off, he fell back on having spit-races down the window and shouting out hysterical poems all about wee-wee and bums.

I much admired Harry's approach to all this : she had obviously got herself into the mental condition of a peasant woman setting out on an eight-day journey to Vladivostok, and simply sat there, hour after hour, in monumental endur-ance. I personally found myself smoking a great deal and every hour or so walking up and down the corridor, mutter-ing.

At long, long last we reached Penzance and drove out to the nursery and Clement became very subdued – of course, he was very tired. We got to the place and a harassed and peremptory Matron relieved us of the children, who imme-diately began to scream and wail; our last glimpse of them was of three tear-stained faces swiftly disappearing through the great portals, three pairs of hands stretched out to us as if we were Mum and Dad.

In silence Harry and I walked down to the water front and gazed at the gloomy sea. We didn't seem to have much to say to each other. After a long quietness, Harry gave a sigh and said : 'Oh, lor, dear mother, is it worth it ?'

'Tired ?' I said.

'M'm. And all that's happened. Another family bust up, gone to pieces. Depressing, isn't it ?'

'Oh, don't get depressed, Harry,' I said. 'I expect those kids are washed and fed and perfectly happy already.'

'It's not now that depresses me, it's the awful years that lie ahead of them.'

'Good gracious, they'll be properly looked after, won't they?'

'Yes, yes,' said Harry, impatiently tapping her foot. 'Everybody will be very kind. It's not that the years ahead will be harsh; it's that they'll be totally incomprehensible. Oh, dear, I always find it so pathetic, to see another batch of children loaded on to a sort of maniac Dodgems.'

I put my hand over hers.

'Cheer up, love,' I said. 'You're imagining they've got minds as sensitive as yours, but I'm sure they're a jolly tough lot really. I shouldn't think they'll come to much harm. Stop getting worked up over someone else's kids.'

'It's my job to, isn't it?'

'Oh, Harry, Harry, you're a pretty girl – you shouldn't have to be driving yourself round the bend over a lot of Crumps. You should be enjoying kids of your own.'

She took her hand away quickly.

'For a graduate in psychology, Charles,' she said, 'you are damned insensitive, aren't you?'

And she gazed out over the sullen sea while her eyes slowly filled with tears.

7

'FOR God's sake,' cried Miss Dashforth, slamming the phone back in its cradle, 'this cannot go on!'

She slumped down in her chair, lit a fresh cigarette, ran her fingers through her hair and gazed with unseeing eyes at her bowl of anemones. But this sort of explosive behaviour was a daily occurrence with her nowadays, and I looked up from the report I was writing only because I wanted to check the date. It was with a faint click of interest that I realized that exactly a year before, I had appeared before the Committee and been appointed to this crazy job.

Nineteen forty-nine was slowly unfolding itself: clothes rationing finished and somebody or other was photographed tearing up those horrid little books. The clocks went forward, and front gardens which I had hitherto only known as smudges in the darkness were revealed to me as full of tulips and grape hyacinths. The rows of flowering municipal cherries suddenly turned pink all along Soil Way. Lamp-lit culs-de-sac and closes, which all winter through had looked romantically shadowy, emerged in summer light bleary and full of old Woodbine packets. I experienced my first unexpected catch of breath on suddenly seeing industrial Westburn under the beams of a late evening sun, when a thousand roofs turn into a golden river. The days grew warmer. Miss Dashforth went for a week's leave but only after much fidgeting and dithering; I think she really wanted someone at County Hall to tell her she couldn't possibly go on leave, she was quite indispensable. However, no one did, so she went off to the Gower Peninsula in a huff.

Her holiday did her good, there was no doubt, for she came back like a spring that's been dropped on a pavement; she bounced through each day, and even when she stood still she balanced on the balls of her feet as if preparing to leap to the ceiling. In this ebullient mood, when she was apparently ready to sweep the entire juvenile population of Westburn off the streets and into Care, she came slap-bang into conflict with what we called the Vacancy Situation.

When she and I, and scores like us, came into this service, we had come to bring a New Deal to what were then known as Deprived Children. What had simply never come into our reckoning was that children were getting deprived faster than we could bring the New Deal to them. We had not expected children to be coming into Care in such numbers. We had not expected the post-war restlessness and austerity and the gross housing shortage. We had not expected magistrates to realize that they had a new thing they could do, and to start committing children to the care of the authority in ever-increasing numbers – Egbert had been one of these, but there were many others, more wildly unsuitable than he was. So, far from our tearing down the overcrowed barrack Homes, and giving the children more individual attention, we were working sixty hours a week and upwards only to perpetuate the crowd and give less attention than ever; and although our trip to Penzance with the Crumps was the longest I ever made, it was very difficult to find accommodation for all the children who were pressing to come in.

Of course, this wasn't altogether a bad thing. A lot of families who came along with a hard luck story and expected the State to rear children for free, and who were told that the best that could be done was for them to take their kids a hundred miles to a Catholic Convent, turned round and made their own perfectly satisfactory arrangements without bothering us further. But it could work the other way, too, and that was what was upsetting Miss Dashforth. The day before she had had to tell a mother who was very harassed and sick that no vacancy could be guaranteed for the daughter. The woman had become hysterical and was now in Six Counties, and the little girl had been taken in by a most unsavoury baby-farmer in Hags Heath.

'No,' said Dashforth, struggling upright in her chair again, 'we can't go on like this; we've got to have more accommodation available. The Government won't allow us to build more Children's Homes, so we'll have to concentrate on foster-homes. If we can get more foster-homes for the short-stay kids, Charles, and if we can get some of those old-established children out of The Rookery and into foster-homes, we shall have a bit more room for manoeuvre all round.'

'O.K.,' I said. 'First catch your hare . . .'

'I know, I know,' she said. 'We'll have a terrific appeal launched to find new foster-mothers, give plenty of publicity to it, and we'll get more homes, I'm sure. After all, Charles, you know, boarding-out is not only the most practicable form of care, but it's also the cheapest and it's far and away the best way of looking after these children. People will flock forward once they learn of the need.'

'Well, I dunno,' I said. 'I can't see people flocking forward to take Sidney Smee, or Herbie Slythe, or half a dozen others I know.'

'Oh, well, they're institutionalized,' said Miss Dashforth, 'they weren't boarded out soon enough. Get the right child in the right foster-home at the right time, and we shall find we have no problems left to tackle.'

So with these stirring words we set to work. Miss Dashforth stumped the whole area addressing Mothers' Unions, Townswomen's Guilds, Parent-Teacher Associations and so on; Harry concentrated on recruiting short-stay foster-mothers, that is, women who would take a succession of young children for periods of up to three weeks; while I was deputed to discuss with the staff all the children in the four Homes in our area, namely, The Rookery, Tots' Glade, Merrythought, and Slag Dell. These discussions were with a view to finding out how many children were suitable for boarding out.

The Homes staff were not in the least enthusiastic. Miss Tooth at Merrythought said : 'Well, really, Mr Mole, I must point out that I was appointed to run this Home as a cosy family; and now you come along and want to break it all up, that's being rather cruel to the wee ones, isn't it?'

Mrs Meredith, Matron of the Slag Dell Nursery, said: 'I cannot understand, Mr – Er – why you wish to entrust the care and welfare of our children to *amateurs*.'

Miss Heaton, at Tots' Glade, said: 'Oh, what a dull idea, Charles – I may call you Charles, mayn't I? Tell me, Charles, are you married?'

Mr Mussel said: 'All I can say, Maule, is that I'm glad I'm getting out in time. The whole service is going rotten – rotten to the core. D'you know, Maule, I've got a lad in here now – father earns fourteen pounds a week, fourteen pounds, Maule, twice what I get – dumped in here so that mother can go to work, too! Iniquitous. The old style Relieving Officer would never have allowed such a thing, it's only you people with your soft ideas.'

'Well, I –'

'And there's another – that Paddy O'Hooligan – six foot tall, armed to the teeth, he doesn't want a Children's Home, Maule, he needs a Reformatory of the most traditional type. He's a constant anxiety to us, and there's no need for it, it's all because of your new-fangled ideas.'

'Well, that's what I'm getting at, Mr Mussel,' I said. 'Perhaps something can be done to reduce your frightening responsibilities if we can get some of these children out.'

'Get them *out*, Mr Maule? Get them *out*? Are you implying that this establishment is a sort of iron cage in which the children have somehow become trapped? This is a home, Mr Maule, the only home many of them have known; they treat it as their home, and come in and out as they please.'

'No, no, Mr Mussel,' I said. 'I'm sure you need take no offence, I was thinking in terms of this new concept of boarding *out*, rather than boarding *in*.'

'New concept? Ha!' barked Mr Mussel contemptuously. 'Are you aware, Maule, that boarding out was encouraged by statute two hundred years ago? Have you read the history of the Foundling Hospital, hey? Have you ever heard of the old Waifs and Strays Society, who went in for Reception Homes and boarding out last century, h'm? New idea, tchah! It's all been done before, Maule; I've seen it all before, and I've seen it fail.'

Dealing with Mr Mussel, I realized, must be like dealing with some Chinese mandarin – you had to watch out all the time for Face. Now, that he'd scored off me and my education ('I'm untrained myself and all the better for it'), he got quite affable.

'I can't see what you expect to gain from boarding children out in foster-homes,' said Mr Mussel. 'Adoption, yes, I can see that provides an unfortunate child with a completely fresh start, but fostering is neither one thing nor another.'

'Well, it gives him his own backyard to scratch round in doesn't it, and an address to bring his friends to, and a life where people don't go on treating him as pitiful,' I said. 'I should have thought those things, and a lot of individual attention and affection, would give a child a much greater sense of security than he'd have in a Home.'

'Rubbish, Maule, rubbish. No child gets security by being plunged into some family who have only taken him for money. If people really love children, why do they ask for payment at all? The child's entire life depends on whether he can butter them up enough to stay there. Pooh! It's better here. We can't give the individual affection, but at least our children know where they are; all the time they're growing up they get the complete security of order and routine, and then they're old enough to start out on their own.'

'Well, really, Mr Mussel, you can't honestly think they're old enough to start out on their own at *fifteen*. Could you do it? I couldn't. And poor old Sidney Smee can't.'

There had been another fracas at the Scatterbreads'. On my last visit the foster-mother had met me with a long face.

'Oh, dear, Mrs Scatterbread, what has he done now?'

'Well, really, sir, it's comical in its way, I s'pose. Y'see, sir, Mr Scatterbread thought it'd help Sidney if 'e 'ad an interest, y'see, so he got Sidney to join the cricket club.

Well, what we dint know, sir, was that the cricket club holds their annual dinner soon after Easter, so o' course, as a new member, Sid gets an invite, an' 'e can take a friend along too, so 'e goes wiv Charlie Spanner from Number 27, Charlie's a good steady lad. Well, sir, we did think a cricket club dinner would be a respectable sort of function, but it seems that as soon as the dinner and the speeches is over, these fellers get to drinkin' an' o' course they're all over Sid, saying come on, Siddy lad, sup up, an' fillin' 'is glass up, course it was only meant in fun, but poor ole Sid 'e don't know when to say No. Comes chuckin' out time, Sid goes out in the cold night air and wallop! 'e's flat on 'is face. Well ...' (Mrs Scatterbread took a deep breath, her little monkey face working as she relived the emotions of that night.) '... Well, Charlie got 'im 'ome some'ow, an' we'd left the door for 'im, an' o' course I was awake in me bed when these two comes in, I could 'ear 'em gigglin' an' swearin', well, then Sid says 'e's not goin' upstairs in case 'e falls down again, 'e's goin' to sleep on the settee. Charlie says all right, get undressed, then, an' 'e 'elps Sid get all 'is clothes off an' then 'e wraps 'im up in me 'earth-rug an goes 'ome. Next minute there's a shriekin' an' a carry-on an' 'is lordship's out in the middle of the street with no clothes on, no clothes at all, Mr Mole, shoutin' come back to me, Charlie, come back, come back! Well, my 'eart nearly failed me, all the way down the street I could 'ear windows bangin' open, and the moonlight full on 'im, full on 'im.'

'My word, Mrs Scatterbread,' I said, unbating my breath, 'how awful for you!'

'Ooh, I nearly died, well: Mr Scatterbread 'ad to go out and fetch 'im in an' once 'e was in bed o' course 'e just c'lapsed an' we 'eard no more of 'im till eleven o'clock next mornin', well, we 'eard a noise, so our Val goes up an' there 'e is, sittin' up in bed strummin' on 'is 'otwater bottle as though it was a banjo an' singin' "Music, Music, Music!" An' 'e calls Val 'is darlin' love an' asks 'er to do the dance of the seven veils for 'im, well, Mr Mole, I mean the child's only 'leven, it's 'er mind I worry about. Well, just at that moment, just at that very moment, there's a knock on the door an' in comes Mr Bland!'

'Ha!' I said involuntarily, picturing the appearance amid the chaos of that calm, immaculate man.

'Well, what was I to do? I couldn't give pore ole Sid away, although I know I'm s'posed to tell the probation officer everythin', but anyway, I got Mr Bland in the back room an' I talks an' talks to 'im about the weather, I believe Mr Bland thought I'd gone mad, anyway, in the end o' course 'e says, excuse me, 'e says, Mrs Scatterbread, 'e says, but 'ow's Sidney? So I says, well, Mr Bland, I says, if you reely want to know, Mr Bland, I says, 'e's upstairs blind drunk. Cor, d'you know, Mr Bland was that took aback 'is moustache nearly come off in 'is 'and.'

I bet so too, I thought. Good old Mrs Scatterbread for rallying round in a crisis, but the situation wasn't all that laughable. Probationers promise to be of good behaviour and in consideration of the promise the magistrates withhold punishment for the offence. Now Sidney had broken the promise with a bout of juvenile drunkenness, and innocent though it may have been, Mr Bland couldn't go on for ever telling the magistrates that Sidney's behaviour was satisfactory. Besides, to make matters worse, Sidney had been overcome with shame when he finally recovered from the Cricket Club Dinner, had felt unable to face his workmates, and rather than face them had packed his job in. Mr Clench, the Youth Employment Man, was trying to get him a new job, but Mr Bland was going to keep a much sharper eye on young Sidney in future; and so was I.

'So you see,' I said to Mr Mussel, as I finished this recital, 'that a kid of fifteen's got to adjust himself to a home and a job all at the same time, and deal with difficulties in both, and I think it's too much for a kid of that age. Much better to get him settled in his home first, a year or two before he has to start in his first job; then he can deal with one problem at a time.'

'Oh, well,' said Mr Mussel, 'another month, and I shall be away out of this madhouse. You decide for yourself,

Maule, it's your responsibility, but if you're thinking of boarding out twelve or thirteen-year-olds, will you inform me where you're going to get 'em from?'

'But surely you've got quite a number who've been here for years?'

'I have, I have. And why d'you think they've been here for years? For a very good reason, in every case. Let's just go through my register. Paddy O'Hooligan – well, it'd be a saint who took in that roughneck. The Nimmo brothers – charming boys, delightful boys, but you put them in a foster-home, and their father will be up straight away to wreck it for you. Willy Mulligan – nice lad, but he wets his bed every night, who'd put up with that? Dennis the Menace, alias Dennis Fogg; he's always wet, too. Herbie Slythe, he's fifteen next month, you've got to do something about him anyway – he wants to work in a hotel, by the way, that's his latest idea. Little Donald, he's set his heart on the Navy, he won't look at a foster-home. The Winch twins – they're going home next month when father returns from his honeymoon. Frank Flash, committed by the Juvenile Court for indecent asault on a small girl – would you like to let him loose on a family? Animoto Unikuwu – the Children's Officer says his foster-parents must be of the Ifni or Kyuwo religion, I'm sure you have plenty of them in Westburn. Egbert Crump, you know him – how about Egbert?'

Yes, well, how about Egbert?

Nothing much had happened on the Crump front over the past few months. Mrs Crump was still missing, though she had been rumoured at different times to be in Widnes, Ryde, and Canvey Island. Mr Crump was also missing, but he had been seen one night when he unexpectedly turned up in the Casual Ward at Stark House. (At least, it used to be called the Casual Ward, but it had lately been rechristened the Wayfarers' Reception Centre.)

The three little uns were presumably settling down in Penzance; when there were vacancies we hoped to ship them home to Westburn again, but at that time it was rather a case of out sight, out of mind. Winston, I presumed, was happy in Tots' Glade, but the housemother there, Miss Heaton, was both big and lonely, and I preferred only to go when I had a witness with me.

Our Baby had been registered and christened; Bebe had decided to call it Bing, confiding to us that she didn't like the name much but she couldn't think of anything else. Mrs Cropper had found Bing to be a reasonably intelligent baby, as far as anyone could see, who flourished with good care and had, therefore, just recently been placed for adoption.

Bebe herself had been taken in hand by the Moral Welfare Worker, who had put her in a simple, protected sort of job, living in as a resident domestic servant in a prep school near Durmston. The pink-haired Gloria had at first gone into a rather dreadful lodging house with an usherette friend of hers, and then, momentarily, into a Girls' Hostel, but for the past month she had been with one of Miss Dashforth's old war-horse foster-mothers. Her hair was still pink, but it was going browner at the roots and she even talked vaguely of joining a Youth Club. Miss Dashforth confided to me that she thought Gloria was 'stabilizing'.

So the Crump family had scattered pretty thoroughly all over the map, except for the three here at The Rookery – Egbert, Myrna, and Cary.

'What about Myrna and Cary?' I asked. 'I mean, if I do find a home for Egbert, will it matter parting him from them?'

'I do not myself think it is ever a good plan to separate brothers and sisters,' intoned Mr Mussel sanctimoniously. 'But you won't find anyone to take three Crumps, and actually Myrna and Cary seem much more attached to each other than to Egbert, and Egbert has very little to do with them. If you happened to be walking round and looking at the children in here, Maule, you would never take those three to be sister and brothers. Different fathers, I suppose.'

'H'm. Oh, well, first I'll try and find foster-parents, and then we'll have another chat,' I said.

As Mr Mussel was showing me out, a dark boy with a

lop-sided face came furtively up the path carrying a bulging sack.

'Ah, inside, Herbie!' stated Mr Mussel. 'Inside and get your bath, lad! That,' he added, as the boy gave a cautious smile and disappeared indoors, 'that is our wandering junk-man, Herbie Slythe; an absolute genius that boy has for dealing in salvage, goodness knows what he has in his sack, scrap metal probably. Yes, don't forget, Maule, he wants hotel work. Good night.'

As the great brassbound door clashed shut behind me, I began pondering about Egbert. I thought it was probably right to try and find a foster-home for him. His own home had obviously disappeared – in fact, the rooms in The Rat Yard now held a nervous Indian family called Civilengineer; he had settled in The Rookery quite well and seemed quiet and easily manageable, and with some individual attention and training, I thought he could be made into a pretty use-ful sort of lad. Certainly I couldn't see what else would offer such good prospects for him in the long run, that is if I could find the right sort of people.

'The right child in the right home at the right time!' I murmured to myself, as a kind of magic rune.

And so in that week's edition of the Westburn *Times-Advertiser* I put the following advertisement:

CAN YOU HELP JOE? If you have a kind heart and a spare room, think of poor Joe, friendless and alone in an Institution when he might be enjoying the loving comradeship of foster-parents. For further particulars, apply to the Area Children's Officer. . . .

By Monday morning's post I received three letters. The first was from Mr Mussel, and even the heading on the paper seemed to have a baleful glare. This letter registered 'horror' and the gravest disapprobation' of 'the ringing slight' afforded to 'a myriad devoted residential admini-strators' by my 'disastrous and, it is to be hoped, unthink-ing' choice of words in the advertisement, which would give the public an erroneous impression that 'in these enlightened times' it was possible to be friendless in a Children's Home, copy to THE CHILDREN'S OFFICER.

The second letter was from Mrs Bloat.

The third was from Mr and Mrs Indwell.

8

MRS BLOAT'S offer of a foster-home had been sent from a house in what the humorous inhabitants of Westburn call Lavender Walk, though the correct name of the alley is The Stifling. It is an odorous and repulsive neighbourhood, an old part of the town in which wooden houses lean out over the Gleeze, where it loiters between scummy piling. This was obviously not a promising venue for the boarding out of Egbert. I sent an acknowledgement to Mrs Bloat and said her letter was receiving attention.

Mr Mussel's letter I put on the end of my table meaning to answer it later. Sometime during the following autumn it fell down behind the cupboard, where to the best of my knowledge it still remains.

The third letter, from Mr and Mrs Indwell, ran as follows:

Dear Sir/Madam,

Ref your advert in the Westburn *Times-Advertiser* of Saturday's date, 'Can you Help Joe?' Hubby and I are interested. We are clean-living, respectable folk. We are very fond of children, but have none of our own. I am sure we have everything here a boy could want, car, wireless, big garden, and he would have his own room and live in like one of us, so hoping you can oblige us with further particulars.

Yours very truly,
Mr and Mrs S. W. G. Indwell

The address was 'Sidanelse', Shakespeare Walk, Alderman Scrowpe Garden Suburb.

Well, no queues of citizens all clamouring to offer a home for Egbert formed outside the office that day, and in fact no other reply was received to my advertisement; so the first step was to go and see the Indwells and investigate their home circumstances.

'Sidanelse' was the semi-detached half of a pair of homes which together presented a façade like a great triangle full of black and white wood. As I opened the gate, the downstairs curtains twitched anxiously.

Mrs Indwell greeted me very prettily, with a sort of roguishly demure air, like a young bride advertising her home for the furniture cream people. This did not go too well with the fleshy jaws and powder packed in creases round her anxious eyes. Her husband was a cynical, small, bald man with a dark moustache. We all sat down on the rexine three-piece and eyed each other.

'Well,' I said, cheerily, 'it's very nice of you to offer a home for this lad of mine.'

'Not at all, not at all,' murmured Mrs Indwell. 'When would you bring him?'

'Oh, good gracious, I can't make any definite arrangement yet,' I began.

'You mean we're not good enough, there's something wrong with Our Home?'

'No, no,' I said, 'no, no, it's just that I have to make some preliminary investigations and so on, fill up a form, you know, typical red-tape and all that!'

'Pah!' said Mr Indwell in a voice that contemptuously put in their place generations of civil servants. He reached for his evening paper and disappeared behind it, but for all that he maintained a very sharp, if covert, interest in me.

'Oh, but surely, is it necessary in our case?' said Mrs Indwell. 'We're people of standing, after all, I mean, we know Colonel Plimm – you know Colonel Plimm, I mean you've 'eard of 'im? – and as for Our Home, well, you can see for yourself . . .'

'Oh, yes, indeed, Mrs Indwell, very lovely,' I assured her earnestly. 'But unfortunately, you see, well, this is the law, you see, there is an Act of Parliament which requires foster-parents to have to answer certain questions. . . .'

'First I've heard of it,' muttered the evening paper.

'. . . and secondly, I have to think of the lad himself, you

87

know he's got no one else to look after his interests, and I have to think of your feelings too. I'm sure you've got a lovely home, Mrs Indwell, I can see that, but is it right for this particular lad? And if it's not right, it'll be a terrible disappointment for you, won't it, not to mention the disappointment to Egbert.'

'Joe!' said the evening paper accusingly.

'I mean Joe,' I said.

'You said Hegbert,' said Mrs Indwell.

I said patiently: 'The boy I'm particularly interested in is called Egbert, but I called him Joe in the advertisement so as not to identify him and cause him embarrassment.'

They were both regarding me, I felt, as though I were a professor of some incomprehensible potty subject, like Early Wheels. At length Mrs Indwell said 'H'm,' rather grudgingly, 'well, all right, what would you care to know?'

'I think that before I start asking a lot of personal questions,' I said, 'I'd like to tell you something about this boy and see if you are really interested in having a lad like that, otherwise there's not much point in the questions.'

Nodding in agreement, Mrs Indwell said: 'Is he a nice boy?'

'Well, er –' I pondered a bit; was he? 'Yes, he is *basically* a very nice boy,' I said safely. 'A bit wild at times, of course, but what boy isn't?'

'Has he been in trouble with the police?' asked the evening paper.

'Yes, he has appeared once in court, on a very minor charge, when he was *much* younger,' I said.

'Pah!' said Mr Indwell. 'There you are, Else, he's one of these young thugs, what did I tell you?'

'You're not keen on trying to redeem a lad like that who only needs affectionate training to make good in life?' I asked him.

'Me? Oh, don't ask *me*. I leave all this sort of thing to my wife. She may want to take him on, why not ask her?' And Mr Indwell retired once more behind the evening paper.

His wife was looking from one of us to the other with a look of pained indecision, like a Pekinese forced to choose between liver and steak.

'Well, I don't know,' she mourned. ' 'E's an orphan, isn't 'e?'

'As good as, as good as,' I assured her. 'He has got parents, actually, but we don't know where they are, and they've been missing for some time.'

'Oh, but they might turn up any moment and snatch him away from us!'

'I doubt it, Mrs Indwell,' I said. 'They're not married, and I think they're both living with new partners, and I don't think either of them has much interest in any of the eleven children.'

Mrs Indwell seemed just to have detected an unpleasant smell.

'Have you any little girls, about three, without any parents at all?'

'No,' I said.

There was a thoughtful pause. Mrs Indwell was stroking the brown velvet cushions with the back of her hand.

'You see, Mrs Indwell, Egbert is a lad who has never had a chance,' I said, using the catch in the voice I had been practising ever since we started the boarding-out campaign. 'He's what you might call the victim of circumstances; so long as he was with those dreadful people, his parents, he would never have gone straight and made good. If he can find real love and security now, he may win through. Will you give him the chance to do his best?'

A tear, loaded with face-powder, rolled slowly along the side of Mrs Indwell's nose. The evening paper cleared its throat uneasily. I was surprised; I thought I'd been too beastly mawkish altogether.

'And, of course, Mrs Indwell,' I added, 'you know, I'm not asking you to take a pig in a poke. I'll arrange for you to meet the lad first, and perhaps he could come here to tea with you so that you could have a look at him and see if he would fit in, and give him a chance to get to know you beforehand, you see, and there would be absolutely no obligation on you.'

'Oh, well, then, in that case . . .'

'Good,' I said, with alacrity, whipping out the Foster-Parents' Particulars form and feeling exactly like a washing-machine salesman who has just produced the hire purchase agreement. 'Now these tiresome old questions of mine! Your full name, Mrs Indwell?'

'Elsie Alexandra Indwell.'

'And your age?'

'Thirty-six – about.'

'And do you go to work, Mrs Indwell?'

'Certainly not. House duties, you put down there.'

'Right-ho,' I said, drawing a line through the wages space. 'Now, Mr Indwell. . . ?'

'Sidney Webster Garth Indwell.'

'And your age?'

'Forty- one.'

'And your profession?'

'Business executive.' (He was actually, I found later, Chief Clerk in the processed cheese division of Plimm's Wholesale Grocery.)

'And your income?'

The evening paper had now been completely lowered. His intent little glance scuttled across to his wife and scuttled back to me again.

'Is that necessary?'

'Just a rough idea, Mr Indwell . . .'

'Ah, well, a rough figure – well, say, roughly, three-fifty per annum.' And again his eyes made a quick check on his wife; but it seemed all right, she wasn't registering any-thing.

We got through the next bit of the form quite smoothly – the bit about the number of rooms and distance from school and does the house have main sanitation, and then we came to 'Reasons for taking a foster-child'. Not much space had been left for an answer here: I usually put either 'money' or 'not money'.

'Well, you see, Mr – Er – I'm not religious, not like some of these so-called religious women who go to church on Sundays, but do the dirty on you the other six days of the week, I mean to my mind religion's more than Church, I was forced to go to Church when I was little and it's made me bitter, but I'm as religious as the best of 'em, I always listen to Sunday Half Hour on the B.B.C. and what I say is, religion is doing good to people, and that's why I want the child, I mean I want to do good to it.'

I put down 'not money'. Under religion I put 'C.E.'

'Now, I have to take up three references,' I said. 'If you could give me names and addresses?'

'You gonna write to them?' asked Mr Indwell, suspiciously.

'Yes,' I said soothingly, 'just a short note explaining what you are thinking of doing and asking if a child would be properly looked after in your home. I'm afraid it's a regulation, and we have to do it.'

'First I've heard of it,' sniffed Mr Indwell. We were ages wrangling about who to give us referees; they started by saying Colonel Plimm and Miss Wepys, but I said I wanted people who knew their home life and how they got on together, was there a neighbour who would know? They were horrified at the thought of letting anything leak out to a neighbour, of all people. Mrs Indwell asked if her mother would do as a reference; I said no, not family. In the end we settled on Mr Indwell's old friend Don, Mrs Indwell's old friend Claire, and the doctor.

After that I had to do my statutory tour of the house, particularly inspecting Where Child Would Sleep and Is Bedding Adequate? Mrs Indwell led the way and as we went upstairs I saw her husband pick up his paper again and turn on Radio Luxemburg. We went first into the small back room Egbert might inhabit, and I must say it was most cheerful and attractive: when I saw the other rooms I realized that they hadn't bothered much about this one, that was its secret. Their own bedroom was very dark, lots of netting over the windows and heavy pink curtains and a lot of satin drapes, and all the furniture and everything having a sinister veiled appearance. I was curious about this emotional hothouse, so instead of retreating obsequiously from it, I walked boldly in and said: 'Oh, you have a lovely view from here, Mrs Indwell!' Actually, I could see half a silver birch and a corner of the next-door Vauxhall.

'Yes.'

'You like living up here?'

'Oh, yes. It's very select, you know, and we find it 'as tone, if you know what I mean.'

'You moved up just before the war?'

'No, we came here in 1940, we was fortunate really, old Mr Crow panicked and the place was going dirt cheap, of course at that time property was a poor investment, wasn't it?'

'Yes. And you never had any children, Mrs Indwell?'

There was a pause. Then she said: 'That's no business of yours, young man. Do you want to see the bathroom?'

After she'd shown me that, and we were starting downstairs again, she suddenly said: 'Course, I'm the surviving one of twins, you know.'

I said: 'Really?' in an interested voice, but she didn't say any more, and I didn't understand, anyway. I thanked her very much for putting up with my questions, and told her I would now take up the references and come and see her again to arrange a meeting between themselves and Egbert, and then I bade good night to Mr Indwell, getting a discourteous grunt in reply, and so eventually I took myself off down the twilit avenues, all full of dog-exercisers.

Next morning, at the office, Harry told me that a Mrs Bloat had called to see me while I'd been out. I sent a note saying I was absolutely rushed off my feet, but would certainly call on her soon, not to worry meanwhile.

I would probably not have boarded Egbert out with the Indwells had it not been for another boy called Neville Chamberlain. Neville had actually hit the headlines of the national Press, no less, by running away from home and going to an American air base in East Anglia and begging for a lift to Kentucky, as he was so unhappy at home. This story had aroused the professional interest of two British tabloids, four American tabloids and Miss Perrett, the probation officer, who had investigated the case and had finally advised the parents to bring the boy to Court as being beyond their control. She hoped that Neville would then be placed in the care of our Department. This was due to happen in about two weeks' time, and with the eyes of at least six sensational newspapers upon us, we felt we had to have a place for the boy good and ready. There wasn't one. Creakings and shiftings of beds occurred through the whole structure of the Department, but there wouldn't be a bed for Neville unless I got a move on, shifted Egbert and made a space in The Rookery. I got a move on.

The references on the Indwells were satisfactory. Don said: 'They are wonderful persons, honest and clean living'; Claire said: 'They keep a good table, and what more would a child want?'; and the doctor said 'Yes'. There wasn't anything to object to in them, not to *object* to, I muttered to myself. I had a talk to Egbert and he seemed quite interested in the idea, though whether he really ever thought of it as affecting him personally I am inclined to doubt. Anyway, a week later I took him up to 'Sidanelse' for tea and let him stay the week-end there. I must say Mrs Indwell welcomed him quite nicely; she had got a special tea ready, luncheon meat and those infinitesimal jellies served in little wax-paper moulds. It all looked very gay; Egbert munched his way affably through it, and I chatted to Mrs Indwell about the quality of coal and the price of butter, and when Mr Indwell came in from work he made some remark about Denis Compton which Egbert seemed to appreciate, so it all started very well, and when I left Egbert, in his grey jersey and very short haircut, was settling down to hear Radio Luxemburg.

I collected him on the Sunday afternoon and while he was getting his things together, I asked Mrs Indwell how she had found him.

'Oh, 'e's a nice boy, isn't 'e Sid?' she said, in a rather surprised voice. 'Oh, we liked him, yes.'

'He's a boy,' said her husband non-committally.

Egbert seemed to have had a good time.

'Did you like the people, Egbert?' I asked, in the trolley-bus, going back.

'Yer.'

'Did you do anything special?'

' 'Elped Uncle wiv 'is car on Sat'day. Went aht to Ded-brough on Sunday to Aunt Else's grandad.'

'Aunt and Uncle,' I thought, 'good.'

'Well, Egbert, do you think you'd like to go and live with those people?'

'Yer.'

'I mean you'd have to be a good boy, you know.'

'Yer.'

'Why do you want to go there, Egbert?'

' 'Cos I can't stand that bleedin' Rookery no longer.'

Well, well, I thought, so much for your theories of security, Mussel, old man, and mentally I raised two fingers to him.

So it came about that a few days later, and one day before Neville Chamberlain was due in, Egbert left The Rookery and went to live with the Indwells, taking with him two of everything, his medical card, identity card and ration book, two-and-sixpence savings, a Form of Agreement for Foster-Parents with clothing listed on the back, and a small whistle he had got from a Christmas cracker.

When I got back to the office, Harry said that Mrs Bloat had called again.

'Oh, blow these Bloats!' I said. 'They can't possibly make acceptable foster-parents, how can I put them off without hurting their feelings?'

Harry said: 'Well, why not tell them about some fictitious boy who is quite repulsive, and say that's all you've got? Then they'll withdraw disgusted, and the onus won't be on you.'

'Good idea,' I said, 'I'll get that over and done with.'

So I went down to Lavender Walk; it was a dampish evening and I was aware of the fungi clustered along the sides of the houses. There was a place down there where they converted garbage into pig-swill, and the air was heavy with the odour of the monstrous soup.

I groped my way into a yard full of dustbins, dockleaves and dog-mess. Several radios were blaring in my immediate neighbourhood, but since all the buildings looked like warehouses, I couldn't tell whereabouts to inquire for Mrs Bloat. Suddenly, however, a woman walked out on to a kind of landing high up on one warehouse and emptied a teapot over.

'Mrs Bloat?' I called.

'Oo?'

'Mrs Bloat?'

'Oh, she's down there. Yolande!' she shrieked.

A door was kicked open, right by my elbow, making me leap a yard, and there stood a very tall, smiling woman with one eye and two teeth, all yellow.

' 'Allo!' she cried. ' 'Allo! 'Allo! Come in, do, come in. 'Ave a cupper tea.'

And before I could stop her, she had picked up a tin mug from the newspaper-covered table, wiped it round with her thumb, filled it with tea from the blue enamel teapot, and topped it up with condensed milk.

'There y'are, 'ave a lovely cupper!' she said. 'Come about the boy, 'ave yer? When can I 'ave 'im?'

I took a deep and rather wobbly breath.

'Well, Mrs Bloat,' I said, 'the only boy I have is a boy who weighs fourteen stone and wets the bed every night and messes his pants twice a day and likes to interfere with little girls and pulls the wings off birds and has bad breath and pinches things from Woolworths, and blows his nose on his fingers and has piles.'

I only stopped because I had no more breath.

'Oh!' said Mrs Bloat, her one eye shining. 'Oh, poor little mite! Bring 'im along, I'll love 'im!'

9

WESTBURN does not offer many opportunities to the boy or girl who wants to make a career in the hotel business. There is the Imperial Station Hotel, which is very dark and sooty and covered with that brown marble that looks like glazed brawn; there is the Victoria, in the High Road, jammed in between MacFisheries and Freeman Hardy and Willis, with a difficult subterranean entry to the garage; there are a few roadhouse places, licensed restaurants really, like the Merrie Highwaymanne, on the Great Circular Road; and a few miles out past Slag End there's a gaunt and expensive country hotel called Cronk's. I tried all of these, but none of them wanted Herbert Slythe; so I went to see Mr Clench, the Youth Employment Man. Mr Clench was a small pale chap, with the habit of constantly licking his lips.

'The hotel profession? Why, yes, the best way to enter it is certainly to obtain first an Honours B.A. with a couple of languages, and then have a year or so in Switzerland.'

I said: 'I don't think Herbie is quite . . .'

'Or for the lad who's not *quite* so bright, there's a full-time course in cookery at several different Technical Colleges.'

I said: 'Herbie is probably not quite . . .'

'Or, of course, getting right down to *basics*, several of the bigger firms offer an apprenticeship with day release classes and the opportunity to specialize in cooking, waiting or management. For the lad who's keen to get on . . .'

I said: 'Look, Mr Clench, with years of training Herbert Slythe might just make the grade as a porter or boots; or he might just stay on washing up.'

'Oh,' said Mr Clench. He drummed lightly on his blotter. 'Have you tried the Victoria?'

'Yes,' I said, 'and Cronk's and the Imperial and the Highwaymanne – they don't want him.'

'H'm. Must he have hotel work, I mean I've got a job just been notified for an assistant car-washer at the garage, couldn't you persuade him to try for that?'

'No,' I said grumpily. Herbie had made up his mind. I felt I must press on for him, even though the Wandering Junkman was being rather tiresome. When we first started talking about jobs and lodgings, Herbie had nearly had hysterics; he hadn't fully realized that he would have to leave The Rookery where he had lived most of his life. He'd spent the next month chewing rhubarb leaves or lead and had managed to push a bead into his ear, anything to put off the evil day when he had to face the outside world. Getting over this stage, he said he wanted to join the para-troopers or else be a frogman. Having failed both on educa-tional grounds, he asked if he could be in charge of a Children's Home, and having been headed off that, he had hit on hotel work. Lodgings he simply would not face, and Mr Mussel – whose own bags, too, now stood packed in the hall – said that Herbie would only strip the valuables from any lodgings he entered, or break the foster-mother's heart, or seduce her daughter, or in some other way bring the Children's Department into disrepute. 'Better string along with his ideas, Maule, you'll get nowhere by opposing him,' said Mr Mussel soberly. So all this meant that Herbie must have a living-in job.

'Well, there's nothing in Westburn in that line,' said Mr Clench, licking his lips nervously and ruffling through a pack of job-cards. 'Canteen hand at Washington and Gru-decker – he'd have to live out. Boy to train as cat's-meat-maker – living out. Wedding cake designer, G.C.E. in Art essential, live out. Salvage operative at sausage factory, live out. No, I'm sorry, Mr Maule, I don't think I can help.'

'Couldn't you try another division?' I said. 'Or even

another county? Herbie's overdue already for a job, I must get him in somewhere.'

Mr Clench said rather curtly that he would ring up his colleagues: he never liked failing to fix anyone up in his own area, even if he had to chase them into something quite different from what they wanted to do. He retired to his own telephone and I settled down to a long wait and the study of a pamphlet on Army Rates of Pay (Revised).

After about an hour, Mr Clench said that his colleague in the southern division had a job to offer, that of vegetable hand and general factotum in the Rod and Gaff at Blethering. This was about eight miles away, a small town clustered at a road junction. I thanked Mr Clench very much and was about to set off when he said:

'Oh, by the way, I've had young Smee in to see me again.'

My heart sank.

'Oh, Lord, is he out of work again?'

'He was, I'm afraid. I'd fixed him up as a suspender-tester at the corset factory, but apparently he kept larking about, pinging people, and then a fortnight ago he went and pinged the Managing Director, gave him a bit of cheek, and got his cards on the spot.'

'Oh, gosh. What a fool youth. Have you fixed him up again?'

'Yes. I submitted him to United Gnomes as a moulder's assistant, and they've engaged him. He's terribly immature, Maule, isn't he?'

We agreed that he was indeed terribly immature, and I said I'd go and have a straight talk to Smee, and then I went off to take Herbie down to see the job at Blethering.

When I said where it was, Herbie collapsed in a heap on the floor, moaning: 'It's too far, it's too far!'

'Oh, nonsense, Herbie!' I snapped. 'It's eight miles and it's on a direct bus route and a direct train route, you can be there in a quarter of an hour by train or an hour if you run all the way.'

'It's not goin' there I worry about, it's comin' back!'

'For goodness' sake, the distance is exactly the same, from whichever direction you traverse it!'

'But it might be dark, comin' back!' moaned Herbie.

I clutched my thumbs.

'It's all right, Maule, it's all right,' said Mr Mussel, who, now that he was actually packing for his retirement, had become quite soothing in manner. 'This is a terrific upheaval for Herbie, you know, after his sheltered life, eight miles must seem like eight hundred to him. We must reason with him, Maule.'

We reasoned with him for an hour and a half: that is to say, we told him over and over again that if he wanted hotel work he'd have to go to Blethering, and if he wanted to stay in Westburn he couldn't do hotel work. In the end, rather pale-faced, he came with me to Blethering by bus. We were there in twenty minutes.

The Rod and Gaff was a very unpretentious-looking Victorian sort of hotel on the junction of two trunk roads; for some unknown reason it had become popular enough with moneyed people to have developed an unusually good cuisine, so that now, in a cramped parlour-dining-room, quite sumptuous meals were served.

'You see, my staff are high-class men,' explained Mr Walton, the Manager, 'artistes in their own line, you might say. I need a lad to do all the rough work for them, peeling potatoes, washing up their saucepans, running errands – rough work, I know, but a keen lad can learn a lot from just watching the chefs, and after a year or so I could probably promote him to, say, stillroom boy or vegetable cook.'

I looked at Herbie, standing forlorn with his lopsided face amid the black and gold of the entrance hall, and decided that even this lofty post would be beyond him.

'Well, Herbie!' I cheerily cried. 'What a wonderful opportunity for you!'

'Yer,' he muttered unhappily.

We saw the little bedroom in an attic which he would occupy, and we saw the chef, a man with scarlet cheeks and orange hair, and his assistant, a man with blue cheeks and black hair, and his assistant, a man with pink cheeks and pretty golden curls. Afterwards, Mr Walton said in a kind voice: 'Well, Herbie, d'you think you'll like working here?'

'It's a long way from Westburn,' muttered Herbie.

'Oh, come, come, it's not far,' smiled Mr Walton. 'And anyway you'll settle down with us and be happy, I'm sure. I'll keep an eye on him, Mr Maule, don't you worry about him!'

It was finally agreed that Herbie should move in on the following Friday, so as to be ready to help with the week-end rush, and that I should come and see him on his day off, which would fall a few days after that, to show him that his friends were near at hand, and that it really wasn't far from Westburn. Of all this, Herbie seemed to remain unconvinced.

I left him at The Rookery, and went on to see Sidney. Sidney, these last few months, had blossomed, in a rather fungoid way; he was no longer the pale, quiet little boy who had thrown the brick through the window; he was a bit of a gay blade in his bright silver-and-crimson tie, thick-soled shoes, and long lank hair.

'I reckon 'e's gotta young lady!' giggled Mrs Scatterbread. 'Orf 'e goes of an evening, up over the Rec, all smarmed up!'

'Like a dog's dinner,' grunted Mr Scatterbread. 'Honest, Mr Mole, you ain't never seen the like of 'im with 'is 'air-cream – puts 'is 'ole flippin' 'and in the jar, scoops out a great 'andful and lobs it on 'is 'air so it starts running down 'is chops like bacon fat, cor, turns you up 'e does, sits down to tea with 'is face all running down with grease, cor.'

The subject of this nauseous anecdote came in at that moment, so the Scatterbreads withdrew and left him to me.

'Well, Sidney,' I said. 'You lost your job at the corset factory.'

'Yer.'

'Now look here, Sidney –'

'Smoke ?' he said, pulling out a long and heavy cigarette-case.

'No, thank you. Now, look here, Sidney –'

'Please yourself.' He lit a cigarette with a flourish of his lighter. 'I gotta nother job.'

'I dare say, but look here, Sidney – what, with United Gnomes ?'

'Yer.'

'What do they make ?' I said, curiosity overcoming the Dutch Uncle stuff.

'Garden figures, boys fishing, that stuff. I'm on mushrooms to start with, one and threepence an hour. Then I'll do frog-on-mushrooms, one and fivepence. 'E sez I can work up to Bambis, one and ninepence.'

'Yes, but look here, Sidney –'

'Well, what's biting you ? I'm getting better money now than I got in that flippin' Cheshire Cat place.'

'Yes, I dare say, good luck to you, but look here, Sidney : you've only got about two months of your probation to go, haven't you ? And one of the conditions of your probation order is that you're of good behaviour and that you stick to your employment. And you've had three jobs already this year and you've been drunk. You know, Mr Bland's patience won't last for ever. If you muck about any more, he'll have to report you to the magistrates for breach of probation.'

Sidney shrugged his shoulders. Taking a comb from his pocket, he ploughed it back through his hair, spattering the wall behind him with rows of oily dots.

'For God's sake, Sidney, I don't want to see you hauled up and put away, lad – nobody does; but that's what will happen if you don't stick to this job and keep out of trouble. It's up to you : pull yourself together, lad, at least for two months.'

'Yer. Can I go now ?'

'Oh ! Yes. Blow. Vanish. Beat it ! Cor !'

I marched furiously out of the house, aiming a kick as I

went at a bit of Sidney's homework simpering amongst the geraniums.

Then I caught an Outer Circle bus, intending to visit Egbert, who had been boarded out for about three weeks at that time. When I got to the foster-home, however, nobody answered my knocks and rings, and then the lady next door told me that the Indwells and the little boy had all gone to Southend 'for the luminations' and wouldn't be back till late.

I was sitting in the office the following afternoon when Mr Mussel rang me up.

'I say, Maule, we're having a time with Herbie.'

'Oh, yes?'

'Yes, after you left him here yesterday he seemed very worried about this hotel job and kept saying it was too far away from his mates. Then soon after midnight I heard a crash, so I went down to investigate and there, outside the Girls' House, was our Herbie, stark naked, carrying a sack full of empty jam jars, and chanting "I must get back to Westburn tonight, I must get back to Westburn tonight!"'

'Exciting for you,' I murmured.

'Just one more example of the constant demands upon our time and nerves,' said Mr Mussel urbanely. 'Well, Herbie was obviously worried about the distance between Westburn and Blethering, so this morning my Housefather has had the lad out with him in the car. He's shown him the bus route, he's shown him the bus stop, he's taught him the bus number, he's taught him how to buy a railway ticket, he's shown him the railway station and the timetable, he's been four times over the main road to show Herbie the way to walk, he's made him learn our telephone number by heart, and he's taught him how to send a telegram. I *think* Herbie's been reassured a little, I don't *think* he'll feel cut off now.'

Good heavens, I thought, thanking Mr Mussel for his trouble, while they were about it they might have built beacon fires along the tops of the hills. A mere eight miles away – of course Herbie would be all right.

I didn't feel quite so confident on the Friday when I collected the hang-dog, lopsided creature complete with two of everything, a tin full of seashells and a box full of old Army badges. However, having said good-bye to all the staff twice and shaken hands with Mr Mussel and gone inside again for his collection of fuse-wire and remembered that he owed the boilerman twopence for cigarette papers and said good-bye to Matron and asked the sempstress for her address and asked Sir to ask Frank to ask Rita, at school, to write to him and said good-bye to Matron and gone inside again for a spare roller-skate wheel he wanted and transferred his sea-shells into a paper bag and his badges into the tin, and asked Sir to write down the full address of The Rookery and re-membered to collect a teapot stand he had made at school and said good-bye to Matron and decided that he didn't after all want his seashells and Little Donald could have them and shaken hands all round with the staff, he came with me willingly enough.

I got him to Blethering by train and we ambled out to the hotel, where the manager was pleased to see us and wel-comed Herbie cheerfully:

'Hallo, laddie. Come along in, son; my word, what a lot of luggage, eh? We'll have to put a special wardrobe in your room, shan't we, eh? Come along, then laddie!' And chattering gaily, he led the wan youth towards the upper regions.

I had decided that my best plan was to leave quickly, as I felt that a prolonged leave-taking would only upset Herbie, and the sooner he faced his new life the better. So, calling after them: 'Cheerio, then, Herb, see you Wednesday!' I set off at a brisk walk to the station. Within two minutes I had boarded a fast train back to Westburn Central, and there strolled out into the station yard with the comfortable feeling of a job well done. In the yard a sports car screeched to a stop, and out of it, having obviously begged a lift, step-ped a familiar figure with a lopsided face.

'Herbie Slythe!' I said in a terrible voice, more of a croak, really.

'Why, 'allo, Mr Mull!' he said. 'I got lonely.'

I got him back to the hotel somehow, back to the

bewildered Mr Walton, and this time I took my time over my departure, not going, in fact, till I had seen Herbie decked in a white jacket and butcher's apron, sharing a joke with the golden-curled assistant chef. This time I got home in peace.

The next morning, Saturday morning, I arrived at the office door at the same time as a person I thought I knew vaguely: he was wearing a charming ensemble, lime-green hat, suit and shoes, lemon-yellow shirt, socks and gloves.

'Hallo, hallo!' he cried. 'Mr – Er – *isn't* it?'

'Why, of course, Mr Smurthwaite,' I said, remembering.

'Oh, call me Anthony, do, everyone does,' he said. 'Is your charming consœur on duty this morning?'

'I expect so,' I said, and led him up the corridor.

As soon as she saw us, Miss Dashforth rose, excitedly jabbing out her cigarette.

'Why, Anthony!' she cried. 'How lovely! Come in.'

One glance was enough to dismiss me.

I went into the other room and fiddled about with date stamps for a bit and presently Miss Dashforth popped her head in. 'Charles,' she said, 'I'm going out for an hour or so, can you hold the fort?'

'Why, of course,' I said, hugging myself gleefully as they trotted off together.

The telephone rang. It was the police. They said they'd just found a baby abandoned on the Central Station, would I please come and collect it, and make it snappy, it's only a few weeks old and *I* can't feed it, said the enormous desk-sergeant in his booming voice. I said no, sergeant, of course not, sergeant, I'll be over right away, sergeant.

I scribbled a hasty note for Miss Dashforth, telling her where I'd gone, and the phone rang. It was the Almoner at Six Counties:

'I say, we've got an urgent case for admission here, a Mrs Freebody, query attempted suicide, symptoms of hysterical paranoia, doctor says she must be admitted today, in fact she's here now, she's got three children under three, and no husband, will you cope?'

I said: 'I can't possibly –'

She said: 'Good, well now here's the address . . .'

I said: 'Look, it's *Saturday*!'

She said: 'Thanks so much. Bye-bye.'

Pushing my mouth in and out, I wrote another note for Miss Dashforth.

The telephone rang. Oh, no, I thought, this really is one of those days. It was Mrs Scatterbread:

''Allo? Mr Mole? 'Allo? Is that you, Mr Mole?'

I said yes.

' 'E's done it this time, sir, Sidney 'as, sir. There's gnomes *everywhere*!'

'What?' I said, in a dazed voice, feeling as though I'd stepped into some Enid Blyton story.

'Can yer come over, sir, only see I can't explain over the phone, sir, only come as soon as you can, sir, Sid got drunk again, sir, and now 'e's got the gnomes.'

It sounded terrible, the way she said it, as though he'd got some dread tropical disease. I promised feebly that I would come as soon as I could get free. As I put the telephone down, it rang again. A faint and faraway voice said:

'Oh, hallo, Maule, it's Walton of the Rod and Gaff.'

'Can you hold the line?' I said, beginning to giggle foolishly.

'Have you got Slythe?' he said.

'No. Oh lord, has he gone again?'

'Yes. Cleared out this morning. Not a word to anyone. I can't go on like this, Maule. If that lad's back here by this afternoon, I'll give him one more chance. Otherwise, no go.'

'I see.'

'You do understand, don't you? I mean, I can't go on like this.'

'No, quite so,' I said. 'I'll do something.'

I put the telephone down, and for a full minute stood there, looking like something off Easter Island. Then the telephone rang again.

'Maule? Look, I don't want to complain higher up, but your telephone has been engaged all morning, that's not good enough, you know, not in an emergency like this.'

'Who's speaking, please?' I said weakly.

'This is Mister Indwell. I want you out here at once, Maule. If you want me to keep that boy, you'll have to come out here, straight away, and beg me to do it!'

And he rang off with the sound of a lid falling on a burial vault.

10

ALTHOUGH it is full of unexpected subsidiary tucks and folds, Westburn, generally speaking, is built on land which falls away in a long slope from the Dedbrough Hills down to the valley of the Gleeze. This slope is very gentle and so much built over that hardly anywhere is there to be found a spot where one can get anything of a view, or even a consciousness of the slope. I know one such spot, however, and for a long time it was one of my favourite places to visit on an evening walk. I used to leave my lodgings in Albert Avenue and walk northwards by various routes, all of them climbing by little and little, crossing the Great Circular Road and then working towards the railway line. Just as the line dives into a cutting and starts threading its way through the hills, there is a little wooden footbridge over, reached by an unexpected footpath in between a couple of semi-dets. You walk down this footpath in between high board fences topped on the one side with honeysuckle and on the other with forsythia, and you walk out on to this footbridge and when you look down the line, as it falls curving towards the central station, you can see more than half the town of Westburn, a great higgledy-piggledy jumble of squares, cubes, triangles, oblongs, cones, the exclamation marks of factory chimneys, the watchful steeples, the red corpulence of the gas-works, and the huge dumb-bells of the power station. A long way away, far away, over the other side of the invisible Gleeze, the land begins to climb again up towards the very faint misty hills around Blethering. This is a scene to linger on, to fall into a formless urban dream about, to gaze at, unseeing, for half an hour at a time. Punctuating one's thoughts with a groundless excitement come the trains, storming huffily up out of Westburn or coasting disdainfully down. As one stands on the footbridge in summer one is aware of the sweet scents of a hundred back-gardens, all backing on to the line in a final flurry of hedges and hollyhocks; one is aware, too, of the small sounds of men pottering amiably about in their shirtsleeves; often, too, one can watch a railwayman bending about on his plot of sooty garden beside the line. On winter nights one is not so aware of gardens, one feels a kind of warming kinship with the railway engines – they storm along through the inhospitable night and so do I, neither of us having anything to do with that glittering cascade of light that is Westburn. Winter and summer, this is a place where I find myself unwinding, relaxing, dekinking. So it was that at the end of that black Saturday I went there, leaning against the sooty railings and idly watching a signal-arm swing upwards and a railwayman go pottering about, tying paper bags round his chrysanthemums.

The first thing I'd had to do that morning, with situations clashing about my tortured head, was to decide what to do first. I couldn't get hold of Miss Dashforth; there had been a violent noise out in the street which I'd recognized as her trying to get her car into first gear, so if she and Beau Smurthwaite had gone off by car they might be anywhere. I decided to deal with the abandoned baby first, as it was the smallest and most helpless, so I rang up and was lucky enough to book a cot for him in The Rookery's nursery unit. I went along to the police station and tried to persuade the sergeant to take the child round in a police car, but he wouldn't, so I had to lug the little bundle awkwardly on to a trolley-bus and go that way. I'm not very good at babies, being scared and gingerly, and this one yelled mightily all the way; and all the way I had the glances of my female fellow-passengers fastened like barbed spears in my flesh.

I walked in through the gates of The Rookery just as a huge hired car rolled out. Its occupants didn't see me, but I clearly saw them – Mr and Mrs Mussel, sailing into retirement, she with a handkerchief to her face, he with his eyes wet with tears.

I handed the baby over to the very efficient duty nurse, and then I went back as fast as I could to the office, hoping that Miss Dashforth had returned. Oh, three cheers, yes, her car was lurking in the gutter. I went in the office and dug her out.

We went together, in her car, to see the Freebody children, and found them in with a neighbour. They all looked identical; pale greasy faces with a sprinkling of hard red spots round the mouth. I suppose there must have been nine months between them, but they'd only just made it.

The prospective task of trying to fix up accommodation for three children under three late on a Saturday morning had, at first, paralysed me with its magnitude. Miss Dashforth, however, sailed cheerily in to close quarters, and I have since learnt that if you do head straight into the problem – and better still, if you sit tight for a few days and do nothing at all – it usually resolves itself. As this one did : for the neighbour, a cheerful, untidy girl with blonde hair done up in a turban, said she would very willingly look after the two older ones, having, in fact, done so at Mrs Freebody's last confinement and on various other occasions. Not only this, but *her* neighbour said she would take the baby if she could borrow a cot. Miss Dashforth had a reserve cot at the office, so she went and fetched that, had a quick look over the bedrooms, approved the arrangements for the moment, and said she'd be in on Monday to discuss finance.

So that was that. The next crisis with a time-limit on it was that of Herbie Slythe, who would have to be back in Blethering by early afternoon if he were to keep his job. I decided that it was a waste of time persevering with that job. Herbie was obviously never going to settle down in it. The main worry was where the devil he could sleep that night – if I found him. Anyway, at that moment he might be anywhere at all, so it wasn't worth while chasing about trying to find him. I'd decided to look in on Egbert next when, seeing that by my watch it was one o'clock already, I realized I was hungry. I went across to Taff's Caff, a rather seedy-looking place on the Great Circular which serves large meals at all times, mainly for long-distance lorry-drivers. As I pushed open the steamy glass door, I saw Herbie Slythe sitting at a nearby table hunched over a cup of tea. For a moment he had the grace to look shame-faced, but only for a moment, and then he was hailing me joyfully: 'Hallo, Mr Mull! Cor, wot a surprise, eh, come an' sit down, ole man, meet my mate!'

His mate, who was eight feet tall and wearing a vast Army Surplus greatcoat, nodded at me, took from behind his ear a tiny piece of cigarette, lit it, nodded at Herbie, said 'See ya', and rolled massively out of the caff. I sat down in his place, opposite Herbie, my face sharpened into a sort of hatchet with hatred.

'What the bloody hell are you playing at, Herbie Slythe?' I gritted.

'Owdja mean, Mr Mull?'

'You know well enough how I mean, doing just as you like, walking out of the hotel, packing your job in.'

'Cor 'blige, Mr Mull, I only slipped out for some fags, I ain't packed me job in.'

'You damned nearly have: Mr Walton rang me up to say he was sacking you if you weren't back by early afternoon.'

'Ooh dear. I better 'urry up, then.'

'I'll ooh dear you, you little — , you mean you're going back?'

'Yer, 'course I am. I like it there, Mr Mull, 'onest, I reckon it's a good place. I'll get weaving back there again.'

'I don't understand this, Herbie,' I said. 'You say you like your job, but then you go and risk it by slipping out for some fags. For goodness' sake, you could have got cigarettes from the hotel, surely, or at least from Blethering, you didn't have to come all this way?'

'Ah, well, see, these was special fags, in a way – three thousand of 'em. I've borrowed 'em off me mate. I say, Mr Mull, could you lend me me fare back to Blethering?'

'No. You got yourself up here, now get yourself back again.'

'Ooh dear. Ooh dear, ooh dear. Well, I don't know where you'll fix me up with a bed tonight, Mr Mull, do you, and I mean I'll lose me job, and it won't sound so good when I have to tell everybody that you wouldn't – '

'Oh, shut up, Herbie, all right, here you are.'

'Twelve and eightpence.'

'It's three and three return, you crook, you. Here's half a dollar, now beat it.'

He gave a terrific, heartwarming grin.

'Cor, thanks, Mr Mull, you're a real pal. I shan't forget this. Cheerioh, then : see yer !'

And he got hold of a large carton, tied up with string, which had been hidden under the table, and strode off whistling. A few minutes later I saw him thumb a lift on a lorry outside.

I got myself a plateful of egg, bacon, and chips and speculated as to how Herbie had, in the space of merely a few hours, changed from the panic-stricken waif in the hall of the Rod and Gaff into what looked suspiciously like a big-time black market operative. However, I realized that I didn't know why, it all sounded much too improbable, and anyway, the main thing at the moment was that Herbie was fixed up – touch wood – and I could get along to Egbert.

Mr Indwell opened the door to me and for some time stood looking me up and down.

'Just about given you up,' he said.

'I'm sorry; there's been a lot happening.'

'So there has here,' he said, 'and I don't get overtime for it.'

'Nor do I,' I said.

For some reason this seemed to soften him slightly, and he ushered me into the front room, where Mrs Indwell was sitting in an upright chair and Egbert was sitting on a pouffe and both looked frightened.

'Well, now, what seems to be the trouble ?' I asked in as jocular a tone as I could, to try and dispel the atmosphere of doom.

'Trouble? Ha! I'll say there's trouble!' cried Mr Indwell. 'I say this to you, Maule, and I say this in front of this boy here, that this boy here is a liar; and if there's one thing I can't abide, it's a liar. Now then.'

'Uh-huh?' I said, giving one of those yes-no-maybe movements of the head. 'Tell me what happened.'

Mr Indwell went into an acid recital of what had happened, standing before me like prosecuting counsel. What it came to in the end was that Mrs Indwell kept a pile of three-penny bits – 'for the charity envelopes' – behind a china pussy on the mantelpiece, and was in the habit of counting these from time to time. On Saturday two were missing, and since her husband had not taken them, she suddenly swooped on Egbert and accused him of the crime, and Egbert, terrified, said No 'E Never. He had gone on saying No 'E Never as they became more and more worked up and made it more and more difficult for him to climb down. 'Just stood there brazen and faced me out, he did, faced me out,' muttered Mrs Indwell. In the end, Mr Indwell had said: 'All right, Egbert: until you own up you don't go out of this house, which means you don't go and watch the United this afternoon.' Within five minutes Egbert had shyly owned up, whereupon the Indwells had forbidden him to watch the United as a punishment, and had rung me up.

'And if that's the way you bring 'em up in your Homes, well, I don't think much of it,' finished Mr Indwell. 'You're producing nothing but liars and thieves, that's all.'

And he took up his afternoon paper and settled back in his chair.

'I see, well, what are you proposing to do now?' I asked him wearily.

'Me? What's it to do with me? *I* never asked for the lad to come here, it was between you and the wife, I fancy. I've done my duty in reporting the facts; it's surely up to you now.'

He went back behind his paper barrier and I addressed

myself to Mrs Indwell. She was looking at me with eyes that seemed to express a mixture of hurt, anger, and anxiety.

'Mrs Indwell,' I said, 'I wonder if you'd mind if I have a quiet chat with Egbert on his own?'

'You gonna give him a good telling off?' she said, suspiciously.

'Er – yes,' I said.

'Egbert, go 'long with this gentleman now – take 'im out in the garden, Mr Maule, no one'll bother you there. Show 'im the way, Egbert, where's your manners, boy!'

Egbert opened the doors for me, smiling apprehensively, and trailed up the garden path after me, a smallish bullet-headed boy with a wide mouth. I chatted amiably for a bit – 'Oh, it's nice out here, isn't it, Egbert – is that your rabbit-hutch? What's your rabbit's name?' – until we'd got well out of earshot of the house, and then I stopped under the laburnam and looked at him and said:

'This would never have happened in your house, would it, Egbert?'

He looked startled. 'No.'

'That's the trouble really, you see; you've come up against a rule you never knew was there. D'you want to stay here, Egbert, really want?'

'Yer.'

'Why?'

'Well, I like it – it's bin all right till yes'day – they bin kind – got me me rabbit – say I can 'ave a bike Chrismuss if I be'ave – I don't wanna go back to that bloody Rookery.'

'M'm. All right, Egbert. Well, I'll do what I can to help you stay here; in the meantime, what you must do, Egbert, is to study them, you see, see what upsets them and what pleases them, keep right out of trouble if you can, and if you do get in a jam let me know and I'll come and sort it out, if I can.'

'Yisser.'

'Now you trot back in and put your arms round your Auntie and hug her and say you're very sorry – never mind what for – and I'll have a talk to your uncle.'

I went back and confronted the afternoon paper.

'Well,' I said, 'I think you handled that awfully well, Mr Indwell, very competently.'

The paper shook with gratification.

'You've got a lot more understanding of children than I have, Mr Indwell. I expect you learnt a lot from your own father?'

'Ha!' The paper was lowered at last. 'Now there *was* a man who understood children, my father, ho yes. Discipline, that was his motto, d'you think I'd have dared to pinch money off my father? What? Cor!'

Ah, here we go, I thought, leaning forward, cheek in hand, elbow on knee, an expression of close attention on my face. Day by day we went through his own childhood, degree by half degree he thawed, and the hands of the clock behind him went past three to four, past four towards five. Mrs Indwell, who'd had a good weep in the kitchen with Egbert, had then pulled herself together and cooked him a boiled egg and sent him out to play. She made us cups of tea. Mr Indwell went steadily on; I only had to say 'Really?' from time to time. Yes, his father was a marvellous man – and presently: of course, nowadays, he'd probably be thought too strict – and presently: cor, if Dad had known the things I did when his back was turned he'd a-killed me – and presently: mind you, I'm not saying he was wrong, but – and at last we came to the really delicate bit, the place where the fish is finally gaffed and landed, and holding my thumbs, I said: 'If you could choose what age was the happiest of all, would you choose your childhood, Mr Indwell?' 'Not flippin' likely,' he said, 'What? Let a kid of mine go through what I had to? Cor! Not flippin' likely!' Before his words had time to die away as he realized what he was saying, I let out a gusty breath and stood up. Now all that remained was to direct his attention from what he'd just said and to attract a little bit of his contempt and bitterness

114

to myself, which I did by being very nice to his wife, and then went off, saying: 'I'm terribly sorry to have kept you so long, Mr Indwell, I'm afraid I do talk an awful lot.'

'Oh – well – ' he said, gruffly, actually accompanying me to the door.

I suppose I should really have rounded off Masochism Saturday by calling on Sidney Smee, surrounded as he was, apparently, by gnomes; but by now I was feeling pretty beat up. I telephoned my landlady and said I wouldn't be in till late, no, I'd eat out, thank you, Mrs Dean; and then I strolled down to the railway bridge, which was not very far from 'Sidanelse', intending to have a quiet cigarette there, unwind a bit and then perhaps go on to the pictures and see *Kind Hearts and Coronets*. So I leaned against the sooty railings and idly watched the railwayman go pottering about, tying paper bags round his chrysanthemums. It was about half-past six on a still evening, the small round clouds all golden underneath, and the air full of scent.

I'd been there for some time, unwinding into a state where I had practically hypnotized myself, when a small perky dog, a Cairn, came scuttering across the bridge and had a sniff round my socks. I could hear its owner coming along the path, so instead of kicking it, I said: 'Hallo, Face-ache.'

'Well, hallo yourself,' said the owner.

'Harry!' I cried. 'Gosh, well, I say, is this your dog?'

'Yes, his name's Gorm,' she said. 'What are you doing up here, Charles?'

'Unravelling,' I said. 'I've had a rotten day.'

'Oh, dear; what happened?'

I told her all about it, while Gorm scuttered about on the banks of the cutting, occasionally barking at a train. She stood very relaxed, I saw, swinging the dog-lead, the strong gold light of the dying sun making her face glow. When I'd finished she said:

'I see, yes; so you've just strolled down here to relax after that lot.'

'Yes. I often come here, as a matter of fact, it's a nice view. But what are you doing here, Harry?'

'I often come here, too. I don't live very far away. I bring Gorm along here sometimes, for his walkies.'

'I didn't know you lived up here, Harry: are you in lodgings?'

'Oh, no: I live with my mother. I'm a Westburn girl, didn't you know?'

'No, I didn't,' I said. 'I don't know very much about you at all, Harry. I certainly didn't know you came from Westburn. How convenient you got the job here; did you take the Child Care Certificate specially?'

'Oh, no,' she said. 'I only accidently drifted into the Children's Department. I really wanted first of all to be a medical missionary, but then I'd only just started my nursing training when there was trouble at home, so I had to pack up.'

I was memorizing every line of her face. A stray petal had drifted into her hair.

'Then, in the end, we got over that, but I thought I wouldn't start a long training, just in case there was more trouble, so I took a Diploma Course, just the two years, you know. Then I had a year at home, and then this job came along, I was very lucky really.'

So was I, I thought, looking at her eyelashes. She was gazing abstractedly away, down the line towards the distant hills.

'Oh, Harry, how marvellous it was to meet you, it's made up for everything!'

One of her wonderful slow smiles crinkled her eyes as she turned towards me. Her eyebrows flared so liltingly, her lips were so red –

'Oh Harry –' I said incoherently.

The next second there was a frightful screaming noise from the end of the bridge. Gorm was being set upon by an angry old tory of a dog, grizzled and gaunt. 'Lay orf, you ole mucker!' shouted a raucous voice as the tory dog's owner came panting along the footpath. She was a rotund

woman, with bright yellow hair all in curlers, and was wearing a pink plastic mac and black plimsolls. She gave us a
knowing wink when she first saw us, but her second glance
was much more alert and wary.

I took a deep breath.

'Hallo, Mrs Crump,' I said.

II

WE just couldn't pin her down, she was evasive and desperate to be off. Oh yes, she lived 'just over there', with an airy gesture towards the setting sun, oh, the kids were all right? Good — cheerioh, then, miss, sir. Harry walked with her a few steps, but short of holding her back by physical force, we couldn't engage her in any longer conversation. She made a vague promise that she would come in and see us at the office on Monday morning, and departed at a hurried pace, followed by her familiar, the old grey dog, Pong.

Miss Dashforth got quite cross about this encounter when we told her about it on Monday.

'Oh, really, you are a couple of coots!' she said. 'Why on earth did you speak to the old faggot? We're well rid of her, we don't want her turning up every five minutes, interfering with what we're doing for her kids, disgusting old party.'

But Mrs Crump didn't turn up; I don't know quite what we'd have talked about if she had. Harry and I both felt somehow that, now we'd found her, we ought to know how she was living and what she was likely to be doing about her children, not that we wanted her to interfere, but she was just part of the whole picture. Still, Miss Dashforth was right in a way, the children were reasonably settled, at least they were being no trouble, and their mother's reappearance would have an unpredictable effect. I think probably both Harry and I were relieved that Mrs Crump didn't come.

Gloria was still with the old warhorse foster-mother, old Mrs Erams in Funnel Lane, and really quite a changed girl; her hair was now in its natural frizzy brown state, she'd got a new job in the station refreshment room, and she was walking out fairly steady with a chap named Jack Muskett. Clark had been licensed from his Approved School and was quite a well-known character round Westburn, being co-lourful but harmless. The flash youths at that time wore very long drape jackets and peg-top trousers, and Clark wore quite the brightest and most ridiculous example of this style in the town: the jacket was so long that only his boots showed below it, and as he walked down the High Road he looked like a toddling toy going down a sloping board.

Myrna had been boarded out by Harry with a sweet old couple in the older part of the town, not far from Lavender Walk. She was a very quiet, but intense girl; I don't know that she was happy, but she was always well groomed and dressed in very plain, good clothes, and I think that she was quite queening it at school, even in those days. Winston was being rather a nuisance in Tots' Glade, Miss Heaton said he was maladjusted; he used to attack other children's clothes with scissors, or try and set light to their toys, apparently this had got worse since his brother Clement came back from Penzance to join him. Anona had been boarded out over the other side of the County, we didn't hear anything of her. Sabrina was in the Nursery Unit at The Rookery, a perfectly adorable little black toddler. This left Celia, who was still away in her Open Air School and we all hoped she'd stay there. Just one big happy family, I used to think morosely, as I visualized them scattered to the four corners of the county. Still, we could say that they were all getting some sort of chance to do well for themselves, and even though Winston was awkward to manage, none of the kids was manifestly unhappy. I think Egbert at that time was the most worrying one.

Still, for a while at least, I seemed to have got Mr Indwell into a more tolerant mood, and there were no more squeaks from Shakespeare Walk. The Boy of the Week was Sidney Smee.

Sidney had obviously been on a right blinder at United Gnomes, according to the story as I pieced it together later on. I'd known, of course, that he had become quite a leading light in café society at the time, one of a select gang of youths who divided their evenings betwen Taff's Caff and the Pop Inn. Apparently, one Thursday night, these lads had been boasting of this and that, and poor old Sid had had really no more to boast about than his window-smashing escapade, and that wasn't much, 'but one o' these days' he must have said, 'I'll make a *real* noise in Westburn.' 'Coo, what?' 'Ah, you wait 'n' see.' But in the end he had to say he was planning to land a brick through the glass roof of United Gnomes. 'You'd never dare!' 'I would!' 'You'd never dare!' 'I would, then!' 'Well, show us, show us, now! Pah! See? He's yeller!' And thus and thus they all trooped round to Droops Cut, collecting on the way, from a builder's yard, an old handled paint tin, half full of solidified paint.

The United Gnomes factory is a tall narrow building, once a corn store, and the glass roof is a good fifty feet up. Sid knotted his tie tightly to the paint tin and swung it round and round at a high speed, released it, and watched it soar most gratifying up and up and over and through the glass roof, a moment of the most intense and enjoyable nervous apprehension. The crash itself, due to some acoustic kink, was disappointingly puny to the listeners down below, and indeed several of them, as they took to their heels, expressed doubt as to whether Sid had hit the roof at all.

Of this, however, there was no doubt, at all when Sid showed up gleefully for work next day, for he was immediately seized, hustled before the Guv'nor, and sacked on the spot. His flying bomb had not only burst through the roof and knocked over a great pile of Nymphs Combing, it had pulverized a most valuable prototype, first of a new series of Humorous Garden Furnishing and showing a knock-kneed horse squinting at a wasp on its nose. The loss of this had given the chief designer what was tantamount to a nervous collapse. What Sid had completely overlooked was that he had happened to be wearing, the previous night, a tie which Mrs Scatterbread had prudently marked with a name-tape: S. SMEE.

Now, United Gnomes operate a wage system commonly

called Working a Week in Hand; that is, you are paid no wages at the end of your first week, your first week's wages at the end of your second week, and so on. It is a curious system, and I have never quite grasped the reason for it. It means, as it meant to Sidney, that you get two weeks' money when you leave. Sid had only just managed to complete two weeks, anyway, but no matter, there he was, rich.

His immediate reaction was to spend his money, so he ate a meal of eggs and chips, bought a bottle of Tizer and a cigar, and, armed with these, took himself to the pictures. Unfortunately, the film was *Whisky Galore*, which gripped Sid's imagination: he rushed from the cinema that evening round to Old Mother Shambles in Gas Lane and bought from her a bottle of what consists largely of methylated spirits and is known locally as Happy Sap. Of course, a thimbleful of this stuff was enough to bring out the beast in Sidney, and as soon as it was really working inside him, and he had a cigar aglow too, he set out on a kind of ritualistic revenge. Forcing an entry into United Gnomes, he filled a sack with about a gross of Assorted Pixies and began to leave them all over the town in various grotesque, not to say obscene, positions. When stopped by a policeman at 2 a.m. emerging from the Ladies in Basin Square, he had about eight Pixies left, with which he bombarded the pursuing posse, but he was finally captured and charged with Making an Affray.

Well, that was pretty well the end of the road for Sidney Smee; he had three charges against him, as well as the offence called Breach of Probation, and over and above this was jobless and homeless, for the Scatterbreads refused to have him back this time. ('Well, you see wot it is reely, Mr Moll, it's Our Val, I mean we can't 'ave this sort of carry-on, it's the effect on the child's mind as I worry about.' Actually, Valerie, who'd failed her eleven-plus, was wildly excited about everything, was now deeply in love with Sidney, and used to collect the Sunday papers to see if he featured in any of them.) Confronted with all this, the magistrates seemed at first very much in favour of sending Sid to an Approved

School, and remanded him for inquiries to be made: but Mr Bland was urging upon them the alternative of a Probation Hostel.

'You see, look at it this way,' observed Mr Bland to me, ruminatively thumbing his moustache, 'if Sidney goes to an Approved School at this age, well over sixteen, he'll go to a senior school and he'll mix with a lot of toughs who've spent most of their lives qualifying for that treatment. Well, when all's said and done, Maule, the laddie's not a criminal.'

I agreed, no, Sid was very foolish and wayward, but not a dyed-in-the-wool rogue.

'So you see, if he goes to a school, he'll mix with types who will do him no good,' Mr Bland continued, 'whereas in the hostel he'll go to work as usual in the daytime and mix with ordinary chaps, and there will be some control over his leisure so that he doesn't go on the booze, which has been his downfall, so far. Yes, I think the hostel may just pull him round.'

I said: 'I'd feel happier about the outcome if I understood what lay behind these outbreaks. Mr Bland, do you think he is fuguing?'

Mr Bland's eyebrows jolted upwards.

I said hastily: 'I mean, do you think he returns compulsively over and over again to his problem of non-existent Mother, creating and then shattering some symbol of her femaleness?'

Mr Bland gave me a long look and then he said: 'No, old boy, I just think he's lonely.'

Gosh, yes, terrifyingly lonely. I knew how it was and yet other boys were alone in the world and didn't react in this way, there must have been some more complex reason to account for Sidney's behaviour. Whatever that may have been, though, the practical problem was that he was jobless, homeless, and a challenge to the Court; and in the end, the magistrates followed Mr Bland's suggestion, as they very frequently did, and Sidney duly departed to spend the next twelve months in a hostel in the London area. I was left

122

pondering on the problem of his isolation and to apply any lessons I had learnt, if relevant, to the problem of Egbert Crump. I was in a quandary with Egbert. I didn't think the lad was happy with the Indwells, but I didn't think it would help matters at all if I took him away.

The trouble is, of course, that almost every one of us, if suddenly challenged, would reply: 'Oh, yes, I'm happy.' Egbert did so, when I tried to tackle the dilemma that way. For the first time in his life he had a pleasant and orderly home, to dance in like a mote in a sunbeam. He did things which he knew he would never have done in any Crump establishment; things like picnicking, having people to tea, and sleeping in ironed pyjamas between sheets. And I think he got a lot of enjoyable attention from the Indwells: I believe that for the greater part of his time there, things went very pleasantly and placidly, they all enjoyed things together, outings, radio programmes, they had a companionship. But for all that I used to worry about Egbert's isolation; it seemed to me that whether a mote dances in sunlight or in shade, its dance depends on rather fortuitous upcurrents of air, and if the air currents fail, there's a long way between one mote and the next and neither is much help to the other. Egbert was of, but not of, the Indwells, invited to be one of the family and relax, so long as he 'knew his place' and did not relax. It was a difficult, unsatisfying position, I thought, like sleeping with a bomb under the bed or being a Jew.

My first thought was to reduce Egbert's isolation by keeping him in closer touch with his relatives, particularly his sister Myrna, who seemed respectable enough; when I suggested this, however, the Indwells became very hostile and simply didn't understand the necessity for it. ''E's *our* boy!' they reiterated. 'This is his home, you musn't unsettle the child by reminding him he belongs somewhere else!' It was during this interview that I learnt, somewhat to my horror, that Egbert now went by the name of Indwell at school; I felt this was quite the wrong thing to have done, but by now Egbert was very loath to revert to Crump. 'We-ell,' he said, 'the kids are always sayin' why's your name Crump and 'er name's Indwell, I get sick o' arguin'. It's not nice neither. I 'eard one o' the masters the other day sayin' I was illedge. That's not nice, is it?'

The whole trouble, I thought, was somehow tied up with the Indwells' marriage, and I felt in a hazy way that if I could by some means reduce the tension between them I would make things happier for Egbert. Without really understanding what I was doing, I began dropping in on Mrs Indwell at about half-past-three-to-four; this gave me anything up to an hour's chat with her before Egg himself came circumspectly home from school. I kept this up fairly regularly through the autumn, had rather a long break over Christmas – we had the most frightful rush that year – and then resumed my calls, at about fortnightly intervals, all through January and February. The clocks went back, the roses died, the fogs came; I ran the usual nervy gauntlet of the housing estates, during the month before Guy Fawkes, when every lurking boy packs a banger; but a good deal of my time, during these action-packed months, was spent on the brown velvet cushions of Mrs Indwell's sofa, listening.

At first I got nothing but strings of complaints about the government and austerity and short supply and so on. Then, very slowly, and encouraged by faint nods and grunts from myself, I got a string of complaints about herself, her health especially, the fool of a doctor, what her neighbour thought of the fool of a doctor, a series of fearful scandals about the local hospital and how therefore, it was no good her going *there*. The way these conversations developed reminded me of the movement of some old buzzard, flapping heavily around and around in the sky, but always drawing nearer and nearer to the wound in the middle. When I went on turning up at the house, amiable, unruffled, never interrupting or counterclaiming, Mrs Indwell began to tell me about her husband.

'Of course, he comes from a very good family, very good family indeed, but he was misunderstood all his life and in

124

the end was cut off with a shilling, I mean it's been a struggle.'

(Egbert at about this time started attending the Boys' Brigade.)

'Of course, he sez – and whether it's true or not I don't know – but he *sez* that actually he is the actual illigitimate son of someone very 'igh indeed – well, I mean, royalty, as you might say.'

(Egbert played a game or two for the school at centre-forward.)

'I can't myself see, if he really is of noble blood, why that means that therefore I must be the one who can't have children, I mean I know he's got a lot of what you might call qualities I'm very grateful for, but that doesn't follow, does it, I should have thought the other way round, really.'

(Egbert went to the Employees' Party at Plimm's, and actually shook hands with the Colonel.)

'Then he starts on this story about me being one of twins, he reckons I must be incomplete, well, I mean, it's as if he was covering up all the time. And he doesn't *do* anything either, if you know what I mean, just lies there, sometimes for months together; and if I make a movement, he sez: "Oh, don't be disgusting!" he sez.'

(Egbert got a plastimould set for Christmas and filled the house with plaster shepherdesses.)

'We could 'ave 'ad children, I believe we *could* 'ave 'ad children, but of course, 'Is Lordship won't even admit it's 'im, let alone 'ave treatment. If I even think of bringing the subject up he shuts up for a month or two, won't speak, just sneers; I tell you, Mr Maule, I've lain in bed at nights and *prayed* . . .'

After this last admission she shut up on me and I never got so far again; I reckoned I must be somewhere near the heart of the trouble. Now I'd got there, I didn't know what to do about it anyway. I asked Miss Dashforth, and she said: 'Well, I suppose it does no harm if you can spare the time, but really, Charles, you're a month overdue on seeing

Johnny Valentino, you must learn to do first things first.' I asked Harry one evening, when we were strolling out for a quiet drink at the Duck and Drake. She thought I was on dangerously thin ice, and that I might go through and be swept away in an emotional flood if I wasn't careful. In my own mind, I felt sure that what I was trying to do had to be attempted if Egbert were ever to settle down in this family; certainly, I couldn't see that I was really doing any harm, for Egbert was still there, still apparently flourishing, the centre of no storms or outbursts, going to school cheerfully, going to Boys' Brigade regularly, nodding affably to me when I called.

Thus, the blow, when it came, was largely unexpected.

The trouble all began over a wet bed. Now, Egbert did not suffer from the all-too-common complaint of bed-wetting which made the task of finding homes for many children so difficult. I suppose it would have been no surprise if he had done it, but in fact, he'd never been known to be wet. Now, when suddenly one morning he woke up soaking, it must have been as big a shock to him as it was to Mrs Indwell; unfortunately, however, he tried to conceal the evidence and Mrs Indwell, when she found the wet sheets crammed into the wardrobe, took the whole thing melodramatically and gave Egbert a rather frightening lecture about 'the evil sin' and never doing it again. I think, from what Egbert later reported of her speech, which was full of lurid descriptions, that she had the wind up over a vague horror called What Boys Do, a subject she knew nothing whatever about, for I'm sure her husband never enlightened her. Anyway, up she blew, and Egbert got scared, and the next night he wet the bed again; only this time he made a bolder effort to conceal the evidence, cutting his wet sheets into small squares and trying to flush them down the lavatory. Result, chaos. Mr Indwell was summoned home from work, arriving in a foul temper as he had arranged to have a big steak-and-brown-ale luncheon with two chaps on the sales side, useful contacts for him. He found water dripping through the hall ceiling and his wife, white with red eyes, moaning at the little cornered rat. How he must have impatiently roared and ranted! Some time about then one or other of them said to Egbert: 'You're just as mucky as that old cow of a mother of yours!'

At three that afternoon Egbert marched into my office; he was also white with red eyes. He sat down with a thump and announced that he was never going back there no more: 'No, Mr Maule, not if you was to go down on yer knees I won't.' After he'd quietened a bit, I realized that he was showing a very steely determination indeed: his mother had been insulted, that was the end. Presently I sent him out to get some buns and took myself out to Shakespeare Walk; I found that Mr Indwell had returned to work, and Mrs Indwell was standing, heavily powdered, by the bags and boxes packed with Egbert's belongings. I had to stand and listen to her side of the affair.

'It's the ingratitude that hurts, Mr Maule, that's what hurts,' she finished. 'After all we've done for 'im, in every way, given 'im our name, stood by 'im, fed 'im, and everybody remembered him at Christmas, Mr Maule, all our relatives sent to 'im – and not a thank you out of 'im, I may say – and then after all that 'e rounds on me an' has the downright ingratitude to say I'm not fit to lick his Mum's plimsolls – that awful old person, Mr Maule – I can never love him again, I could never love a boy who could say a thing like that, never!'

She had suddenly broken; a large powdery tear rolled out of her eye and fell with a splash on the corner of Egbert's Dan Dare Space Race.

'And I so wanted to, Mr Maule, I so wanted to!'

'Well – ' I said awkwardly. I collected Egbert's things together and stood up with all the bits clustered in my hands. 'Well . . .'

What on earth could I say? I said I was sorry things had turned out this way. I said it was all my fault for bringing the lad in the first place. She didn't listen. Nor did I.

'Well – ' I said. 'Well, cheeroh, then, Mrs Indwell.'

As I left she was still just standing there quietly, as though she was standing at a bus stop. But I think she must have known that the last bus had gone.

12

THE new people up at The Rookery were called Mr and Mrs Boatwright. They were a youngish couple, the first I'd known who had taken the new Home Office training for Home staffs: he was a tall, bony fellow with a large nose, gawky both physically and mentally; she was a brisk and energetic midget. They both came from Yorkshire. They'd made some changes at The Rookery – for instance, I could walk in any time and have a chat with them. Also they allowed the children to wander in and out of the kitchen as they pleased, and the Cook had resigned.

One afternoon, about two months after Egbert's return there, I went up for a chat about two of the boys who were due to leave at Easter: Paddy O'Hooligan was going to Elysium House, the hostel for working lads, and Little Donald, who was entering the Navy, was involved in a welter of forms, eye-tests and Guardian's Consent. We talked over the details of all this, and then Mr Boatwright, warming his big hands at the gas fire, said:

'Y'know, Mr Maule, Ah'm a bit worried. About our Egbert.'

'Oh?'

'Ah. Ah reckon he's going a bit mental.'

'Good gracious, really? What does he do?'

'Well, it's not so much what he does. See. It's more like what he is.'

This was about as clear as mud.

'Well. It's a bit hard to say. See. 'E goes vacant.'

Pot calling kettle black, I thought to myself.

'Ah. And then there's this enuresis.'

'Does he wet the bed still?' I asked. I'd assumed that he'd clear up as soon as he was out of the Indwells' house.

'Oh ah. 'E's a chronic wet bed. Every night, every night. You ask the wife.'

Mrs Boatwright was sitting working a queer sort of rocking machine, a mechanical sock darner. She had a great basket beside her full of about four hundred grey and holey socks.

'Egbert?' she said. 'Ah, 'e's a terror, a fair terror, wet bed every night.'

'Yes, but lots of your boys wet the bed,' I said. 'You don't call them all mental?'

'Oh, naw, naw. It's more what Egbert is, like. 'E walks about as though 'e were shell-shocked.'

'Ah,' said Mr Boatwright. 'That's right enough. Ah tell you. 'E always reminds me of someone who's had a thump on the head.'

'And terrible rages at times,' said Mrs Boatwright, shaking her head at the memory. 'Oh, terrible. Ah tell yer what, Egbert reminds me very much of that lad, what was his name, when we were doin' our practical at Bleacham, Freddie Drax-Cave-Chetwynd.'

'Oh. Ah. Ah,' nodded Mr Boatwright. 'An' we know what 'appened to 'im.'

This aristocratic-sounding youth meant nothing to me, not even that he was aristocratic. Many of our children collect surnames as fast as their mothers collect 'husbands'.

'Yes, I think I see what you mean,' I said, 'though it doesn't sound very serious to me: surely this is just regression following a mild trauma accompanied by sibling rivalry and ambivalence towards the mother figure?'

The Boatwrights gazed at me.

'Ah. Ah,' he said. 'So what do we do about it?'

'Oh, that's your job,' I said primly. 'I've no experience of residential work, my task is merely to observe and report.'

'Ah, well, Egbert's flippin' okkard to live with, any road. You can report that.'

'What do you suggest, then?'

'Well, Ah've been wondering. If he shouldn't see one of these 'ere psychiatrists.'

We talked around it for a bit and I took the idea away

with me. I was sure Egbert wasn't mentally deranged, but come to think of it he had been through a bewildering, pointless experience and perhaps skilled treatment would help him to sort himself out a bit. Anyway, if he were examined, we should have a bit more information about him, and it wouldn't do him any harm, I presumed. I asked Miss Dashforth about it next morning.

'Oh, well, if you believe in that sort of thing, Charles, personally I think it's an overrated pastime,' she said, scattering some cigarette ash into her hair. 'All that lad needs is a good foster-home, the right home at the right time – '

'Dashforth's Law hasn't worked with him, has it?'

'Of course not! You got the wrong home at the wrong time, that's perfectly obvious. I should let well alone, Charles, after all, Egbert's getting on for fifteen now, and I doubt if they will even see him at the Clinic before he leaves school, let alone give him therapy.'

'Yes, that's why I thought perhaps we ought to try and get him seen before he has to face the world, he's making rather heavy weather of life at the moment without the extra strain of employment. And, of course, there is my own diagnosis of mild trauma and regression to consider.'

'Oh, all right,' she said. 'Bung up a chitty to County Hall.'

Getting a child seen at the local Child Guidance Clinic is a complicated, long-drawn-out procedure, something to do with medical etiquette and something with the great demands made upon the service by anxious parents. I sent off to the Chief Welfare Officer a request that Egbert's name be brought to the Clinic's notice, together with some notes on his life and present behaviour, and expected to hear no more about it for months.

About a week later I was passing a dark grocer's shop in the High Road when out came a fat, sad-looking woman, Miss Niff, the Social Worker from the Clinic. When she saw me she hailed me with a mournful hoot.

'Hilloo, Hilloo! I vos going to tiliphone you!'

'Oh, yes?'

'Our leedle friend Egbert,' she said, falling into step beside me and nodding her head sagaciously. 'Yiss. Vell, ve haf seen through *him*!'

'Oh, have you?' I said, disappointed. I'd known him for a couple of years and I couldn't see through him. I felt ashamed and chagrined that Miss Niff could do better than I could.

'Ho, yiss,' she said, still nodding. 'Hev no fears. Shall I tell you vot ve propose to do? *Ve are going to put Egbert on the vaiting-list.*'

'My word!' I said, adding cautiously: 'Is that good?'

'Ho, very good,' she said. 'Very effective, it is a method of treatment with a very high success-rate: ve put them on the list and by the time they are actually seen at the Clinic nearly ninety per cent are cured.'

About ten days after this – it would be towards the end of March – I had a surprising telephone call from the Clinic. There was a lot of measles about, several children due to attend the Clinic had it, and so there was an unexpected opportunity later that morning for Egbert to be seen by Dr Pike. It was absolutely vital we were at the Clinic on time, the whole timetable would be disrupted if we were a moment late. I promised I would do my best to get him there, and at once trotted round to Smirch Street Secondary Modern and abstracted Egbert. He came out looking rather surprised, and gave me a number of hard sideways glances.

'Where we goin'?'

'We're going to the Clinic, Egbert,' I said, cheerily.

'Wha' for? I've 'ad me teeth done, an' me eyes.'

'Well, er – look at it this way, Egbert,' I said, gravely. 'A mind is just as much a part of your body as your tummy, you know, and just as likely to get a bit out of sorts sometimes, a sort of collywobbles you know, eh? Well –'

Egbert stopped dead.

'Are you takin' me to a bleedin' trick-cyclist?'

'Yes,' I said, 'I'm terribly anxious to do anything I can for you and –'

'If 'e shrinks my 'ead, I'll sue you!'

'He won't shrink your head, Egbert, for goodness' sake be your age! He only wants to talk to you; and I want you to talk to him.'

'Hah!'

We walked the rest of the way in silence, hurrying so as to be there in time.

The Clinic was in Gibbet Hill, a short road of large detached houses, mostly used as branch offices by insurance companies and the National Assistance Board. No. 4 was distinguishable by its neglected garden and the three dead trees with mutilated trunks. We went into a very small waiting-room where there were a dolls' house and a table covered with dismembered magazines. I was pleased to see we had got there dead on time; we wouldn't have to wait long. Egbert slouched down in a chair, and began reading a Tarzan comic; the only thing I could find to read was an old copy of *Woman's Own*. Twenty minutes later, when I'd got to the recipe page – 'Be Bold with Rhubarb!' – a large woman with untidy hair came in and said: 'Hallo, Walter!'

Egbert gave her a look of pure hatred: 'Me name's Egbert.'

'I see, we're Egbert this week, are we?'

I said: 'Excuse me, his name really *is* Egbert; he's a new one.'

'But Walter *always* comes at this time on Tuesdays!'

'Excuse me,' I said, 'this is Wednesday.'

The woman gave us a most suspicious look and went away.

Half an hour later, a rather smelly girl with a faint moustache came in and said: 'Mr Albert Crump?'

I said: 'Egbert Crump.'

'It says here Albert. Are you Mr Crump?'

'No,' I said, 'my name's Maule, I'm the –'

'Oh, you're the stepfather! How nice!'

'I'm the boy's welfare officer,' I said firmly.

'Oh.' She wavered for a moment, and then went away, I

suppose to check up at the office, for she soon came back and said : 'Yes, this is the one. Come along, Albert, dear !' She stretched out a hand to him, but he stumped stubbornly past her, giving me a slit-eyed look as he went.

An hour later he came back, looking squarer than ever; slumped down in his chair and pulled out Tarzan again. The smelly girl smiled fleetingly at a point a yard behind my shoulder and disappeared.

By that time I'd read two copies of *Beano*, a chapter of a musty book called *With Gordon to Soochow*, and an article on crochet work called 'Dramatize That Little Black Dress !' I began moodily chain-smoking.

A little later two mothers arrived, a large competent one, obviously an old hand at this, for she settled down with a novel and her knitting, and a small one with a tic who began telling me that she was Going Through the Change and what it felt like.

Half an hour later a gaunt man with glittering eyes came to the door and silently beckoned with one finger. Egbert went to him as though sucked, and disappeared down the passage.

I dived out to the nearest stationer's and bought a Pan Book, something about escaping during the war; I was half-way through it before Egbert returned; it was then half past two.

At three, Dr Pike came to the door again and beckoned me. He took me to his office and for a full minute looked at me in silence.

I had to say something : 'Ha – er – quite a nice lad, I think ?'

The doctor nodded. Silence fell again.

'I thought mild trauma and some regression ?' I said, chattily.

Again the doctor nodded. There was another long pause. Then he reached across his desk and moved a paperweight about a quarter of an inch.

'Toilet-training ?' he muttered.

'I don't think he's had any,' I said.

The doctor reached across his desk again and moved the paperweight to its original position. He was silent for another long minute. Then he nodded. Then he stood up and bowed to me.

'Yes, but – but – ' I said, bewildered.

The doctor bowed me out of the door.

'About the sibling-rivalry – ' I tried, but the door had shut behind me.

It was half past three when we came out into the street again, and we hadn't had our lunch. 'Egbert,' I said, 'I'm going to buy you a slap-up dinner now.'

'So you bloody well should do,' said Egbert. 'Cor.'

Ten days later I received from the Clinic the report on Egbert. Some years afterwards, the boy himself told me what had happened during his interview, so that I can put two and two together in this way:

'Findings of the Educational Psychologist (Miss B. Cleech).'

(This was the smelly girl who'd had Egbert for the first hour.)

'Egbert was hostile, silent, and depressed throughout the interview, and in spite of the examiner's friendly reassurance, failed to warm up at all.'

(Egbert said he thought this revolting tart was trying to make a pass at him.)

'In view of this it was thought advisable to use a non-verbal Passalong Test, in which he showed a wide scatter of successes, ranging from a failure at the seven-year-old level to a success at the eighteen-year-old level.'

(Egbert was given some shallow boxes filled with red and blue blocks and was told to slide them about until he had reproduced a design he'd been shown. He was about to begin with contemptuous efficiency when the examiner got a message to say that her morning coffee was getting cold. Egbert instantly put on a maddening slowness, completing the first and second boxes minutes outside the time limit. The third box he did by accident and couldn't cover up. When he got to the ninth, he was asked if he'd like a cup of tea; he completed the test in seventeen seconds.)

'A similar scatter was revealed on the Binet-Simon test; at times he did not bother to answer at all. Tested for educational retardation he showed marked backwardness in arithmetic.'

(Egbert was asked to add up a lot of sums. He got the first right and she said: 'Good, good!' He got the second wrong, and she said: 'Good, good!' He got the third wrong and she said 'Good, good!' Obviously it didn't matter; he got the rest wrong too, blow her.)

'Findings of the Psychiatrist (Dr Hamilton Pike).

'This boy is markedly disturbed, fearful, and inaccessible.'

(Egbert was frightened out of his wits, he had never met anyone like this, he thought the Devil had got him.)

'There is a deep-lying anal fear and noticeable dreams of power.'

(After mentioning his mum and dad, Dr Pike muttered: 'Ever wanted to defecate in their bed?' 'Wot?' said Egbert. Dr Pike explained. The incredulous Egbert offered to change places.)

'Nevertheless, I believe this boy is recoverable and potentially he has a strong and effective personality and very considerable insight, as shown by the drawing he did for me.'

(All right, I'll show you, thought Egbert savagely, seizing a pencil and paper and reproducing clearly and exactly page 23 from a book Rudolph had brought back from Alexandria.)

'Summary of Case and Disposal: That he be deemed to be maladjusted and placed in a school for the emotionally disturbed.'

I gave a strangled yelp at this, and Harry looked up with one eyebrow lifting.

'It's this report on Egbert,' I explained. 'It says he's seriously maladjusted and needs to go to a Special School.'

'And don't you believe it?'

'No,' I said. 'Well, at least – I dunno. I suppose they can judge ?'

'Don't ask me : you're the one who's mad on pshycho-analysis, aren't you ?'

'Yes – no – well, I mean, this is a chap I *know*, it's a bit different.'

'Perhaps you don't know him well enough,' said Harry. 'Perhaps you haven't spotted that his mother-fixation has got mixed up with a fetish-sublimation.'

'No, don't fool about, Harry, this is a human being. What's maladjusted mean ?'

'Not fitting in with his environment.'

'Yes, that's what I thought,' I said. 'But he'd be a bit wonky if he *did* fit in at The Rookery, wouldn't he ? It's not exactly a natural place. Perhaps Egbert's all right and we're all a bit batchy ?'

'That's possible,' she said gravely.

'I suppose if he really needs special treatment I ought not to prevent him having it.'

'You sound a bit dubious, Charles. Suppose they were talking about your own son, would you accept this report ?'

'No !' I said at once. 'But that's not a fair question, Harry, I'd be personally involved then, and if my son was maladjusted I'd try and change myself to provide what he needed.'

'In fact, you'd stick up blindly for your own son, Charles; so why don't you do the same for Egbert ?'

'I'm not paid to stick up blindly for anybody,' I said. 'I'm supposed to see clearly and act rationally. I thought I had been, but that Child Guidance lot make me feel like a two-foot toddler trying to see what's on top of a wardrobe.'

'Good : that makes you a bit more normal.'

'Anyway, I can hardly think that a son of mine would get into the situation in which Egbert finds himself,' I said, primly.

'It depends on who you marry, dear, doesn't it ?'

'I know who I'm going to marry.'

Her eyebrows lifted again.

'You,' I said.

There was a sort of tightening round the angle of her jaw, that was all.

'I think you'd better go and see old Dash about Egbert,' she said, evenly.

Old Dash jammed a cigarette into the corner of her mouth and let the smoke pour into her eye while she skimmed through the report. When she had finished reading she said:

'Pah! Stuff and rubbish. I told you not to go near that daft place.'

'Don't you believe this?'

'No! I expect old Egbert was sickened to death with the lot of them, well, so should I be, so would any self-respecting kid, good luck to him if he did give old Pike a few rude answers, for two pins I would myself.'

'I thought that perhaps with their twenty years' experience they might be able to understand Egbert better than I do,' I said humbly.

'Pah! That lot's only had one year's experience twenty times,' she said. 'Anyway, don't worry about it, Charles, nothing'll come of this, like all their ideas it's impossible.'

'How?'

'Well, look at the kid's age, nearly fifteen and he's not overbright. There's not a special school that'll look at him.'

'How about this chap Smurthwaite?'

Miss Dashforth made a great show of lighting a new cigarette and then stubbing out the old one.

'H'm. Yes. Anthony might take him, if I asked. D'you really want Egbert to go to The Cottage by the Creek?'

'I want him to have the best available opportunity; the trouble is, I don't know what that is.'

There was a pause. Then Dash said: 'Anthony's a peculiar cove, you know. Lots of things that I think are important he doesn't seem to care about at all, and yet he can see further into people's hearts and minds than anyone else I know.'

I was feeling too perplexed at the time to take umbrage. 'Has he got glittering eyes?' I asked uneasily.

'No, you know he hasn't, don't be silly.'

'All I wanted in the first place was some clue about how to help Egbert sort himself out.'

'Well, if he'll take him – and if Education will pay – and if Central Committee will approve – and if Health accept this report – what was I saying? Oh, yes: look, Anthony can get much deeper and help Egbert much more than ever those Boatwright creatures could.'

'Couldn't he just tell me what to do?'

'What can you do, Charles? You can't have him living with you round in Albert Avenue.'

No, that I couldn't. No, that was the whole damned trouble, I couldn't have Egbert with me to make or break him all by myself, I had to rely all the time on half-understood substitutes. What *did* I want for Egbert? What did Egbert want for himself? He was half-understood, too. I struggled to make my mind pierce his, and cursed myself when I found I couldn't do it. Were there people who could pierce in deeper than I could, could Anthony do it, how did he do it? Why couldn't I do it? Should Egbert be rushed off somewhere else, to the back-end of nowhere this time, because I couldn't yet get through to him?

I had a fortnight of this irresolute mental panting, and what made me feel worse was an encounter I had with Mr Bland, one morning when I was just leaving the Court after an adoption hearing.

'Ah, Maule!' he hailed me.

'Hallo, Mr Bland: how's things?'

'Terrible; up to our eyes; it doesn't matter what happens in this town, they seem to send the probation officer to see to it first. I say, Maule: friend Smee.'

'Oh, yes? How's he doing?'

'Silly lad!' said Mr Bland, shaking his head. 'Silly foolish lad. Up before the beaks again, two charges of take and drive away, four others T.I.C.'

Sidney had been stealing cars, I translated; six of them, apparently.

'The hostel won't have him back. It means Borstal this time, I'm afraid.'

'Oh, the silly dope,' I said. But I felt terribly sorry about it, another little sparrow fallen. Was Egbert to fall the same way?

When I got back to the office I found that a decision had been made for me. Miss Dashforth, with the air of a conjuror producing a rabbit, laid a letter on my table. It ran:

LOVE, LTD

Dedicated to the proposition that children
are born free but are everywhere in chains.
President: The Earl of Wull
Administrator: A. J. Smurthwaite
Schools: The Cottage in the Sun
The Cottage on the Heath
The Cottage on the Wold
The Cottage by the Creek

Cheques should be crossed and endorsed 'A/c Payee'

9-4-50

Agnes, my dear –

Delighted to hear the Committee agree – of course send us the Crump child. I think we shall be able to help and release him. Will you be bringing him down yourself? I hope so – any old time – what about Friday?

Ever yours,

A.S.

P.S. Attached is my account for Crump's fees for this term, payable in advance – would you see that it is passed for payment before the child arrives?

A.S.

13

'CHARLES –'

'Yes, Miss D. ?'

'Charles, about Egbert going to his new school –'

'Yes ?'

'Well, I – know you want to take the lad down yourself, understandably, but I – er – wondered if I could come too ?' said Miss Dashforth, shyly.

'But, of course, Miss D., that would be splendid.'

'We could go in my car !'

'Oh.'

'Actually, you need a car to get to that place,' she went on. 'Trains only run as far as Strickworth, and it's eight miles beyond there and buses on Saturdays only; you have to get a taxi and by the time you've paid for it to wait – well, we may as well go by car all the way.'

'Yes.'

'You've never been there, have you, Charles ?'

'No.'

'I haven't been down for three years. It's a fascinating place; we can have a good look over it, if we take the car we shan't have to rush away. Now, when shall we go, how are you getting on ?'

'Well,' I said, 'the main hold-up is over these clothes. I've been sent a list a yard long and I'm supposed to get everything from Harrods.'

'Let's have a look.'

I brought out the foolscap sheet entitled : 'Love Ltd, Clothing List. The following are the minimum clothing requirements of boys attending any of our schools. Parents and guardians should note that any child arriving at school without minimum clothing will be liable to be sent home again.' There followed a list of clothes amounting in value – at a rough guess – to £150.

Miss Dashforth skimmed rapidly through this:

'Trun, trun, trun – one suit black formal, one suit grey Sunday, three jackets grey school, three prs trsrs school, one blazer orange and cherry, two caps orange and cherry, three ties orange and cherry, all above obtainable from Harrods; boots, wellingtons, plimsolls, shirts, hose, half-hose, shoes, jerseys (one blue, one white, one orange and cherry), shorts, gym kit, hanks, belt, braces, fourteen towels – fourteen? – sheets, blankets, pillow-slips, counterpane, good heavens, don't they supply anything, whatever are the fees for? H'm. Formidable, isn't it?'

'Yes.'

'Well, look, leave it with me for the moment, I'll perhaps ring up Anthony and see if there's a way round this.'

About half an hour later Miss Dashforth came into my room, looking slightly pink.

'I've rung Anthony,' she said, 'and it'll be all right if we just get the everyday things, Anthony will get the rest from Harrods next time he's in Town, so we can go down any time. Would Friday suit you?'

'All right,' I said gloomily.

'You don't sound very keen: are you still not sure if Egbert should go?'

'I'm not sure about anything any more. What does this Smurthwaite fellow think he's going to do to my boy?'

Miss Dashforth considered, pinching her lower lip.

'Well, as Anthony puts it, every human being has the right to function fully and gloriously at every level – physical, psychical, and libinal. And if they don't, he feels they are just as much cripples as legless people. He thinks that children especially are likely to be crippled in this way, because of the harsh treatment meted out to them by insecure parents.'

'I wouldn't call old Ma Crump insecure,' I said. 'I thought she was rather monolithic.'

'Ah, no, it's The Rookery that's done for Egbert,' said

142

Miss Dashforth. 'That's where his bed wetting has started. Anthony says that bed wetting is a terrible cry for help from a submerged soul.'

I suppressed various indelicate thoughts and said: 'Well, what's he going to do about it, then – fool about with hosepipes?'

'Nothing so crude, don't be horrid. Anthony aims to evoke and redirect the libidinal harmonies – he describes his role as that of conductor of the endocrine orchestra. He is very good at going about – well, releasing people.' And Miss Dashforth confusedly stubbed out a cigarette she had only just lit.

'This sounds a bit odd coming from you, Miss D.,' I said. 'Now, if I talked like that, you'd tell me to come down to earth.'

'Well, it depends who – well, I hope I'm as quick as anyone to learn from others,' said Miss Dashforth. She sounded a bit huffy. After a pause I said placatingly:

'So long as Egbert ends up happier through going to this place I'm sure it's worth doing. I still can't see how he can be described as maladjusted, though; he seems to me remarkably well-adjusted, seeing all the things we've done to him.'

'Yes, well, I do think that after all that, Egbert must be emotionally disturbed.'

'So what? I'm emotionally disturbed, too,' I said, listening to Harry's footsteps in the corridor outside, 'and I thoroughly enjoy it.'

'Oh, tut, Charles, you are being difficult this morning. Run away now and prepare Egbert for his move, and we'll all meet at The Rookery at nine on Friday.'

It was not difficult to prepare Egbert for a change, as he was by now fully adjusted to the fact that life was full of quite incomprehensible changes, as though his own life was a chaotic journey across the London Underground system. Me he regarded, I think, as a sort of maniac train announcer, paid to be helpful, but appearing only when it was necessary to announce that the train he was on wouldn't be going as far as he thought it would. Indeed, I think that Egbert's mental state at this time was very like that of a railway passenger, hurtling along, deep in a newspaper, oblivious of the scenery, oblivious of his fellow-passengers, and certainly oblivious of the marvellous technical skill that made his journey possible.

Egbert seemed to show surprisingly little concern for the other members of his family, though they were all scattered far and wide. Of Mr Crump, Mrs Crump and Bebe there was no news at all; nor had we tried to find them. Rude had briefly reappeared in the office to ask if his own baby could be adopted. Clark was still to be seen around Westburn, still in a long drape jacket, but with a new hairstyle, the first D.A. I had seen. Gloria had just gone out of Care, her hair a pretty light brown; she used to come and see Miss Dashforth every month to talk about her wedding arrangements, she was getting married the following March 'to claim the Income Tax'. Myrna was still in her foster-home, still looking dark, compact, smouldering, walking to school and back in her good dark clothes, a cat who walked by herself. Cary, after one false start, had achieved a wildly successful foster-home in the outskirts of the town, with a great fat couple who ran a scrap metal and general junk business – Cary had never been happier in his life than when he rooted round the yard with his dad on a Sunday morning. Winston, who had always been an unpredictable rogue, had been found to be very unintelligent and had been sent to a boarding school for backward children, where he had become miraculously tractable. Clement, in a foster-home over our border, was driving the foster-mother straight up the wall and presumably, Miss Van Tromp thought, would follow Winston to boarding-school all in good time. The littlest uns were all fostered peaceably enough.

None of these children showed the slightest interest in the others, although we all occasionally threw out hints about inviting brothers and sisters to tea. This was surprising to me – I am an only child myself – for I should have thought that children in such circumstances would have clung on to their brothers and sisters; but not a bit of it, with the Crumps, anyway. Miss Dashforth used to say: 'Oh, well, it's probably all for the best; wipe out the past and give 'em all a completely fresh start, let 'em avoid the mistakes their parents made, that's the thing. We're building for the *next* generation, Charles, the next one more than this one,' which I supposed was all very well, except that Egbert had had three fresh starts so far, was rising fifteen and still had nothing to anchor himself by.

Next Friday at nine we met at The Rookery and Egbert came down the steps looking square and resigned to whatever was to happen this time. He climbed into the back of the car and immersed himself in a thick comic-book. I got in beside Miss Dashforth. The Boatwrights hovered around outside, ducking their heads and goggling in at us like fish; Mrs Boatwright had her hands wedged in between her knees.

'Ah've given 'im a couple of Kwells,' she called. ''E should be all right. Bye-bye, then, Egbert!'

'Hrrmph!' muttered Egbert; but when we were half-way down the drive he suddenly turned and waved to them out of the back window.

We settled down to the journey; at least, Egbert did, deep in his comic or gazing indifferently out of the window, occasionally grunting in reply to the remarks we kindly dropped to him, crumbs from the grown-ups' table; and Miss Dashforth did, giving considerably less than half her attention to her driving, but talking incessantly, making little darting movements with her head, suddenly scrutinizing her face in the driving-mirror, occasionally joggling the steering wheel to and fro to emphasize what she was saying. I didn't settle down at all.

We got to Strickworth at about eleven and stopped for coffee. Then we went off along a minor road over the level crossing and then after three miles turned left down a lane. After four miles of weaving about in a maze of lanes, Miss Dashforth confessed that she was lost and we stopped to ask a jovial red-faced man who was trimming the road verge.

'*Where?*' he asked, puzzled.

'The Cottage by the Creek.'

'Ar, now you've got me, me dear; an' Oi thought Oi knew all around hereabout. Is it a pub, then ?'

'It's a school,' said Miss Dashforth. 'The Headmaster is a Mr Anthony Smurthwaite.'

His face seemed to become affected by a sharp frost.

'Oh, *that* place !' he said, looking at us keenly, as though at least two of us ought to have been in strait-jackets. He gave us some curt directions and stood and watched us out of sight.

After a bit we came to some massive gates, standing open. Just up the drive was a notice : 'Beware of children. Drive slowly.' In the grass verge beyond the notice lay a trades-man's van, overturned with all four wheels in the air.

We lurched slowly up the pot-holed drive and presently emerged by a large, oblong mansion made of mud-coloured brick. A group of girls in faded pink dresses were hanging round the front door, occasionally standing on their hands and rearing their blue serge knickers skywards.

We got out of the car a bit stiffly and Anthony came out to meet us.

'Agnes, darling !' he cried, taking both her hands in his, and gazing at her with his head on one side. 'Darling, *did* you pass my account through for payment ?'

'One for £200 I did.'

'Oh, good, good, yes, that was for this term, d'you see; oh, good, well, you can come in.'

He led us across a large hall furnished with a Gauguin print and a moth-eaten sofa and into his study. This was a huge room, very well decorated in off-white; Egbert stump-ed along with me, sat down on the edge of a delicate chair covered with *petit-point*, and eyed a bronze statuette of a naked gladiator.

'And this is Egbert !' beamed Anthony. 'We're delighted to have you join us, Egbert. I expect we shall get on. You'll find this is a peculiar sort of place, nothing like anywhere else you've ever been in, thank God. And I'm rather a pecu-liar chap, you in your funny way would call me the headmaster, I expect, but I'm actually the administrator and everybody calls me Anthony. Smoke? Try a Turk.'

He held out a heavy cigarette-case, but Egbert refused in a surprised way and shifted his glance to a print of a ruminative nude on the far wall.

'This is a community, you know,' went on Anthony, lighting a cigarette, but not offering me one. 'It's not a school, not a Home, not an Institution. It's a place that *lives*. You'll see, when you go round: I'm going to ask another boy to take you round in a minute and show you where to stow your gear. This is a community where you come and go as you please, working out your own ambit in the constellation: there are no lessons, until you choose to seek out your own; there are no set meals unless you wish to attend them.'

'What about pocket-money?' asked Egbert.

'Threepence a week,' said Anthony. 'Money plays no part here, there is no cash-nexus, love and freedom are the bases on which our community is built.'

'Cor!' said Egbert.

A girl in a smock and a queer spaceman haircut came in and asked:

'Anthony, excuse me, may we do reed-pipes in the conservatory for the next hour? The Lower Sixth have just come to me and particularly asked.'

'Of course, Sylvia. You see?' he said to Egbert. 'As they feel the need to express themselves, so we provide the means. As we shall do for you, as we shall do for you. Agnes, we're doing some vivid pioneer work on reed-pipes, most exciting. I've managed to get TV interested in us. Now, Egbert, have you any questions to ask me?'

''Ow long shall I be 'ere?'

'Ah, now. I say to you, as I say to every child who joins us, that this is the end of the road for you. No matter how perplexing and bewildering the road may have been, here in our funny way, we understand and learn to love. And here we help you, no matter how long it may take us, until you return to the world a fuller, freer and more exciting individual than you would ever believe possible.'

'Cor!' said Egbert.

Anthony went to the door and called: 'Boy!' Presently a foxy-looking boy in khaki shorts appeared and said: 'Yes, Anthony?'

'Steve, this is Egbert: will you show him round and settle him in? Good. Run along then, Egbert, and I shall see you this afternoon again.'

Egbert tore his gaze from a detailed representation of the Rape of the Sabine Women, and went meekly out with the foxy boy.

'Ah, well,' said Anthony, rubbing his hands, 'he'll settle in, I feel sure. It'll be a long job though, Agnes, there are certainly fixations there, are there not? Quite a marked sex-guilt syndrome, I thought, though by no means pathological. Steve will help in that direction, I fancy; a dear good fellow, Steve, though once the most repressed individual one has ever met.'

'How do you manage to sort them out?' I asked curiously.

'Do you know, it's really quite fantastically simple. These bairns have simply never known love – pure love, allknowing and forgiving love. We love them.'

'Sex seems to be a little – er – intrusive?'

'But, my dear fellow, doesn't it enter into everything, don't you find that?'

Dashforth gave me an ironic glance that made me blush like a schoolboy.

Anthony said: 'Of course, sex is a major preoccupation here. After all, most personality difficulties are rooted in sexual misusage, and again a sexual relationship is the first, most primitive blossoming of the higher love. It is a means to an end, and therefore we are very tolerant of sexual experiment. But as experiment proceeds, so crippling guilt disappears and one comes to the realization of the body as the very wonderful functional mechanism that it really is.'

Anthony leant back in his chair and ran his fingers complacently over his fat pink jowls.

'You mean you just let them go around fiddling with each other?' I asked, shocked.

'Oh, my dear, what a painful thing to say! Of course not; it is merely that in an atmosphere of complete mutual trust and frankness the whole thing dwindles to its rightful and healthy place. Boys come to see girls as persons, not obscene receptacles. Besides, we're not obsessed with unbridled licence; we have an intensely therapeutic community life, and every child has individual counselling, given by myself. We aim to re-create the entire personality, not merely the bit below the waist.'

Anthony broke off to look at his watch:

'Well, now, do look over our little community while you are here, we have time before lunch.'

He took us up to the bedrooms first; a lot of iron bedsteads had been jammed into attics, where the wallpaper was peeling away from large brown patches of damp. A bearded man was painting one of the doors scarlet.

'Ah, Michael! How splendidly gay!'

'An improvement, I think,' said the man shyly, dripping paint on his sandal.

'Prefects' Room,' announced Anthony, throwing open another door. A boy and a girl sprang from each other's arms and gazed blushingly out of the window.

'Ah, Frank, Magdalen!' nodded Anthony.

We went down a very steep dark staircase, where Miss Dashforth missed her footing and stumbled. There were twenty beds in the room below, all covered with brown Army blankets. In one corner a small boy was in bed, reading a comic.

'How are we, Stuart? Soon be up and about again, eh?'

'Me pain's worse,' grumbled the boy.

'Yes, yes; yes, yes,' said Anthony soothingly.

'Psychosomatic,' he told us as we went out. 'Very interesting, you know: he insists that he's swallowed a marble, which, of course, we know stands for his mother – the jolly old elemental O, y'know, it's very clear in his case.'

'Shouldn't he see the doctor?' I asked doubtfully.

'Heavens, no: he's seeing me this afternoon and he has

sufficient insight to be helped to recognize the real cause of his discomfort.'

Round the corner we met a curvy blonde girl with a sulky mouth and long eyelashes, looking as though she featured on most of the covers of the paperback shockers.

'Ah, Matron!' cried Anthony. 'Matron, may I introduce Agnes Dashforth and Mr – Er – from Westburn.'

Matron gave us a cool stare and said:

'Anthony, that lot in the Blue Room want to make a fire this afternoon. Is that school clothes or play clothes?'

'School clothes, dear.' To us he said: 'Zoroastrianism is quite the rage here at present. Did you see my article in last month's *Totem* – the one on Teen-Age Fire Dancers? Oh, do read it – you should read it, it was awfully good. I've just sold the American rights.'

We went into a large room downstairs where there were some boys and girls, all wearing jeans and tee-shirts, and a dishevelled woman winding up a large horn gramophone. She put on a noisy jazz record. A girl and a boy minced down the room arm in arm and two other boys sprang on them, pretended to cosh the boy, who fell groaning realistically, seized the girl, clapped a hand over her mouth, and hustled her into what was apparently a car, which drove off noisily.

'Dance Drama!' said Anthony proudly. 'Diana is doing some extraordinarily exciting work in this medium, you know – I'm writing it up now for TV.'

'Where are the classrooms?' I asked, timidly.

Anthony looked at me as though I were a cheese-mite on the end of his nose.

'I see you are still horridly trammelled by conventionality,' he said. 'In the world as a whole, how much part does a classroom play? Hardly any; a classroom is a mere convention; and so it is here, so it is here. We are a community engrossed with the true relationships, not the mere imposition of teacher upon passive class. Relationship, after all, is the true educative reality.'

We went in to lunch, in a rather dark, small room, and each collected from a gravy-stained serving hatch a plate containing a small piece of liver and a large quantity of swede. Anthony talked a great deal about Group Therapy, Identification of the Individual, and Ego-Absorption. At intervals he was interrupted by harassed looking staff, with whose queries I must say he dealt briskly and efficiently.

'Anthony, I'd bagged the Quiet Room for Percussion this afternoon and now Cyprian says he's got it for Junior Boys Flower Arrangement. I don't know what to *do*!'

'Tell Cyprian he must use the Glass Lounge, dear, that's quite empty, I know.'

'Anthony, I must ask you to accept my resignation, I – I –'

'Calm yourself, old chap: what is the problem?'

'Anthony, I – I – in a moment of madness I struck a child.'

'Oh, yes. Oh, dear. Resignation will merely be a guilt-ridden flight, Marcia: like Cain, you know, like Cain. You must submit yourself to the School Parliament, dear, and accept their judgement.'

When we left, an ominous cloud of heavy sulphurous smoke was rising from the brushwood down by the lake. I could see Egbert among the crowd, conspicuous in his good grey suit.

'Say what you like, Charles, it is a stimulating place!' cried Miss Dashforth, as she sped through lanes crowded with gigantic agricultural machines. With my tongue cloven to the roof of my mouth, I could have wished it had been less stimulating.

I managed to say: 'Materially it was pretty awful.'

'Yes, it was, wasn't it? And that worries me. Yet on the other hand, the man seems so energetic and purposeful, the Boatwrights seem just dead compared with him.'

'I wish I knew what he was being purposeful about.'

'He's transplanting those young growing things into a really rich and nourishing soil.'

'Like a bloody compost-heap,' I said. I was still jealous, I suppose.

Miss Dashforth subsided into a huffy silence until we were

through Strickworth. However, we were too good friends to stay like that for long. She began to chat about the work again. Then she said :

'I hope old Harry's been all right by herself, and no crises.'

'She'll cope all right.'

'Oh, yes. Poor old Harry. I feel awfully sorry for her.'

I raised an interrogative eyebrow.

'She has a rotten time at home, you know,' said Miss Dashforth confidentially. 'Her mother is mad.'

I stared straight ahead through the windscreen.

'Oh, not absolutely raving, I mean,' she went on. 'It started when the old chap died, old Colonel Harrison; his wife got frightfully depressed at the time and Harry had to chuck up nursing and come home. Harry's an only child, you see, there isn't anybody else. Well, after a couple of years, Mrs Harrison seemed to have got over her mental illness so they got a companion for her and Harry went off and did her Social Science. And then suddenly everything collapsed again, Mrs Harrison got suicidal, and some wretched surgeon gave her one of these pre-frontal lobotomy things, you know ?'

'Oh yes. But – aren't they any good ?'

Miss Dashforth circumnavigated a roundabout before replying.

'Well,' she said, 'Mrs Harrison's much happier, much, much happier, not a care in the world; but she's quite devoid of a moral sense. She'll take anything from a shop, walk off without paying, bring all sorts of things home. Most people know her by now, of course, but poor old Harry just never knows what may be happening while she's out at work.'

'Good heavens !' I said. 'I never knew, never had an inkling, Harry never said a word.'

'Well, why should she, after all,' said Miss Dashforth, and sighed. 'Oh dear. Poor Harry. And, of course, she has to stick by her mother, she hardly goes out; and she can't possibly consider getting married.'

I sat very still for the rest of the journey. Somehow Anthony and his school and even Egbert seemed to have become very small and a very long way away.

14

ONE morning in the late autumn of that year, when it was very wet, I went in to see Miss Dashforth about something and she was deeply involved with the telephone. I hung around waiting for her to finish and fiddled with some papers on the end of her table, and found myself scanning a report on some people called Parchment who wanted to become foster-parents. They lived in a village called Much Furbish, about five miles out, and Miss Dashforth had been to see them herself. Presently she put down the phone, and I asked her about them.

'The Parchments? Oh, yes, I saw them, didn't I? Oh, they're rather a sweet old couple; they wanted to have a pretty little girl, but they're much too old. I shall have to turn them down.'

'Are they absolutely hopeless?'

'Well, no; well, yes. I mean they're much too old, they're both about seventy. I couldn't put a little girl there, even if we had one. Why Charles, do you want them for one of your great oafs?'

'I was wondering about Lenny Lumb,' I said.

Lenny Lumb was a boy whom I had first met soon after I started to work in the Department. He was a boy whose mother had died when he was a baby, and as there had been no father named, he had come into the care of the old Guardians Committee. They'd sent him to a little Charity Home in the depths of Suffolk, and there, as the years went by like shadows, Lenny Lumb grew up, a mere name and case number to the Westburn office. Then suddenly, when he was a boy of twelve, correspondence began to flow about him; he wasn't doing at all well at school, he was retarded, he was dull, he had been referred for a psychologist's report, and finally it was agreed that he was really incapable of benefiting from education in a normal school. This meant that he needed a school where the teaching process was slowed right down to a pace he could cope with. He was deemed to be Educationally Sub-Normal, and arrangements were made for him to be transferred to our residential school for E.S.N. boys over at Melcombe.

He was brought down to London by one of the Home staff and I met him at Liverpool Street. He had never previously ridden on a train and had never been out of Suffolk; to him, life was the cool, grey house, the soft-shadowed dormitory, the lined face of Miss Teed, the dear, unchanging routine as one year flitted by after another.

'He hasn't brought any clothes,' said the housemother, doubtfully, 'only what he stands up in, is that right?'

'Yes, that's right,' I said. 'We see to everything at Melcombe Hall, he'll get rigged up there.'

'Oh, ah. Well, I must get off if I'm to get my train. Cheer-oh then, Lenny: be a good lad, won't you, and don't forget to write to us.'

She marched off through the crowds like a grenadier. Lenny looked after her as might a dog left at the boarding kennels.

In those days I used to talk a lot to the boys, chattering away jovially and plying them with interested questions. I got very little response from this one. He fixed his earnest brown eyes on mine and seemed to be trying to understand a lecture in Greek; if he answered at all, it was in a faint, blown-away whisper. He held my hand for the journey across London. The escalators terrified him, we had in the end to walk down the stone steps in the middle. When we were settled on the Westburn train, I said:

'I like your little suitcase, Lenny.'

He had a tiny toy attaché-case, from Woolworth's, I suppose.

'What have you got in it? All your treasures?'

'Ss.'

'Can I see?'

'Ss.'

He brought out from the case, one by one, a marble; a broken propelling pencil; a birthday card with 'You are 7' on it; a cigarette-card portrait of George Arliss; and an empty picture-frame. After thirteen years of life, that was all he had.

Lenny was a meek child, and though he was totally un-used to a large all-male school, he seemed to settle in at Melcombe without any severe disturbance. Soon, however, we came up against the problem of holidays; Melcombe was a boarding-school which closed down for the three main holidays each year. I used to go over there to see the boys about twice a term, and on my second visit Lenny said:

'Sir, I'm going to Miss Teed for Christmas, sir, aren't I?'

'I expect so, Lenny, I'll write and ask.'

But my note to Miss Teed brought a reply from the Secretary of the Home, who regretted that Lenny's place had now been filled, perhaps in the summer . . .

'I'm sorry, Lenny. Miss Teed hasn't got room this time, you're going for Christmas to a very nice place called Tots' Glade.'

At Easter Miss Teed still hadn't got a spare bed.

'I can go to Tots' Glade, then, sir?'

'I'm sorry, Lenny, Miss Heaton hasn't got room this time, you're going to a very nice place called The Rookery.'

Lenny wasn't very happy at The Rookery. He was used as a cat's-paw by the other boys, and somebody stole his propelling pencil.

In the summer there wasn't room anywhere and Lenny went to a holiday foster-home with a lonely spinster named Miss Eldridge. She took him out for treats – the Church Fête and two whist drives – and the rest of the time they just sat and looked at each other. I saw Miss Eldridge again about half-way through October.

'Ay don't think Ay'll persevere, Mr Mull.'

'I'm very anxious to get him anchored somewhere, Miss Eldridge, the poor chap never knows where he's going next, and he badly needs a reliable friend for the holidays.'

'Ay don't think Ay should raise his hopes, Mr Mull, there is no affinity between us. He seems to have no resources. Have you a little orphan girl, say about nine?'

'No,' I said, in a surly voice.

The school broke up a week before Christmas that year and I had nowhere for Lenny. Then the Tankheads rang up. Mr Tankhead described himself as a Company Director, he said he had one child, a boy, who was lonely, and there was everything there a boy could wish for. When I went to have a look I could see that Peter Tankhead did indeed have a bike, a crystal set, a tape-recorder, an electric train, a gramophone, and a huge Meccano set. He was a silent, haunted child.

Mr Tankhead said: 'A boy coming here could regard this home as his own, Mr Er ... We'd make no distinctions. The right boy could have a marvellous opportunity here, and I tell you what – when his time came, I'd take him into the firm with *me*.'

'Well –'

'Oh, if you're not interested, of course – in my humble opinion any child would be grateful.'

In despair I sent Lenny.

'Where am I going for Christmas, sir?'

'I've found you a lovely place, Lenny, with a boy called Peter Tankhead, you'll have a lovely Christmas there, and lots of things to do.'

On Christmas Eve a white-faced Lenny was brought into my office.

'I asked for a boy, Maule, not a blasted lunatic: here, take him. He tried to sit on my wife's lap! He's a potential sex maniac, that's what he is, aren't you, Lumb? Yes, look at him, he knows. Fondling her all over. There'll be a report about this going in to the Clerk, he's a personal friend of mine. If that's what you get for doing somebody a good turn –'

Lenny spent that Christmas with Mrs Cropper: she managed to buy him a box of sweets before the shops shut on Christmas Eve.

By this time Lenny was fifteen, a tall, well-built lad with a large head; special school children have an extra year at school, and Lenny was due to leave at Christmas 1950. The plan was obviously to find him foster-parents who would have him when he left school and to let him grow accustomed to them during the next two holidays.

'Where am I going for Easter, sir?'

'I'm trying to find you a nice auntie and uncle of your very own, Lenny; I haven't found any yet, but I expect I will.'

He looked disappointed.

'Wouldn't you like that, Lenny?'

'Sir, couldn't I go to a 'Ome, sir? When yer boarded out, sir, yer miss the boys, sir.'

'You feel lonely, do you, Lenny?'

'Ss.'

'Well, you see, Lenny – ' But I couldn't make it clear to him. He looked as though he'd been kicked once too often.

There wasn't room in any of the Homes at Easter. About a week before, a boy at the school called Charlie Jinnings said his parents would love to have Lenny for the holidays. I knew the Jinnings family vaguely, there were about fifteen kids, their father was a dustman. It was by no means a registerable foster-home, but the Jinnings were warm-hearted, slap-happy folk and Lenny seemed glad to go with them.

Half-way through the Easter holidays, the District Nurse called on the Jinnings and found Lenny sleeping on a mattress with three little Jinnings and covered with an Army greatcoat. She called the N.S.P.C.C. before she called me, and Lenny spent the rest of the holiday in the Reception Centre.

'Sir, I don't like foster-'omes, sir.'

'No, Lenny?'

'Sir, you never know where you are, sir.'

There was a place in The Rookery that summer. I thought perhaps it would be safer. Lenny had a much nicer time there, he went on holiday with them to Littlehampton and conceived a great affection for Mrs Boatwright: they used to peel the potatoes together.

'Sir, could I always go to The Rookery, sir, for every holiday, sir?'

'Oh, but Lenny, you see, when it comes to Christmas you'll be leaving school and then you'll be getting a job and you see, working boys can't stay at The Rookery. I shall find you a nice place where you can settle down and save your money and be a rich boy.'

'Ss. Where will I live, sir?'

'I don't know yet, Lenny, but don't worry, you know I'll do my very best.'

October and November faded past.

'Sir?'

'No, I don't know yet, Lenny, don't worry.'

Miss Dashforth looked very dubiously at the reports.

'Well, I don't know, Charles; it might be worth a try, but they're awfully old.'

'Shall I go and see them, anyway?'

'Yes, do that: go and form your own conclusions. I haven't taken up references yet, by the way.'

The middle of Much Furbish, thatched cottages standing round a green, was very pretty and inhabited by artists, motor traders and radio script-writers. The Parchments lived down a side-lane, in rather a plain, slate-roofed cottage, one of a severe block of three. They were very pleased to see me and made me a cup of strong, black tea.

I'd decided to take my time over this, and for a while we talked about the old-age pension, the clash between Liberals and Conservatives in 1902, and the best way to preserve runner beans. Mr Parchment liked pottering round the long garden at the back. He was a short, slight, silvery man; his wife was large and round, like an old-fashioned loaf. They had a bedroom upstairs as was never used now, it seemed a shame not to put it to some use, like.

'For meself Oi'd loike to help a liddle gel, if so be as she'd settle, but that other young ooman as called, she thought we was too old for it, din' she, Walt?'

'Ah,' said the old man, squinting at his pipe.

'Not that she said so, mind, but Oi could see the way she was thinking. Oh, she was very noice, and o' course Oi quite see it, we're not gettin' any younger.'

I began to talk idly, pensively, about Lenny Lumb. They listened to me attentively, there was no change in their attitude, no cries of sentimental pity.

'Ah,' said the old man. 'What would 'e be thinkin' o' working at, sir?'

'He hasn't much idea yet, Mr Parchment,' I said. 'He might do quite well on a farm, perhaps, he's very gentle and kind with animals.'

'' 'E don' want to be gentle with they bloody ole cows,' chuckled the old chap.

'Now, Walt, you moind your language,' said Mrs Parchment, placidly.

The old man winked at me over his pipe.

'There's not much goin' in farming this toime of year,' he mused. 'Oi moight 'ave a world with Mr Honeydew if Oi sees 'im about.'

Imperceptibly we had begun to talk as though Lenny were coming.

'He may get a bit lonely,' I suggested. 'He's so used to living with a crowd.'

'Ah, well, there's Min's boys just down the lane, they'll be company for 'im.'

Min, Vi, and Rose, their three married daughters, were all settled round the village. The three sons had moved away, one in Australia, one in London, and one in the Navy.

'One o' Min's boys 'as a bike as 'e's finished with, Lenny could 'ave that.'

We went up to see the bedroom the boy would have: I wasn't too pleased with it, it was rather dark, bare, and neglected. But by this time I'd made up my mind that this was worth a try for Lenny, these people wouldn't lightly give up a job they had once undertaken. We arranged that

Lenny should come to them for the Christmas holiday, and that if there was no startling incompatibility he should stay on with them and get a job.

'I think you'll find him a nice, quiet lad,' I said, as I was leaving. 'So long as you don't rush him.'

'Lor bless yer, sir,' said the old lady, slapping her thigh, 'can yer see us folk rushin' anybody?'

Westburn seemed more than usually loud and vulgar when I got back to it that night.

I wrote to the people whom the Parchments had given as referees and all the answers said much the same thing, that these were excellent old people, but didn't I think perhaps they were a bit too old. By this time, however, the memory of Lenny's imploring eyes had made me decide that he must go to Much Furbish as arranged and I took him over there the week before Christmas. He was very quiet on the way. A burnt child fears the fire.

But as soon as we got in the door, Mrs Parchment said: 'Hallo, lad, come and get your tea,' and she produced from the old-fashioned oven a vast steak and kidney pudding and set it before him and then sat by the fire with her hands folded in her lap and twinkled at him.

'Come up an' see 'is room, sir,' said Mr Parchment, in a hoarse whisper. When I got up there I paused in the doorway, staggered by the transformation. The room had been newly decorated with a pink rosebud wallpaper and bright white paint and there were new curtains and shining lino on the floor.

'We thought we'd like to 'ave it proper for 'im,' said the old man.

Goodness, I thought humbly, all this has been done out of the old-age pension.

I didn't see Lenny again for a while as we were terribly busy with Christmas, but I sent him a card with icicles on it, and a postal order, and went up again in January. He wasn't in when I arrived, but the old folk told me that he was getting on all right with his job, he was rather slow and he didn't always grasp an instruction the first time, but once he knew what he had to do, he went right on with the job till it was finished.

'And how is he with you at home?' I asked.

There was a long silence and then they both screwed up their eyes, nodded and said together:

'All roight.'

And Mrs Parchment added: 'Seems loike 'e's bin 'ere all 'is loife.'

There was the sound of loud whistling outside and a bike was cheerfully clattered about, and in came the lad himself.

'Ah, Mum! Dad! Sir!'

I hardly recognized him. He was bigger and heftier and ruddier and happier. We didn't have much to say that evening. I sat and beamed and nodded and Lenny glowed at me over his enormous supper, and what talk there was was largely monosyllabic. The old folk sat and regarded him with that peaceable loving pride that a carpenter shows for a long tried tool. I began to recognize in myself that bitter-sweet feeling that I was an intruder, that they wondered why I bothered to come. Lenny had dropped anchor.

In the middle of February I got a telephone call from someone I didn't recognize.

'This is Mrs Bean speaking,' she said. 'Mrs Bean from Much Furbish.'

Ah, yes, of course, this was Rosie, Mrs Parchment's daughter.

'Good morning, good morning!' I hailed her.

'Sir, I'm sorry to bother you, I thought you should know, sir,' she said. 'My mother died last night.'

'I – I – I'm so sorry, I'll come at once,' I said, and as I put down the telephone, I could feel the blood ebbing from my hands and feet.

I got out to the cottage as fast as I could, and Rose took me through to the back room. The old man was sitting in the front room, reading his Bible. He bowed to me gravely as I went past.

'I'm terribly sorry about this,' I said to Rose. 'I feel as though I have lost a friend.'

'It must come to all of us,' said Rose.

'I can take Lenny back with me now if you wish,' I said. 'I'd like to try and find a home in the village for him, but of course you won't want him here at the moment.'

'Why, sir, you don't mean to say you're taking him away? Our Lenny?'

'Well, I – surely you – I assumed –'

'Sir, my husband and I will move in here to look after Dad and Lenny. But of course we shall, sir. Lenny is one of the family now.'

15

Of all the boys I've taken responsibility for, Herbie Slythe was the one who made me feel most like throwing a brick through a plate-glass window. He seemed to alternate unpredictably between helplessness and cold self-sufficiency. When he was running round the petty Westburn underworld, he seemed possessed of a delicate sensitivity to relationships, he knew when to lay off a geezer because the geezer was hot, when to look the other way and when to be as wide as wide could be. All this he did with untaught skill. But in the matter of living in somebody else's house he was totally incompetent.

He had lasted six months at the Rod and Gaff, spending rather more time off duty in the black market than on duty in the kitchen, and it was only Mr Walton's compassion that staved off his dismissal for so long. When he was finally – and sorrowfully – sacked, one of the hotel domestics took pity on him and had him for a few months until she found him one morning in the market, selling some of her nighties off a barrow. I fixed him up again back in Westburn with old Mrs Holland in Exhibition Terrace: she was a good old soul who fed her boys like fighting-cocks and disciplined them gruffly, but the one thing she couldn't abide was smoking. So this great clot of mine started smoking in bed and puffing the smoke into an empty hotwater bottle, intending to carry it out next morning, I suppose, and empty it. So there was a fire.

After that Herbie disappeared for two days, until I found him in Taff's Caff, which was a transport place offering sleeping accommodation to long-distance lorry-drivers. He'd got round the proprietor to let him stay. I said he couldn't. He said I'd get him out with tear-gas, nothing less. I said he was to come out this minute and go into respectable lodgings. He said, where? That had me, I hadn't got any. For six sweating weeks he stayed there while I wondered who the hell he was sleeping with. Then he got done on a motor-bike deal, couldn't pay his rent, and got slung out; he arrived in my office weeping and swaying about, I didn't know whether to spank him or stroke him.

I hadn't got a damned thing for Herbie, we were terrifyingly short of lodgings; I sent him back to work while I searched, and I went so far as to ask Mrs Indwell to have him, but there was nothing doing anywhere. In the end a Mrs Blackham said she'd have him for one night only, which would give me more time, so I pushed him in there, told him to report to me first thing in the morning for further instructions, and went to sleep with my fingers crossed. This was going to mean an early start for me next morning.

I'm supposed to be at the office by nine, but seeing the hours I spend every evening rushing about, I usually wend a pretty leisurely way in the mornings. That morning I felt more than usually shell-shocked, going off with my mouth tasting dark brown, and I'd cut myself shaving. I scrambled on to a bus and stared blankly about me. The chap opposite was deep in a paper with flaring headlines:

GIRLS STRIPPED IN SEX-SCHOOL DRAMA
(*Exclusive*)
Police swooped last night on ...

☞ Back Page

I've been exposed to this sort of thing all my life and I know I ought to be contemptuous of it, but I still felt that damned unseemly twinge of interest in the story. Oh well, I thought, it would probably turn out to be some feeble anecdote about a headmistress removing a schoolgirl's jewellery. I switched my gaze to the woman in front, who was reading:

TEENAGE VICE RING SMASHED
(*Exclusive*)
Screaming women rushed last night from

☞ Back Page

That meant nothing to me either, so I started concentrating on yawning and blinking my eyes to get the juice flowing, and then I saw that my neighbour was reading the editorial page of his paper and I read:

IT JUST NEEDED THIS!

Well, haven't we always said it?
For years we have said to the Government: Probe this special school racket!

NOTHING HAS BEEN DONE ...

And now it's happened!
A hundred innocent kids – kids like yours, kids like ours – have been found trapped in a foul den, the so-called progressive school of Anthony – beg pardon, MISTER –

And there, covering the rest of the story, was my neighbour's broad thumb, but I'd seen enough. I scuttled off the bus at the next stop and bought the rather sedate paper I favour; it took me some time to find the story, but I finally found it on page 13, next to the radio programmes:

SCHOOL 'IMPROPRIETY' ALLEGATION

—

POLICE INTERVENE

—

Investigations have been instituted by the Chunts. Police into alleged irregularities in the running of 'The Cottage by the Creek', a school for orphans near Strickworth. The Headmaster, Mr Anthony Smurthwaite, 36, will appear before the Strickworth magistrates this morning, charged with keeping a disorderly house.

I marched into the office and silently laid this story before Miss Dashforth. She was gazing hollow-eyed out of the window, the morning's mail unopened beside her.

'I know,' she said. 'County Hall have already been on the phone. All the kids have to be removed forthwith; you'd better go down straight away and fetch Egbert.'

'Isn't it worth our going all the way by car?' I said maliciously, immediately regretting the remark.

'No,' she said tonelessly. 'Get a taxi from Strickworth.

County Hall have warned the Boatwrights: Egbert can go to them until you've fixed up a foster-home for him.'

I felt sorry for poor old Dash, but I didn't know how to express anything to her, so I just nodded competently to her and strode out. I was half-way to London before I remembered Herbie; I rang up from Victoria.

'Children's Welfare Office.'

'Hallo, darling,' I said, and heard her draw her breath in sharply.

'Where are you, Charles? I thought you were Creek-bound.'

'My train goes in ten minutes. Are you doing the telephone, Harry?'

'Dash has gone home with a headache.'

'I forgot all about Herbie Slythe, Harry, has he turned up?'

'Not yet, no. What shall I do if he does?'

'I dunno. Give him five bob and send him back to Taff's Caff, unless you think of anything better.'

'Oh, you can't, Charles!'

'Well, what the hell else is there? This is an emergency. But perhaps he won't turn up.'

'If he does, I'll ring round for a hostel.'

'I'm sure he wouldn't go to one, but still, thanks, love. G'bye now.'

'Bye, Charles. Look after yourself.'

I found my platform. Several dispirited-looking Welfare Officers were drifting on to the same train; they came from various Home Counties and I knew them slightly by sight. It was a depressing prospect, to travel down with them, social workers not being sociable characters, but I couldn't walk away gauntly, so we got into a compartment together. Conversation on the journey was jerky, since the men only wanted to talk about salaries and service conditions, and the women only wanted to discuss casework and the London School of Economics, and all the common ground they found was in comparing the respective performances of their cars.

167

We decided to share taxis for the last bit, and I walked out of Strickworth station with a Miss Hogginshaw, a worried-looking north-country girl with a drip on the end of her nose. There was a group of taxi-drivers outside and when we appeared one of them said: ''Allo, 'ere's another lot of 'em.' I always feel cross when I am instantly recognized as a Social Worker, so when the man said: 'Goin' up the Creek, sir, ha ha?' I just nodded curtly and swept Miss Hogginshaw into the taxi as though she were swathed in mink. Not that she played up much, she spent most of the journey saying: 'Well, I don't know what I'm going to do with my Rita.'

'Reception Home?'

'No, she's been floong out of every Home in the county, no one'll have her back. Say what you like about this place, Mr Maule, but at least they hang on to their kids. Ee, I don't know what I'm going to do with my Rita. Send her home, I suppose. There's no time in this work, Mr Maule, no time for careful casework, it's all wrong. I never get time for my private life.'

The poor thing wouldn't know what to do with a private life if she had one, I thought, but I knew she'd hang on to her Rita, red-nosed and dogged, till Judgement Day if need be.

The Cottage by the Creek looked unexpectedly forlorn when we got there, unclaimed suitcases in the hall, a few staff behaving like hens with their heads cut off. There were some uniformed policemen about too, but they couldn't tell us much about what had happened; they were large, heavily-married men who hinted at the most frightful scenes of self-expression, and they were all kind and patient with the children.

Egbert was all ready for me.

'Is this all the luggage you've got, Egbert? Where the devil are all your clothes?'

He just shrugged.

'I got some pottery in the shed, can I bring it?'

'Yes, do.'

We all climbed into the waiting taxi, feeling vaguely as though we were retreating from Moscow. Rita turned out to be a heavily-built girl with a teeny, high, gigglying voice; she trotted out all the catchwords from the radio shows, and tried to stir up Egbert by tumbling against him when the taxi lurched. I think she was a lot more frightened than she pretended. Miss Hogginshaw and I decided to travel up to town in separate compartments.

Conversation between me and Egbert was desultory.

'I'm taking you to The Rookery for the time being, Egbert.'

'Uh-huh.'

'It'll give me time to look around for a decent foster-home for you, where you can start out to work.'

'M'm.'

'Any idea what job you'd like to do, Egbert?'

Pause.

'No.'

I gazed out at the fields for a while.

'I suppose you feel happy about settling down in Westburn, Egbert?'

He shrugged his shoulders; there, anywhere, what did it matter. He returned to his Tarzan comic and I to agricultural contemplation.

'Can I see your pottery, Egbert?'

He fetched it down. The first item was a queer, vaguely horrible head, the features smeared on in red.

'Oh, yes, very nice,' I said. 'Who is it?'

'Oh, nothin' – a mistake.' He was embarrassed. He fetched out another model, a sow with her farrow about her, quite good, heavy, and fleshy.

'That's good,' I said. 'That's good, I like it. Is it for anybody?'

'I might give it to me Mum.'

'Have you heard from her, Egbert?'

'No.'

'Nor have I, not for a long, long time.'

'She might turn up. Or I might give this to Myrna.'

He fetched out another piece, a crinoline lady.

'Oh, very nice, yes,' I said, but I said it too quickly, and he knew I was insincere. He said there wasn't anything else, and put it all away quickly.

'Myrna seems to be doing all right,' I said. 'You'll be able to see her, now you're back in Westburn.'

He shrugged his shoulders indifferently. The moment for intimacy had passed.

I regarded Egbert covertly as we sped between the washing-lines of south London. He'd changed in the last few months from a chubby schoolboy to a very young man. It was difficult to say how, precisely: the planes of his face had altered, or perhaps only his habitual expression had changed, the jaw was squarer, the nose more prominent and the mouth less so. He seemed more cagey; he'd never been a gay child, but even his seriousness seemed more controlled and deliberate. Somehow, he seemed to be changing before my very eyes into something I hadn't expected, although he was still quite unmistakably Egbert Crump. In fact, at that time he looked slightly less cared for than when he first came out of his own home. His dusty hair needed cutting, his shoes needed cleaning, and he was dressed in a khaki windcheater and blue jeans. I never did find out what happened to the clothes we'd supplied. Egbert couldn't explain Matron's house-keeping arrangements.

The Boatwrights were not pleased to see Egbert.

' 'E'll 'ave to sleep in t'sick bay tonight,' said Mr Boatwright. 'Till tomorrow. When Gordon Cronk goes out. When can yer move him out again, Mr Maule?'

'As soon as I can, Mr Boatwright – within a week or two, if I'm lucky.'

'Ah can keep him goin' with jobs in the garden. But Ah'd like him out. As soon as you can.'

Working lads are rather an embarrassment in a Children's Home; they have extra pocket money, and they smoke and occupy a demoralizing position half-way between staff and children. I hoped to do something quickly but not then, not at ten o'clock in the evening. I wondered where Rita and Miss Hogginshaw had got to; probably Miss Hogginshaw had taken the girl to her own home for the night.

I spent an uneasy night myself, wondering what on earth to do with Egbert and every now and then recalling with a guilty start that Herbie Slythe was also on the loose somewhere. As soon as I got to the office next day, Harry greeted me with the words :

'Your chap Slythe never turned up.'

'Didn't he ? Where the devil is he, I wonder. Oh, well. How's Dash ?'

'She hasn't turned up either.'

I had to do a quick report for the Children's Officer on what had happened at The Cottage, so I did that. Then I tried to find Herbie, who had last been heard of working in some mysterious capacity at the abattoir, but I found he had been sacked from there. Mr Clench hadn't seen anything of him; nor had Mr Bland, who had one or two of Herbie's mates on probation. I didn't try any harder : Herbie had apparently vanished from Westburn and I secretly hoped he'd joined the Norwegian Merchant Navy.

This state of affairs went on for three weeks. In the meantime I got Egbert settled in with a youngish couple named Slazenger : the man was foreman at a garage, and through him I got Egbert fixed up there, too, as a trainee mechanic. The pay wasn't very good, but he seemed to enjoy the surly, contemptuous way they all banged expensive motor-cars about.

Somewhere around Easter that year I took one of those useless leaves we had then. I had about a week of my holiday entitlement left, which I needed, but by the time I'd worked myself into a state of near-catalepsy clearing up before I went, and then nearly had a nervous breakdown catching up when I got back again, it was no rest to go at all. However, I got things more or less squared up, though for a couple of days I was away from the office altogether, flitting round the suburbs like a sheepdog at a Trial.

171

When I got back to the office on the Thursday morning, Miss Dashforth waylaid me.

'Charles, where have you been, I've had the N.S.P.C.C. in.'

'Who for?'

'You. They've found Herbie.'

'Oh, hell! Where?'

'With Mrs Bloat in Lavender Walk.'

'*What?*'

'Yes, it's true.' Miss Dashforth was wanly smiling. 'Herbie turned up there on his beam ends, and she's taken him in. Mrs Bloat is now one of your foster-mothers, ducky!'

'Hell's bells and buckets of blood!' I thanked Miss Dashforth very much for this heartening information and retreated into my own room where I found Harry standing by the window in grave composure. She gave me a quick but troubled smile.

'Oh, lord, Harry, I've got trouble, you've heard about Herbie?'

'Yes. I may as well tell you, Charles, I've got trouble too. Myrna Crump's being thrown out of her foster-home, after all these years.'

'Gosh. Oh, I am sorry, Harry, whatever has she been up to?'

'She's been caught soliciting in the High Road,' said Harry.

16

'OH, let's pack the whole bloody job in, Harry. Blow it, blow the work, blow the blooming kids.'

'What are you going to do instead?'

'I dunno,' I said. 'Perhaps I could go into Industry.'

'Could you do it?'

'What do you mean, could I do it? Of course I could do it. I'm used to responsibility, I'm ready to take charge of any job and work like mad at it, if only I was responsible for, oh, I dunno, plastic toast-racks, something that stands still for a minute.'

'Why did you take up social work, Charles?'

'Well, I – I – I wanted to leave the world a bit better than I found it, I suppose.'

'Would you really like to leave it richer by a few plastic toast racks?'

'No, don't lark about, Harry, you know I wouldn't. But this is a maniac sort of job, isn't it? Taking parental responsibility for people who behave like demented swallows, getting all the kicks when things go wrong and none of the ha'pence when they go right and all for a measly eight quid for a seventy-hour week.'

'Money isn't everything,' said Harry, absently.

'Not when you've got it, it isn't, but when you get an unfair share, you don't half feel small. Damn me, there's a bloke in our road, a plasterer's labourer, he's just bought his second new car since the war, and I can't even afford new shoes.'

'Well, there's a housing shortage, he probably contributes a lot more to human happiness than we do.'

'What?'

'Oh, calm down, Charles!' said Harry, giving me that

slow smile that makes my heart turn over. 'Why are you so worked up, anyway ? Nothing desperate has happened, all your lads are under cover at the moment, and they're not tiny babies likely to die of exposure and neglect. Relax !'

'Yes, I'm sorry, Harry,' I said, rolling my thumbs over and over each other. 'I shouldn't have started beefing, I know things are much worse for you, at home and all.'

'Hey, wait a minute, what's this ?'

'Oh, Harry, forgive me, I shouldn't have said that.'

'Has Dash been gossiping about me ?'

'No, not gossiping, Harry, I'm so sorry, forget it.'

Harry looked down at her clasped hands.

'Dash had no right whatever to say anything, what she knows about Mother was told her in confidence. And there's nothing at home that I can't handle, there's nothing really wrong anyway, for months sometimes we go along splendidly and if you start being sorry all over me, Charles, I shall burst into tears.'

'No, no, I'm not being sorry, Harry. I just – well, I care for you an awful lot, you know that.'

'Yes, I do, Charles, and I'm grateful. But you must understand that if I marry, I shall want to give myself to my husband completely, and I can *not* do that while Mother's entirely dependent on me to keep the house going, oh, and in every way. So that's an end to it, Charles.'

'Oh, Harry, darling, I –'

'Don't, Charles, *don't*, you're making it worse – '

I had got to my feet in considerable tension and Harry was clamped to her chair with her hands making fists, and at this inopportune moment in strode Dashforth running her hand through her hair and noticing nothing.

'Well, Harry, what are we going to do about Myrna Crump ?' she said, perching herself on our table and beginning to swing her thin legs.

I managed to cover up by elaborately lighting a cigarette, but Harry just sat there for half a minute with her head bowed, looking like a Madonna.

'Well, I've seen the girl,' she began slowly. 'She's in a very madamish mood, all head-tossing and shoulder-shrugging and "oh what business is it of yours?"'

'Poor thing. Poor silly thing,' said Miss Dashforth.

'It was quite a long time before I got her to talk at all; she just stood there with a look of cunning rapture on her face and making me feel a thorough old maid. In the end I made up a story about a fictitious girl who Came to a Bad End, and then I think Myrna attended, and in the end talked a bit, but I'm sure she didn't relate what I was saying to herself.'

'Is she v.i.?' asked Miss Dashforth.

'No, she's not,' said Harry. 'The doctor examined her, and Myrna admitted to the doctor that she'd had intercourse with three boys at various times, on the bombsite behind Plimm's warehouse. Apparently several of the girls go there.'

'H'm. Well, I'll tell the policewoman, shutting the stable door after the horse has bolted. She didn't name the boys?'

'No.'

'And she didn't show any remorse?'

'None at all; I'd say what she'd done was just a business deal. She's a hard little thing.'

'Oh, dear,' sighed Miss Dashforth. 'What a silly girl, and she had every opportunity to better herself with those nice Badstocks. Thrown it away, thrown it all away. Well, I don't think we can consider boarding her out again, do you think so?'

'No,' mused Harry. 'I think she'd go on the streets. I can't feel really confident that anything will pull her up, but I'm wondering if a sharpish shock might help her.'

'A Training Home? Well, there's quite a good one at Gerrards Cross. They took Maureen Flannery for me, and she was a bit like this. Shut her up for six months to cool off? H'm. I must say I can't think of anything better. Did you mention the possibility to her?'

'Yes. In fact, that prompted her longest speech. She said: "I shouldn't bother, miss. You know I'm going to be a tart whatever you do, so why waste your money on a Training Home ? Spend it on setting me up in a flat in Droops Cut !'' '

'Well, why not ?' I said. 'We're supposed to develop each child's aptitude and ability, and poor old Myrna's only got the one.'

Miss Dashforth drew herself up, outraged Methodism in every quivering muscle.

'One day, Charles,' she said, 'your facetiousness will land you in serious trouble. Don't let any newspaperman hear you saying things like that, even in jest.'

'No, of course not,' I apologized. 'But seriously, Miss D., what are you worried about with Myrna ? I mean, would it really matter if she had an illegitimate baby ?'

'It would have a shattering effect on her,' said Miss Dashforth.

'It would have a shattering effect on the baby,' said Harry.

'All right, then,' I said. 'But it's surely not the end of the world just because a girl loses her virginity ?'

'We're not treating it as the end of the world,' said Miss Dashforth. 'But we know, as apparently you don't want to, that that way only brings unhappiness.'

'It's a question of the interests of society, isn't it ?' I said.

'It's a question of sin,' said Miss Dashforth firmly. 'Now, what about Egbert ?'

'Oh, he's all right with the Slazengers,' I said. 'So far. Oh, dear.'

'What's the matter ?'

'I don't know,' I said. 'I wish I knew where I was going with Egbert, all this picking him up and plonking him down again, it doesn't seem very constructive.'

'Well, what else can you do ?'

'That's what I don't know ! It's just that ever since this kid came into Care he's had nothing but mess and muddle.'

'Nothing to the mess and muddle he had at home,' said Harry. 'Can't you remember The Rat Yard ?'

'Yes, he had to come into Care, Charles,' said Miss Dashforth.

176

'Did he?' I said gloomily. 'What for? In what way is he any better off?'

'Oh, for goodness' sake!' said Dash. 'Why, his home was absolutely ghastly. Everybody tried to improve the standards there, it was quite hopeless.'

'All the same,' I said, 'Egbert's had one, two, three, four, five, six homes in under three years, and every change was an upheaval for him, an extra strain on him.'

'We'll win through in the end,' said Miss Dashforth. 'I still feel that the answer to every problem we've brought up this morning is the right child in the right foster-home at the right time. What we've got to do is to increase our knowledge of children and foster-parents until we are so good at assessing them that we can avoid the mistakes we've evidently made with Myrna and Egbert. And Sabrina.' (Sabrina, the coloured Crump, had just been returned by her foster-parents because the neighbours gossiped.)

'My knowledge of Egbert has, if anything, grown less over the last two years,' I said. 'I don't know what goes on in his head, I feel quite baffled in knowing how to help him, I feel I must be missing something perfectly obvious. I don't think I'm any good whatever at this job.'

'Reaction,' said Miss Dashforth, in her brusque, labelling tone. 'Don't worry, we've all felt like this and we've all got over it.'

'Maybe,' I muttered. 'But if only there was some plan, so that Egbert and I knew where we were, it's this vagueness and uncertainty that gets me. We haven't had a plan at all, we've had six different ones and they've all turned out wrong, especially that ghastly special school.'

Miss Dashforth rubbed her nose agitatedly, she had left her cigarettes in her own room.

'Yes,' she said bravely, 'we all backed the wrong horse there.'

'Anyway,' said Harry, 'how many people's lives really go according to one plan from start to finish? Well, I suppose they do, according to God's plan, but you don't know God's plan for Egbert, Charles, perhaps it's all coming out just right.'

'With the Slazengers,' said Miss Dashforth.

'I don't think that's going to work,' I said gloomily. 'I don't think it's a very good idea to put a boy with his foreman; if there's trouble at home, it spills over into work, and vice versa, I think it's putting too much strain on the kid.'

'Ah, well, press on!' declaimed Miss Dashforth, springing to her feet and raising her hand dramatically. 'That's the answer to all this: we don't know the answer, so – press on, chaps!'

After Egbert was boarded out with the Slazengers, it was eight weeks to the day that I had to remove him. I found a certain wry pleasure in finding that I had made an accurate forecast, marred by the realization that I hadn't been able to do anything about it, anyway.

We were in June 1951 then, and towards the end of the month we got one of those really blazing spells, inexorably hot. I was steaming when I tramped down to the Slazengers. Galsworthy Road is a red-brick road, red-brick houses with little red-brick walls round the front gardens, the whole street was like an oven. Nearly all the people had doors and windows open and were sitting out for a breath of air; only at Slazengers' was the front door ominously closed.

I was told that the trouble had begun at the garage the previous afternoon. It must have been frightful in there under the glowing iron roof, and, of course, all the customers had decided together to have their cars got ready for the week-end. It was a mad scramble and the mechanics in their heavy overalls changed into a mob of angry megalomaniacs. Towards the end of the afternoon, Egbert, in a mood of unusually contemptuous carelessness, backed somebody's Vauxhall into somebody else's Hillman. Out leapt Mr Slazenger the foreman, drawing Our Saviour's attention to Egbert's lack of brain, moral sense, and father. Egbert listened in a dull rage, and stalked home from work by himself.

He had hardly set foot inside the door at home than he

trod on the smallest Slazenger's plastic tank and broke it. The smallest Slazenger hurled a metal cap-pistol at Egbert, and Egbert smacked his head. Out leaped Mrs Slazenger the foster-mother, flaming hot from her oven, and informed Egbert he was nothing but a black-damned, cream-faced loon – or words to that effect – and to come and 'ave 'is tea for 'eaven's sake. Egbert told her where she could store her bacon and chips and retired in a royal sulk to his bedroom and *Reveille*.

I believe that even at that point tempers might have cooled by morning; but Egbert wet his bed. More, he attempted to conceal the fact by bundling the bottom sheet into the wardrobe, but the smallest Slazenger saw him and reported him. Egbert got out of the house quick, but Mr Slazenger followed him to work with his wife's complaints ringing shrilly in his ears, to be confronted at once by last night's dented Hillman. After twenty-five minutes of mutual abuse, cast in the lowest possible terms, Egbert, his cards in his pocket, took himself to the pictures.

The sweat was trickling down inside my shirt as I spent an hour trying to heal the breach and finished up trembling with frustration and nervous reaction : for an hour I'd had to watch every syllable like a hawk. But the longest respite I could win, and grudgingly at that, was one more night; then Egbert had to be out.

It was in a sultry yellowish light that I got to the office next morning and slumped into my chair. Egbert had already arrived with his suitcase, and was slumped in the waiting-room.

'I couldn't stand that ole hag a minute longer.'

'No, all right.' I lit a dampish cigarette. 'Ever thought of joining the Army, Egbert ?'

'No, what for ?'

'I just thought maybe you'd got fed up with all this chopping and changing in lodgings, and would like to get settled in the Services.'

'No. I'll get called up when I'm eighteen, that's soon enough, innit ?'

'I suppose so.' I relit my cigarette; it tasted like horsehair.
'Merchant Navy ?'

'No.'

'Farm school ?'

'No.'

'Hotel work ?'

'No.'

'Hostel ?'

'No.'

'Lodgings in Westburn ?'

'Yer.'

'Oh, blimey. All right, then, Egbert; wait here, I may be some time before I can fix you up.'

'Orright.'

I went back to my room and started to riffle pretty hopelessly through our card-index of foster-mothers. It was so hot my fingers left marks on the cards. Mrs Indwell, Mrs Erams – Mrs Erams ? No, she had two wild Catholics – Mrs Slazenger, Mrs Bloat – help !

'Suggest something, Harry ?'

'M'm ?'

'For Egbert – he's broken down again.'

'Oh ?'

'I'm absolutely stumped, can you suggest anybody who might take him ?'

'Eh ?'

I glanced sharply at her. She was looking awfully pale, and there were smudges under her eyes.

'You all right, Harry ?'

'What ? Oh, yes, yes. I'm sorry, Charles, what, you want a foster-home ?' She leaned her head wearily on her hand and drew small circles on her blotter. Presently she said :

'Egbert's not really a hooligan, is he ?'

'No, no, he gets his moods, but he's rather passive really. Why ?'

'There's a Mrs Urmston Smith in Cold Acres Lane. It's an extremely nice house, her husband's a further education tutor or something; the standards might be much too high for Egbert, but I must say I liked her very much. Would you like to go and see?'

'Yes, I would. Thanks very much. You sure you don't need her for anyone?'

'No. You're welcome. Number Twelve.'

'Thanks a lot.'

I went out with slightly less flagging feet, leaving Harry still drawing circles. Her head looked as though it weighed a ton.

I found Egbert and said: 'Look, son, I think I've got a place for you, but I shall have to go and ask the lady first. I want you to go and see Mr Clench and get fixed up with a job, and I'll meet you back here again as soon as I can, all right?'

'O.K.'

Like a fool I hadn't brought my mac with me that morning; when I was half-way down Cold Acres Lane, the hot spell broke up in a savage storm with torrents of rain. You could see the water rise in sheets across the grass verges. I was like a drowned rat when I bolted into Number Twelve. Cold Acres Lane is a very unexpected place on the outskirts of Westburn. For a long time it was a genuine lane, skirting an orchard; then a shrewd builder got hold of it, and put up long, low detached houses in the orchard, preserving the hedges and many of the wayside elms and creating a secluded, leafy and extremely expensive oasis.

Near the bottom end I found an attractive timber house, one of those post-war designs which were just beginning to find favour here and there. It had a roof of cedar shingles, I think, and a lot of plate-glass windows, and the garden was laid out in lawns with unusual shrubs, individually treated. Propped up in the grass verge by the gate was a huge slab of oak, carved in plain forthright letters: NUMBER TWELVE. It looked very costly, madly beyond what any Education person could afford. I found out later that Mr Urmston Smith had made a pile in industry, and this present tutoring lark was just a hobby for him.

I shot in under the porch with water pouring out of my clothes. Mrs Smith had seen me arrive and opened the door before I rang.

'Good heavens, man, you're soaked,' she said, unnecessarily.

'I'm awfully sorry to arrive like this, Mrs Smith,' I said. 'I was taken quite unawares.'

'So I see.'

'I come from the Children's Department,' I said.

'Oh, yes. Oh – you want to come in.'

'Well – er – not like this, Mrs Smith, I couldn't ruin your carpets with all this lot.'

'Oh, pooh, come into the kitchen; it's a tiled floor, you'll do no harm there.'

That was a bizarre interview, that morning, with me standing by the Aga with steam pouring upwards from my clothes, and Mrs Urmston Smith sitting, in her glittering kitchen, in an aged rocking chair. I started sneezing halfway through, so she made some coffee and her husband came in – a tall, shambling, white-haired man – and lent me one of his dressing-gowns while my trousers were taken to drip into the bath.

I've often thought since that at that particular moment of my life I must have been needing parent-figures myself, and I suppose that being coddled in the kitchen just rounded off the situation: anyway, I found myself talking to Mr and Mrs Urmston Smith in a way I had never used to any other foster-parents. Gone were my watchful choice of words, my professional poker-face, my ploy of drawing the other chap out before he drew me. I just talked about Egbert and me, and I was amazed to discover how much I knew about both of us.

The Urmston Smiths began by contributing rather knowing remarks like 'Oh, well, it was the same with our son . . .' but after a while, when my story took one or two unexpected turns, they fell silent, and later still they took to looking at me with what I was startled to recognize as admiration. At the end of my long narrative they thought for a bit, and then exchanged one bright look, and then Mrs Smith spoke for both of them :

'Well, Mr Maule, we'll have a try, and we can't say more than that. I do quite see what you mean about the difference in cultural standards. I do understand that Egbert may be unhappy here, or fit so badly that he makes me unhappy. But we'll try and meet him half way, and if it doesn't work out, well, it doesn't, that's the only way to look at it, isn't it ?'

I felt an overwhelming gratitude and affection towards them for what they were going to do, which I could hardly express to them, though I did my best.

They showed me over the house; it was beautifully furnished. The big living-room was on the open plan and also on two levels : at the far end, up a bit, stood a white baby grand, and on this stood the only photograph in the room, a portrait of a young man in R.A.F. uniform who had obviously just sewn on his wings.

'That was our boy,' said Mr Urmston Smith, and his eyes crinkled quickly at the corners.

I paused by the piano and said hesitantly :

'Look – I'm – going to say something rather impertinent and rather unkind, but I think I have to say it. You do know, don't you, that Egbert can never replace your son ? He'll always be somebody else's son ?'

'Oh, yes,' said Mrs Smith, softly.

Well, it was fixed up for Egbert to come, and I replaced my rather damp trousers and hurried joyfully back through the gleaming streets to the office. Harry wasn't there; Egbert was.

'Well, I've fixed you up,' I said. 'And look, lad : this time I think you've got a real chance to get on your feet. These are much nicer people than you've met before and if you mind your p's and q's, I believe you'll have a really happy time with them. Look, Egbert, it's not my way to ask boys to make promises to me, but can I anyway beg you, this time, not to let yourself down ? Or let me down ?'

'Orright,' he said.

I don't know if he understood; I don't know if he cared

By the time I'd done something about a job for him – as a trainee in a radio repair shop – and got him over to Cold Acres Lane, it was teatime; I saw him start, perching rather awkwardly on a settee with his cup balanced on his knee and looking in an awed way about him, and departed feeling thoroughly pleased with myself.

Next morning I bounced into the office.

'I say, Harry, thanks so much for – oh.'

She wasn't there.

She didn't come in at all while I was in, and she wasn't there the next morning, either.

'I say, Miss Greave,' I said, 'is Harry due in this morning?'

'Oh, no, Mr Maule, I'm sure she won't come in, haven't you heard?' said Miss Greave. 'Her mother died, the night before last.'

17

I DID not see Harry again for three weeks; she took what leave was due to her, sought out an old college chum of hers, now married, and went to stay with her, playing with the honorary nephews on the banks of the Thames. And oh, how I missed her.

When she did come back to the office, I found that we were on rather more distant terms than before. I simply wanted to sweep her into my arms and love and comfort her; and she knew this and wasn't very sure how she would cope with me if I did it; and I knew this, too, and hung back for fear of harassing her. She became graver and quieter than ever, and often kept out of my way; and when I was with her I would use the old backchat and endearments in far too loud and casual a voice, which sounded horribly jocular to me. And so we went on for a bit in an uneasy hush, not daring to say what we really wanted to. If Harry was in the office when I was, I would become so conscious of her that I would stare unseeingly at a report for five minutes together; and if she wasn't there when I expected her I used to get the feeling of real physical hunger, a great empty O under my breastbone.

Not that we had a great deal of time just then to see to our own emotions; we had a frightful time during the school holidays. Parents confronted by their offspring's being at home for eight long weeks made fast tracks for the nearest mental hospital. Monarchic doctors casually issued little notes, saying (so far as we could read them): 'Mrs A is suffering from nervous debility and must rest, kindly remove her children until she is better.' Other doctors, lolling about in even cosier surgeries, wrote: 'Mrs B is suffering from nervous debility. Kindly allow her to adopt a child to cheer her up.' Elaborately maladjusted little toughs, whom we thought we'd parked in special schools up long, long drives, suddenly reappeared in droves demanding love and accommodation for the holidays. The local magistrates went to a special meeting, came back and made fifteen Fit Person Orders in five days. We couldn't put children into Homes because the Homes were closed while everybody went off to the seaside. Approximately half our regular foster-mothers had gone off to the seaside too. It was a horrible time altogether.

Although, in the heat and burden of the day, we didn't recognize the fact, the situation as a whole was beginning to grow a little easier. To start with, we'd all got tougher about taking children into Care, in fact we had no longer to say we 'took' them: we 'received' them. Even Miss Dashforth, who used to delight in sweeping bewildered kids out of the gutter to give them a fresh start in life, was beginning to think twice before she interfered. Harry and I had begun painfully to learn that it was often better to sit back and do absolutely nothing and let people sort themselves out. My great friend, Steve Cannon, who was working from County Hall at that time, used to say: 'Well, people got on perfectly well before there was ever a Children Act; let 'em get on with it now. Don't knock yourself up for that worthless lot, Charlie.' Except for seasonal spates, the flow of children coming in was beginning to diminish.

And then our efforts to find foster-homes were suddenly bringing rewards, as though we had planted a lot of seeds over the years and they were beginning to come up. Some people in the Government had found out about boarding out and were saying shrilly that it was not merely the best but the cheapest form of treatment for deprived children. Of course, in a time of austerity and dollar gaps, something that is both good and cheap is quite irresistible in Whitehall; the Home Office made an appealing film and sent down a lot of posters. In one week I interviewed seventeen women and each one wanted 'a little girl, about three, with no parents'. However, good foster-homes were being found and a lot of children were being very happily established in them, and

186

there was more room in Children's Homes. In fact there was so much room in some of them that the horrid word redundancy began to be bruited about. A whisper reached us that Tots' Glade would be closed down next year; Miss Heaton hastily joined a Trade Union and there was a lot of grumbling about what we were doing.

We used to address a lot of women's meetings that year, appealing for foster-mothers; I can't remember if we ever recruited any. I didn't do much of that, I'm a terrible public speaker. I got caught once, when Miss Dashforth unexpectedly fell ill and I had to deputize for her at the Bethesda Four Square Citadel Women's Bright Hour, in Temperance Row. I decided to make an emotional appeal to this lot, so I began by thundering against dreadful irresponsible parents – cruelty, dirt, neglect, disease – children locked in cupboards, children attacked by stepfathers – ghastly tragedy, innocent mind warped, trust shattered – but you can help, your country needs you, enrol as a substitute mother *now!*

As I sat down, sweating, I was gratified to see a number of ladies rise and come forward, but they only said to me things like: 'My daughter was removed by the N.S.P., ever so nice he was,' or 'Do you know my son, Irving? 'E's in a 'Ome,' or 'Ooh, I did like your story about the unmarried mother, did you mean me?'

One way and another the pressure on us was imperceptibly lessening; we could spend a little more time on a decision here, a few minutes longer in a foster-home there, even sometimes manage a whole evening off. I once took Harry to Stratford-on-Avon. I think that some time around then I began to realize that I was not Westburn's Albert Schweitzer, and that if I went on at this rate I should end up a crashing, prematurely aged bore. Several times I swore to myself that I would take up some creative leisure-time interest to take my mind off The Work. The difficulty was to find anything half so vivid and enthralling as the work I was doing. In the end I didn't take up anything. I used to go home, flop into bed and read a thriller a night.

As the months went by it became clearer and clearer to

me that one problem I could shelve for the moment was Egbert's. It hadn't been easy going at first. I think that when Egbert arrived at the Urmston Smith's he found himself overawed by the material splendours of their home, and in this state of feeling he kicked up. I suppose he was registering some unformulated resentment against life in general and, in particular, against people who had so much when he had so little. Or maybe he was just growing fast and couldn't control his arms and legs. Anyway, he began in a surly boorish way, swinging his boots up on the settee, stubbing out his cigarettes on the bedside table, speaking in an un-naturally gruff and uncouth voice, even for him, kicking pouffes out of his way. Twice he wet his bed, though I am not sure if that was part of the pattern. He was trying to test out the Smiths by outraging them, I think. Fortunately, the Smiths didn't let him see they were outraged; but they were hurt and perplexed in private, and I spent a lot of time with them when Egbert was at work, trying to interpret his be-haviour. They were people who felt much more confident if things were rational and understandable, though fortunately they both had a charming irrational warmth about them that in the long run was worth more. Anyway, they went on calmly as they had always gone on, leading their own lives by their own standards, never forcing Egbert either to do or not to do anything, and trusting in the example they believed they were setting him. He nearly mucked every-thing up in October, when he came home one night messily the worse for drink; but he had such an appalling hangover next day and looked so piteous, like a lemur, that Mrs Smith saw the funny side of the episode and got over it. In Novem-ber, one pay-day, Egbert brought home a bunch of flowers for her and thrust it gruffly at her, saying ' 'Ere y'are.' In December he began to call her Mum. In January they began to listen to The Archers together and shared their enjoy-ment. In February Egbert remembered Mother's Day. In March he called Mr Smith 'Pop', which tickled the old boy so much that he rang me up to tell me. In April Egbert had a girl fall in love with him and used to rush home to laugh with Mum over her antics. In May I knew, with triumphant disappointment, that I was no longer wanted.

I could not say the same for Herbie Slythe. When Herbie first arrived at Mrs Bloat's he wasn't far off his seventeenth birthday, an event which, for various technical reasons, considerably weakened my power of control over him. Herbie, who knew the law as well as I did, or nearly, knew that so long as he prevented me from finding out what he was up to, he was pretty well safe to do as he liked.

Through an acquaintance of his, a homosexual waiter, he'd got a job at the Imperial as a general factotum. What with free meals and tips he wasn't doing so badly, but Herbie never had enough money, especially now, when he was mad keen on driving motor-bikes, although disqualified. He did what he could with the wine-cellar, but in the first six months only three bottles of port found their way into Taff's Caff.

This was about the time Harry went off on compassionate leave. It was also a time when, in general, things were getting steadily more prosperous; rationing had all but disappeared, money was a little more plentiful and the black market was dwindling. Herbie turned his attention to more expensive things.

The sumptuous pigskin briefcase he got from a car in the hotel garage very nearly did for him at Mrs Bloat's, because when he got it home he found it was full of little bottles. He emptied them into a bowl and Mrs Bloat's pussy got at it. In the middle of the night Mrs Bloat went down to find her pussy, twice its normal size, trying to gnaw through the wall of the house, and when she got hold of it, it bit her in the leg and died. The case belonged to a Soft Drinks manufacturer; Herbie put it in the Gleeze in the end.

This was about the time I took Harry to Stratford-on-Avon.

A while later, I had an unexpected visit from Mr Mussel, who was nostalgically revisiting some of his old haunts. He'd taken on a spare-time job as Organizer for the

Residential Staffs Association and was on his way to a protest meeting.

'I ran into Herbie Slythe in town,' he said, when we had exchanged reminiscences.

'Did you, Mr Mussel ? How did you find him ?'

'Oh, the same old Herbert; seemed rather scared when I hailed him and we had but a few words together. He's getting very fat, Maule.'

'Is he ?'

'Well, not about the face, perhaps, but he's putting it on round the tummy. If I were in your position I should arrange for a medical check-up. He might have a growth.'

'I'll do that, Mr Mussel, thanks.'

I found out later that Herbie had been smuggling in a pair of sheets, wound round under his trousers.

This was about the time I took Harry to the S.S.A.F.A. Ball and kissed her good night.

What did for Herbie in the end was the day the Children's Officer came down to the Imperial to address Rotary, and Herbie stole his hat. Our bare-headed boss was just telling the manager he was going to sue when Herbie emerged from the staff door wearing his best suit, beige with a silver thread, and the black homburg rakishly tilted over one eye. There was an elaborate row, nobody knew who was suing whom. I put Herbie with Mrs Cropper till the row blew over; she didn't like boys much but she was very loyal. He was there a month. Then he got a job as an engine-cleaner and went to live in the railwaymen's hostel, but not long afterwards he was sacked, so he went back to Mrs Bloat. I told him he ought to be ashamed to live there, and he said why, and I said, well, look at the place, it's like a dustbin, and next day Mrs Bloat came up threatening to do me for defloration o' charickter.

This was actually on the day when Harry and I announced our engagement. We told Mrs Bloat and she instantly became very sentimental and promised to give me an art pot for a wedding present.

Soon after this Herbie decided that Mrs Bloat was really

a bit too grim, I don't think he got much to eat there, so he left without knowing where he was going and had to sleep rough in the park for a couple of nights. I had a visit then from a huge police sergeant who produced the tattered body and demanded to know what sort of care I thought I was giving the poor little waif.

I gave Herbie a real rollocking that time, but I had to do something, so I got him in with a rather neurotic couple I didn't like but who kept pestering me for a little orphan girl about three. Of course it was dicey, so what I did was to get Herbie registered for National Service, and then I persuaded the Ministry of Labour blokes to get him an early call-up to the Army, and they said they would as soon as they could. About this time the old warden of Elysium House, a crabby old devil, an ex-Petty Officer, retired and was succeeded by a young keen chap anxious to make a good impression. Herbie's foster-parents were getting very restless, so I got this young chap, whose name was Christmas, to promise to take Herbie temporarily if the worst happened and hold him until the call-up came through.

So this was the situation, with Herbie very near his eighteenth birthday, and I reckoned I'd got enough defence in depth to save us from any further embarrassment. We hadn't done much for Herbie, he wasn't a shining jewel in the diadem of Care, his future was, to say the least, twilit; but we'd got him through to eighteen all in one piece, we hadn't lost him, we'd given him opportunities to get on and prosper, even if he couldn't take them, and we hadn't been criticized in Parliament over him. There are occasions when even that is quite an achievement.

I wasn't panic-stricken, therefore, when Miss Greave came in one morning, while I was writing to book a hotel for the honeymoon; I was feeling very contented.

'Shan't be long now, ducks,' I hailed her.

'Lucky beast. There's a boy outside, Mr Maule; he's got all his luggage with him and says he's been thrown out and must see you.'

'Oh, yes, well, that's only Herbie. Plan B will now spring into operation. Wheel him in.'

But it wasn't Herbie. It was Egbert.

18

'No, I'm not goin' back!' snarled Egbert. 'Bleedin' ole bag, all over yer one minute wantin' to adopt yer, next minute yer out on yer ear. I'm fed up. *I'm fed up!*'

This is a pretty strong reaction, I thought, as I watched him; he was fond of Mrs Urmston Smith, I'm sure he was, and what he was saying now was just a loud wounded cry. I tried to keep our conversation to as practical a level as possible, what was he going to do now, how was he off for money, was his job safe; the rest I knew I would find out in due course, and I did.

The breakdown between Egbert and the foster-parents was not something which just happened suddenly for one specific reason. There was a whole complex of factors at work and they all acted and reacted one upon the other until, speaking for myself, it was almost impossible to see where the relationship had begun to break and, thereafter, which factors were of primary importance. In these circumstances very often analysis proves sterile and one has to think in terms of vague concepts like emotional climate. The first point of stress one could isolate was the moment, a couple of months earlier, when Mr Urmston Smith had a mild heart attack, nothing very much in itself, just a tiny flutter and a little discomfort. Maybe a year earlier, or a year later, the old boy would have taken it in his stride; but as it was he went to his doctor for a check-up, and he was told that there was a murmur there, that he might have a series of increasingly severe attacks or equally that he might never be troubled again, but he was advised that he ought really to play safe, cut down on his activities, and take life easy for a bit.

Now, the Smiths had had only one child, the son who had

been killed in the war, and they had no close relatives after that. They were deeply in love and to both of them their marriage in that period was immensely satisfying; they had a lot to lose. And however bluffly reassuring their doctor may have been, there is something special about the word 'heart' which tends to disturb one's sense of security. I suppose that as one grows older one becomes increasingly aware of the old pump beating away there, and subconsciously perhaps one begins to listen more acutely for any irregularity in that dependable rhythm. However that may be, the Smiths drew closer together at that time and their relationship became just that shade more exclusive.

And here again one could say that maybe a year earlier or a year later Egbert would have cared more than he actually did. But he was going through the pendulum phase of rebellion against Father and had not yet begun fully to model himself upon Father and find increasing areas of sympathy. Of course, with Egbert it was a bit more complicated because as far as we knew he'd never previously had experience of an effective father. Who knows, maybe he had, in fact, begun to take a delight in this new relationship and was deeply upset by the sudden threat to it. But why ever it was, the result was that when the Smiths created a faint air of exclusiveness, Egbert sheered off a little farther and a little more rapidly than one might have expected.

Now, one cannot separate the activities of the human mind, but I believe that while emotionally Mrs Smith was unknowingly moving away from Egbert, she was intellectually moving in on him. She began to think and to plan what might happen if her husband became seriously ill or died, and in her plans Egbert had an important place. She was a conscientious, responsible woman, and she was fond of the boy. She knew that a situation might arise when Egbert would have again to face the world alone, and she began to think of what ought to be done to equip him for this. Imperceptibly she began to think and then to hint at things like evening classes, trade training, savings, endowment policies;

and equally imperceptibly she began to think and then to hint of adoption.

A year earlier or a year later, all these things might have appealed to Egbert; but not then. Young people of around seventeen are not the most far-sighted group of citizens at the best of times, and Egbert had known for a long time that everything's ephemeral anyway. He had reached a stage where he *knew* he was independent, in tangible things like the wage he could command and in the intangible things like mental vigour and self-sufficiency. So Mrs Smith's hints and plans produced not acquiescence but resentment; and the more resentful shrugs she encountered, the harder she pressed. So when adoption was brought in, Egbert saw it not as a means of release, but as a ball and chain.

And then into a situation that was beginning to tremble marched a rather dreadful girl called Doreen Slattery. She was three years older than Egbert and she threw herself at him.

Up to that time I'd never stopped to consider Egbert as a sexual proposition, but now that I had to I did quite see what Doreen saw. He had filled out over the past year, still wasn't very tall, but had big shoulders and a deep chest, and he moved about with grace and confidence. This was the time when the flash youths went in for very conventional clothes, expensive but formal suits in clergyman grey, just before the Edwardian style burst on the scene. Egbert liked dressing well at week-ends, any old jeans would do for work, but for the dance hall it took him an hour and a half to get ready. He was good at jiving, as he could combine frenzy and stamina with the grave dedicated air so necessary in the cult. At this time Robert Mitchum was still something of a model for the lads, and Egbert could effortlessly convey the necessary aura of sleepy menace. The fact that he looked to me like a sulky child looking for a spank didn't matter in the meretricious world he swam in; Egbert really was somebody when he paused by the dance-hall floor, immaculate in his sombre clothes, running a sleepy, sidelong glance over the girl's breasts.

I cannot imagine that anyone attending The Cottage by the Creek came away without physical experience, but in Egbert's case I don't think this could have meant much to him, judging principally by the obsessing effect Doreen had on him. Maybe at school Egbert had been through the routine naughtiness in an uninvolved sort of way; Doreen got him in deep. Not that she was merely a whore; she rarely thought of anything but her own secondary sexual characteristics; she liked gender better than sex, she liked the chase better than the kill, and she already was expert at prolonging the chase. Egbert became absolutely obsessed with the idea that one day he would possess her; at work, or in the evenings at home, he would suddenly go still, or else pace restlessly, in the grip of a fevered imagination that physically stimulated his whole body. To him Mrs Smith's advice and pleas and friendly warnings suddenly became like a gramophone record spun too fast, an irritating squeaky jabber.

Thus the inky clouds drifted up over the horizon, and when the storm came it was sharp and sudden. One Friday night after a dance, Egbert stayed out wrestling with Doreen and came home very late indeed, about two in the morning. He had a latchkey but he banged into something going upstairs and Mr Urmston Smith woke up with a jump and a moan and a bumpy heart. Mrs Smith was already awake, furious and fearful. Next morning she went full tilt for Egbert and instructed him to mend his ways rapidly. Egbert went out sullenly and in his mind, over and over, beat the words: 'Who does she think she's talking to, who does she think she is, she can't talk to me like that.' But it went deeper than that; Egbert's way of life, and therefore his precious personality, was being challenged, and he knew he had to assert himself now or in some half-guessed way he'd be lost. That night he came home very late and he came home tipsy, and he came home with Doreen; and when Mrs Smith came fiercely downstairs, there they were on the settee, no shoes on, looking up at her with sardonic challenging sneers. . . .

I liked Egbert less than I'd done before, but that didn't have to show.

'H'm. I see. All right. Now what about your job?'

'That's all right.'

'Yes, but do you intend to keep at it?' I asked.

'Well, yer, it's all right.'

'Well, then, you've got to live near it, haven't you?'

A shrug of the shoulders.

'I don't know where I'm going to find lodgings,' I said.

'Oh, I'm fed up 'o lodgings; turn yer out as soon as look at yer, don't do this, feet orf my sofa, no smokin' in front o' the children – phoo!'

'Well, yes, I understand that, but if you don't go into lodgings, boy, where are you going to sleep tonight?'

A shrug of the shoulders.

'Look, Egbert,' I said, 'there's only three alternatives, as far as I know. The first is to join one of the Services, or the Merchant Navy; you get food, clothes, a roof over your head, and a crowd of lads to muck in with, that's not like lodgings.'

'Think I'm daft?'

Sometimes, I thought, morosely.

'Sign on for twelve years, for fourpence a week and some ole sergeant-major bellerin' at yer? Phoo! No, thank you.'

'All right,' I said. 'Secondly, there's the hostel: you live with a crowd of lads and you go out to work.'

'I don't fancy it.'

'Quite nice conditions, a few rules, but they're the same for everyone, and no young children under your feet.'

'I don't fancy it.'

'All right. Thirdly, hotel work, a job where you live in and get your food and shelter provided.'

'Coo, no,' he cried. 'I know about them jobs. Slythe told me. You 'ave to work all day long and ever so late at night, never no time orf, I couldn't ever go jivin'.'

'You get your time off all right.'

'Yer, on a flippin' Thursday afternoon, no thank you.'

'All right, then, it's lodgings.'

'I'm fed up o' bloody lodgings!'

'All right. Here we are again, you name it, we haven't got it. It's one of those or sleep rough, my cocky.'

A shrug of the shoulders.

I thought in silence for a minute and then with great trepidation I asked:

'I suppose Doreen's family couldn't take you?'

A glitter went all over his face, but he said:

'Cor! No. There's nine in 'er family, no room, see.'

Thank goodness, I thought. I got out my cigarettes and gave him one and we smoked silently. I suddenly decided to leave the next move to him; blow him, he'd got himself into a homeless state, now let him do something about it, even if it was only speaking first. I smoked on. He was hunched forward in his chair fidgeting his feet about. The minutes stretched out. It was agonizing, I wanted to do anything to shatter this horrible, unnatural silence; but I didn't even cough or shuffle. I just smoked; and he just smoked; and the cigarettes were about three-quarters gone when he suddenly stirred and mumbled:

'Wot's this 'ostel like?'

I was surprised to find myself exhaling a long breath.

'Elysium House?' I said. 'Well, to be honest, under the old warden it was pretty grim, you just had to knuckle under to him. What it'll be like under this new young chap who's come I don't know, but it seems to me that he wants to give the lads a square deal and decent accommodation. At the moment there's twenty-two boys there, it can hold twenty-five; they've got their own boys' club and some of them keep pigeons and that. It's not home, I suppose, but it's not too bad.'

Silence fell again. I stubbed out my cigarette and he tramped on his. And then he suddenly pulled himself up, stretched and gave me a cheeky amiable grin.

'Well, they can't kill me, can they?' he said. 'I'll go.'

'Where? The hostel?'

'Yer. I'll 'ave a bash.'

So I rang up Mr Christmas and asked if I could substitute Crump for Slythe, and he sounded a bit dubious but in the end he said: 'Well, bring the lad round and let's have a look at him.' So I did.

Elysium House was a huge detached house, in a road full of similar houses, tall and sombre and surrounded with laurel bushes. At one time the leading tradespeople lived in this road – this house used to belong to a Plimm – but nowadays the houses are occupied by dentists and Friendly Societies. The hostel was first opened by a Rescue Society during the Depression, to cater for homeless unemployed lads, and old Hellion had been the warden all the time. He'd never really moved with the times and to the end thought he was dealing with grateful waifs; and he had run a house, which, with its trim garden, silent mealtimes, and No Smoking, had been a bleak place.

Now that Mr Christmas had been here a month I noticed there were already slight signs of seediness. Hellion had taken great pride in his garden, but now there appeared to be a cycle-track down the rockery. A top-floor window was broken; in Hellion's day that would have been mended and the culprit expelled within ten minutes.

Mr Christmas came out to meet us in the porch.

'Hallo, sahib, how goes it? And this is Crump, is it? How do, lad: we shall have to call you Crumpet, ha, eh?'

Egbert recoiled slightly, but managed the ghost of a polite smile.

'Well, enter, enter,' said Mr Christmas. 'Sit ye down and let's have a pow-wow. So you're Egbert Crump, eh? Good. Well, Egbert, and you think you'd like to join our gang here, eh? And my word, Mr Maule, they are a gang at the moment, there's some very lively spirits here, my word! But they're a wonderful crowd really, a wonderful spirit, we have some grand fun, I think you'll really enjoy yourself here, Egbert, do you box?'

Egbert would have said no if he'd been given a moment. But Mr Christmas went on:

'We're reviving our Boys' Club you know, Mr Maule,

five nights a week, very hard work but it keeps the lads off the streets.'

He gazed vaguely out of the leaded window at what looked like a tumbledown coach-house full of dismembered bicycles.

'You know, Mr Maule, you'll laugh at me, I suppose, but I have great plans for this place. I believe it can become far more than just a home for these lads, I believe it can become a dynamic community of shared cultural interest. D'you know Miss Wepys? She's going to give us a series of record programmes, everything from Stravinsky to swing, ha, eh? And we've formed a camping club and I'm taking a few of the lads on a week-end camp next month. Oh, the lads are rallying round splendidly, there's a new atmosphere altogether here now.'

'Good,' I said. 'Well, now –'

'Yes, well, Egbert can come straight in now, I can see he'll be all right with us, won't you, lad?'

Now, how the devil can you see that, I thought, when Egbert hasn't opened his mouth since he got here?

'Dump your stuff down there for the moment, Egbert, and I'll get one of the lads to show you around: there's a couple of them at home today. Come along.'

Presently Mr Christmas came back and said:

'Quite a decent lad, Mr Maule; I think we'll do something with him. Does he enurete, by the way?'

I said no.

'Not that I mind, only I've got four chronic wet-beds already. I put them all in one dormitory, that's my method. I can cure bed-wetting, you know, just a little patience and system.'

The hell you can, I thought; oh, well, you'll learn, mate. Somehow, this nervous, bounding man rubbing his bony hands together made me feel old and wise and cynical. I called cheeroh to Egbert and took my leave.

I would never have expected Egbert to settle down in that hostel; I would never have sat down and consciously planned it as the ideal place for him. Nevertheless, settle he did, that is to say he gave no trouble, mixed amiably with the other boys, conformed with the regulations, and didn't bring Doreen in. Actually, Doreen seemed to fade out of the picture quite soon; not that she gave Egbert up, for she used to hang round hungrily near the hostel, but Egbert seemed quickly and rather surprisingly to throw off his obsession for her. I thought at first it was just because he blamed her for the breakdown of his foster-home, but I wondered afterwards if he found it impossible to preserve the magic of the affair in the clamour of hostel life. Most of the boys there boasted loudly of their amatory exploits, but they all knew it was romancing because they were scared stiff of women. I suppose Egbert couldn't romance, knowing reality, and when he spoke of Doreen factually the magic of her was lewdly jeered away. No, I don't really know how it was, but anyway Egbert ceased to be haunted and settled down peaceably.

Personally I had rather a rotten time clearing up behind him; I had to go and see the Urmston Smiths and hear their story and watch the new lines of anxiety and disappointment round Mrs Smith's lips. She was distressed about her husband and I felt terrible about it; I reckoned the old boy wouldn't have had the heart-attack if Egbert hadn't been there and Egbert wouldn't have been there if it hadn't been for me. Steve Cannon had an awful job talking me out of that.

'Well, for crying out loud, Charlie,' he said, 'you're the sort of bloke who blames himself for a bus crash in Glasgow because you weren't driving the flipping bus.'

'No, don't be silly, Steve; I put the kid into that house and it had that effect.'

'You offered him, but it was Mr Urmston Smith who accepted him.'

'I put it in such a way that he couldn't refuse, and therefore I hold myself responsible.'

'Come off it! These people are mature adults twice your age, they're not flipping pawns in your game, what sort of God do you think you are? Have another brown ale.'

I thanked him, and when he brought the drinks over, he said :

'The whole trouble with you, Charlie, is you're too damned narrow. For four years you've thought Child Care, talked it, dreamt it, ate it, supped it, you haven't got another thought in your head.'

'Oh, come, Steve. I sometimes think about Harry.'

'Yes, yes, yes, but then when you're together I bet all you talk about is The Work.'

'Well, why not? What do you want me to do, raffia?'

'Yes, if you want to, but anything that's not social work. Charles, if you don't develop your own personality and follow some entirely different interest, you'll have damn all to offer these kids, you'll be nothing more than a flipping deprived kid yourself.'

'I've been that all my life, Steve.'

'Oh yes, I'm sorry, Charles, I shouldn't have said that. But you do see what I mean, don't you? A chap who's only expert in child care is no good in Child Care. Be an expert on something else, horse brasses, ichthyology, anything. Get something to *offer*.'

'I know what you mean, Steve,' I said, moodily swirling the beer round in my glass. 'I've thought about it myself. It's all very well, but what honestly can measure up to the infinite fascination of human behaviour? I can sit here tonight and genuinely want to be a good boy who plays golf and breeds dogs and trims his blooming privet, but tomorrow something will come crowding in to drive every good resolution clean out of my mind.'

It did, too.

When I got to the office next morning there was a letter on my desk. It was from an obscure County Borough on the coast, and it ran as follows:

COUNTY BOROUGH COUNCIL OF BLIQUE

Neville Forster
Clerk to the Council

Duncan Sipp, B.Com. (Hons.)
Children's Officer

Dear Sir,

ZSA ZSA MIMMANY (born 3.3.52)

Mother: Mrs Mavis Nazimova 'Mimmany'

The above-named child has been received into the care of this authority, having been abandoned by her parents in a common lodging-house at 69 Rutts Common, Blique.

The parents, who are not married but have been co-habiting for several years, first came to the notice of this authority when another child, Marilyn (31.5.50), was found to be neglected and was committed under a Fit Person Order in 1951. The family then lived in a tarpaulin shelter on the beach, having previously been evicted from an address in Leeds. Efforts to rehabilitate the family met with no success, and Marilyn was eventually boarded out with a view to adoption.

Soon after Zsa Zsa was born the mother handed her to a woman in the lodging-house, saying she was slipping out to get some cigarettes. Since then all trace of both Mr and Mrs Mimmany has been lost. Yesterday, however, it was quite fortuitously discovered that 'Mrs' Mimmany is now living at 4A The Gun Site, Slag End, Westburn, and I would be greatly obliged if you could arrange for her to be visited to ascertain her plans for the child.

From a remark passed by this woman on a previous occasion, I feel it possible that she may be known to you, as it appears that she may at some time have resided in Westburn under the name of Crump.

I shall be happy to reciprocate in similiar circumstances.

Yours faithfully,
DUNCAN SIPP,
Children's Officer

19

MISS DASHFORTH was leaning against the door-frame looking at me with amused crinkles round her eyes.

'Over to you, Mister Maule,' she said.

'Good lord, Agnes, this has put the cat among the pigeons,' I said, tossing down the letter from Blique. 'What are you going to do?'

'We shall have to go and see her, we can't just ignore a letter like that,' said Miss Dashforth. 'I think you ought to go, Charles, you might get more out of her. Something gives me the vague impression that she quite likes men.'

I shuddered. 'If I go, I shall go in broad daylight,' I said. 'I think it's rotten of you to send me, I don't want to take a load of vermin with me on my honeymoon.'

'You've got a week to get cleaned up before the ceremony,' said Miss Dashforth unfeelingly. 'Thank your stars you *are* going off, leaving me stuck here all alone to cope with La Crump. Though I must say it's quite like old times to have her around the place again.'

'Surely she won't trouble you, will she?'

'Charles, a woman like that always means trouble.'

'Well, she's got rid of all her kids here and there, and she's never bothered with any of our lot.'

'No, but I can't help wondering why she's come back to Westburn after all this time. Maybe she's remembered that some of her Westburn family are able to earn good money; maybe she wants her cut of it. This means complications of some sort, I'm sure.'

'Well, who, I mean –'

'Lets have a think,' said Miss Dashforth. 'Rudy's disappeared; Clark's back in the clink, so I hear; Bebe's earning good money, but she's some way away, she might be safe.

204

Gloria: oh, dear. I don't think Jack Muskett ever knew how terrible Gloria's Mum is, he'd get an awful shock if she turned up there.'

'Still, she's married and I shouldn't think Mrs Crump would have the brains to trace her.'

'I shouldn't put anything past the Crumps of this world,' said Miss Dashforth. 'I'd better go and have a cup of tea with Gloria and warn her who's come. Oh, dear, and Gloria's doing quite well, seeing what she's come from, but she's not a very good manager, it'd finish that marriage if Mum moved in on it. I don't like this. What about Egbert?'

'Well, now, Egbert,' I said. 'I'm not sure if this need be a bad thing. I think if she turned up Egbert would go to her and I couldn't stop him. But after all, he wouldn't come to a great deal of harm now, and though he's no trouble at the hostel, I can't see there's much future there for him.'

'You're not going to *encourage* the boy to go home, I hope?' said Miss Dashforth in a shocked voice.

'Oh, no; all I mean is that if the worst came to the worst it wouldn't be the worst that could happen – if you see what I mean.'

'I think I do; let's hope you're right. Now, Myrna we needn't worry about –'

'Where is she?' I asked.

'Goodness knows. She's absconded from about six different Training Homes and Approved Schools, and about four months ago she absconded from a real tough one down in Devon, and she hasn't been heard of since. I suppose she's lorry-hopping somewhere. Who's next: Cary?'

'Cary I would be sorry about, if his mother interferes,' I said. 'He's really happy in that foster-home of his, I think it would be a great shock to him if he knew his mother had turned up again.'

'H'm. Well, all we can do there is to keep quiet about it and hope for the best. Now, what about Winston and Clem, they're both at Melcombe, aren't they?'

'Yes. And they'd have got there anyway, whether Mum was here or not. I suppose Winston remembers his mother vaguely, I don't think Clem does at all, he'd probably throw a fit if she turned up. What about that other girl, what's her name, the one in the Open Air School?'

'Celia? Oh, she's in a foster-home now, in Area 4. She's been away so long I don't think she ranks as one of the family at all. I'll warn Miss Bailey that Mum's turned up, but with any luck Mum's forgotten she ever had a daughter called Celia.'

'Then there's Sabrina,' I said.

'Mrs Crump can have Sabrina with pleasure,' said Miss Dashforth. Sabrina had been boarded out three times unsuccessfully, had developed a fierce temper and was driving the staff crazy at Merrythought.

'Well, it's not too bad,' I said. 'Cary's the most vulnerable if Mrs Crump really does try to interfere with them.'

'If she gives any hint of that you'll just have to give her a straight talk and frighten her off.'

'I couldn't frighten pussy,' I said. 'You know, lots of people have given that woman Straight Talks and told her to Pull Herself Together, it doesn't seem to have done much good, does it?'

'For heaven's sake, what do you want to do, give her a bouquet? She's just a wicked old hag, that's all, best out of the way.'

'No, but I mean I wish I understood why she behaves like this, nobody's ever tried to understand her.'

'Let's get the Honours Psychology notebooks out, shall we?' sneered Miss Dashforth. She was getting slightly bitter these days, now that her rescue stunts weren't turning out so well, and she always had been touchy about her lack of a good qualification.

'No, seriously, Agnes, you know I've been worried all the way through about Egbert and his Mum, there seemed to be something between them that I've never been able to replace. And you know as well as I do that though we see people doing daft and irresponsible things, we very rarely meet somebody who's wholly wicked and useless. I think human beings are mostly rather nice.'

'A woman who abandons a tiny baby and just shoves off is as near wicked as makes no difference to me,' said Miss Dashforth. 'I'd never trust any kid to a woman who'd do that.'

'Yes, you see, it's *so* unnatural that I feel there must be a reason for it somewhere.'

'Do you mean to say you want her psycho-analysed so that she turns suddenly into a radiant mother-figure and has all her happy, laughing children home again to a nest of love ?'

'No, really all I'm saying is that shouting at her hasn't done any good,' I said. 'But if it were possible to get down to the root of her trouble we might just prevent the next kid from being dumped somewhere.'

'Well, you handle her as you think fit,' said Miss Dashforth. 'Only don't forget there are at least three who I think are in jeopardy. The *next* kid ? Gosh, surely she's past it now ?'

'I'll give her certain advice,' I said leeringly.

'You'd better have her sterilized,' said Miss Dashforth.

I knew the gunsite at Slag End quite well, it was rather a happy hunting ground for us. There were about a dozen old Army huts out there; squatters had moved in soon after the end of the war, and over the years the huts had housed a series of feckless families who were always making great inroads on our time. I remembered that I had been to No. 4A before, when it had a wild woman in it called Mrs Daggar, who used to keep her children away from school and throw things at welfare officers. I think she moved to St Albans in the end.

I went to the gunsite that very afternoon, and I was mincing along the squelchy path between the huts when round the corner waddled a figure surprisingly familiar for all the years that had passed. I stopped and regarded her with a mixture of trepidation and pleasure. Her hair was now bright yellow, though still covered with curlers. She was wearing several layers of cardigan, and instead of plimsolls she had big black wellingtons on.

' 'Allo, dear !' said Mrs Crump.

'Hallo, dear !' I replied.

' 'Ow are yer ? Come to see me ?'

'Yes, I have, as a matter of fact.'

'Ooh, good !'

'I'm sorry to come without an appointment,' I said, as I followed her towards her hut. 'I hope I'm not intruding.'

She giggled; my approach was evidently funny. 'No, duck, I like 'avin' visitors. I bin quite lonely without 'em.'

She hurled herself bodily at her door, which was apparently swollen with damp and shrieked excruciatingly open. She had half a hut, divided into two rooms; the one we were in was painted dark green and contained an iron coke-stove, a few bits of old furniture, and a large television set.

'Sit down,' invited Mrs Crump – I couldn't think of her as Mimmany. I shot a cautious look round: the only place to sit seemed to be a sofa, suffering from alopecia and covered with heaps of dark grey washing. It looked a bit buggy, and I would rather have stood, but I was again invited so firmly to sit that I lowered myself on to the arm of the sofa. My ankles immediately began to itch like mad, I think it was imagination.

'And 'ow's my dear children ?' asked Mrs Crump.

'Oh – er – all right,' I said. 'I hear you've had one or two more ?'

'Yer !' she cried. 'Owjer know that ?'

'Oh, the – er – Government told me,' I said.

'Ah, yer, they'd know,' said Mrs Crump, nodding sagely.

'As a matter of fact, I've come to see you about one of them, little Zsa Zsa,' I said.

'Yer, it's nice to be back in dear ole Westburn,' she said.

I opened my mouth, shut it again, and then said :

'What brought you back this way ?'

'To be near my dear children,' she said. We looked each other straight in the eye and I could have sworn we exchanged winks. Oh, well, if that's what she wanted me to believe. . . .

'But you're not a Westburn girl, are you, Mrs Crump ?'

'Don't you call me that, don't use that name, don't ever use that name,' she said, her mouth pursed into a little shocked O. 'I'm known 'ere as Mrs Mimmany, why, if they 'eard some other name called, wot *would* the neighbours think of me?'

Judging by the terrified screams that were searing the air outside, the neighbours were at that moment minding their own business.

'I'm sorry, Mrs Mimmany, I quite understand your feelings,' I lied. 'Er – excuse me, is there a Mr Mimmany?'

'O' course. 'E's about somewhere. Fetchin' in some wood, I b'lieve. 'E don't go to work, see, 'e's 'urt 'is back.'

'Oh dear. In Blique?'

'No, in the First World War. Sometimes 'e can't 'ardly move, Mr Mimmany can't.'

'Dear, dear,' I cooed, thinking he'd been lissom enough to father two kids on her, nevertheless.

'Well, now, about Zsa Zsa – '

' 'Ow's my dear Gloria?' asked Mrs Mimmany.

'Oh, she's all right; she's married, you know.'

'Oooh! Is she? Oooh, fancy! Any children?'

'Yes, one little girl,' I said. 'Now – '

'Tha's nice. It's nice 'avin' children. An' 'ow's my Egbert?'

'Very well, he's a fine boy now. You see – '

'I was always *very* fond of Egbert. *Very* fond of Egbert, I was. You know, dear, it near broke my 'eart when they took 'im away from me, near broke my 'eart, it did, in fac' I'll tell yer something, dear: when they took that boy away, when they took that boy away – it, well it did, it broke my 'eart.'

'Yes, well – '

'Call me a liar if you like, go on, call me a liar, but I tell you, true as I'm standing 'ere, when they took that boy away, not a word of a lie, it broke my 'eart. Oh, 'ere's Mimmany.'

I was rather pleased to have any sort of interruption. There was the thud of a body hurling itself against the door, which screeched open, and in scuttled Mr Mimmany, his nose well in the lead of the rest of him. He was a small man, wearing Air Force battledress. He had a conical hat, steel-rimmed spectacles, and no teeth at all.

'Ah?' he said.

'This is the Welfare,' said Mrs Mimmany, proudly, 'come to see me.'

'Ah. Nyingnyingingingmumumumumnnying,' he said.

'And I'm very pleased to meet you too,' I guessed. 'I've come to see you about Zsa Zsa.'

'Ah?'

'To see if she ought to be adopted,' I said.

'Ah! Myingumumumumum ummunying sumshumchurn-shurm ummen!'

'Good!' I cried, helplessly. 'Er – what do you think, Mrs – er – Mimmany?'

Now that we'd got her trapped into the subject, she stood quite still for some time, her eyes creeping cunningly from side to side.

'I'd want to see the people oo'd 'ave 'er,' she said finally. 'Tha's only nachral, innit, a mother's love demands such assurance.'

Where the hell had she picked that up, from something on the telly, I supposed. Aloud I said:

'Nothing's arranged yet, Mrs M – er – Cr – er, I only want to know what you think?'

'Ah, well, that takes thinkin' about, that does, dunnit? I mean, that takes thinkin' about.'

'Well, Mrs Mimmany, do you intend having the child home?' I said.

There was a pause.

'An' 'ow's my little Sabrina?' she said. 'It's all right to talk in front o' Mr Mimmany, we 'ave no secrets in this 'ouse.'

'To get back to Zsa Zsa,' I said firmly.

'D'jou know,' she said, 'Sabrina was a 'leven poun' baby? I 'ad the 'ell of a time wiv 'er, Bebe 'ad to sit on me I was that agonized, I dint know wot I was a-doin'.'

It was at this point that I mentally put my head down and went doggedly in, feeling like a fox-terrier going down a haunted rabbit-warren. But I could get nowhere; every time I firmly got back to Zsa Zsa, Mrs Mimmany firmly swerved off to another child, and as she had about eleven to choose from she could keep going longer than I could. The most I could get out of her was that the adoption of Zsa Zsa needed thinking about. Mimmany wandered in and out, occasionally rolling himself a very thin cigarette with wisps of tobacco hanging out at both ends. Once I got side-tracked into a very difficult conversation with him about something that once happened to him when he worked as a mortuary attendant, I couldn't make head or tail of it. I sat there itching and nodding my head to him in an imbecile way, and thought that if this wasn't a dream – and it seemed terrifyingly like one – then what the hell did I think I was doing there on a sunny afternoon a week before my wedding. My eyes went boggy under the sheer weight of the unreality of the situation.

After a bit I pulled myself together and switched round to inquiring about their mode of life and what their plans were, but 'plan' was a word absent from their vocabulary. They didn't seem to be aware of why they had come to Westburn; they seemed to have been in some sort of trouble through fiddling the N.A.B. in Blique so they had to go some-where, and as Mimmany was being 'looked for' in Leeds, Westburn was the only other place they knew. So they wandered in and spent several nights in various public parks, and then they'd heard of this hut by the uncanny telepathy that exists down there among the submerged tenth. The address had only leaked back to Blique because they'd sent there for the television set. They were at present officially existing on National Assistance and a very small pension Mr Mimmany had, but there were various mysteri-ous transactions going on which somehow allowed them to smoke and invest fairly heavily in the Pools. They were already some weeks behind with their tiny rent.

I had gone there with the vague idea in the back of my

mind of discovering why Mrs Crump-Mimmany behaved as she did, and I tried to steer the conversation back to her original desertion from The Rat Yard. I was met with fairly determined evasion, but I learnt a little, and as far as I could see she had originally become infatuated with a pantherine West Indian named Sylvester Wellington – Sabrina's father. She had gone with him to Leeds, and when he presently left her she took up with a Pole named Prszyl. I think he must have been psychotic, and after he went back to the mental hospital she said she slept rough for a bit. Golly, I thought, how rough can you get? She lorry-hopped back to Westburn and took up with a widower living alone with his old grey dog in a crossing-keeper's cottage on the railway, and that was when Harry and I met her, that summer's evening so long ago, when Harry stood with a petal blown into her hair ... I missed the next bit, and when my attention returned to her, she was back in Leeds with Mimmany and protesting her undying interest in her dear son Egbert. I did a bit of swerving myself, because I didn't want to discuss Egbert, the only one of her family in receipt of a regular wage-packet.

'How did you come to live in The Rat Yard?' I parried.

'Oh, when we was bombed out in Leytonstone,' she said absently.

'Really? Are you a Leytonstone girl?'

'Yer. Dint you know? Yer. I was brought up in a 'Ome there. Lovely place. Lovely place. I wanted to get my Myrna in there, but there wasn't no vacancy. Well, the ole Matron would 'ave taken 'er, I know, cos ole Matron was always very fond o' me. Very nice, ole Matron was. Very strict, mind you, cor, not wot they're like now, very strict. I s'pose she needed to be, with four 'undred of us.'

I was flabbergasted.

'I didn't know you were brought up in a Home, Mrs Mimmany?'

'Cor, yer. Yer, that's where I was brought up. I know all about them places, I do. I 'member – 'ere, less 'ave a cupper tea, eh?'

I suffered a sudden schizophrenic agony: I was interested in what she was saying, but I could not face a cup of Crump tea. I had the idea of saying my doctor had forbidden me to drink tea, but then I noticed Mimmany furtively wiping a cup on the tail of his shirt, and the hut swam before me.

'I'm afraid, excuse me, excuse me,' I gulped. 'I'm already late for another appointment, I must fly!'

I stood up, feeling apprehensive itches shooting over my chest and into my armpits.

'I've very much enjoyed our little chat,' I said. 'I'll call and see you again some time.'

'Yer. Come when yer like, dear, it's Welcome 'All 'ere, eh? We're not fussy.'

'Oh, thank you. Cheerio, then. And you'll think about Zsa Zsa?'

'Oh, yer. Oh, yer. Cheerio, dear.'

'Cheerio, dear,' I muttered, hurrying away.

I went and found a decent teashop and sat down as far from the other customers as possible and ate an enormous high tea. Over it I pondered on the interview, and thought of a number of extremely clever things I might have said to Mrs Mimmany and a number of revealing replies she would have made and of how beautifully cut and dried everything would have been at the end. But as far as I could see I had achieved precisely nothing that afternoon except a few bites and some nausea. If anyone had asked me what I did for a living I could only have said: 'Well, I sit down and then I stand up again.' I was feeling very despondent.

When I was refreshed I did one more visit in Slag End, a rather mucky home, and then I headed bathwards. While I was on top of the bus I had a fortuitous glimpse of Egbert. He was standing outside the cinema, wearing a light grey suit and a bright tie, his hair long but neatly oiled, his face moody but scrubbed. As the bus moved by I saw him greet a good-looking girl in a white bell-shaped frock who was prettily apologizing for keeping him waiting. With sleepy-eyed masterfulness he swept her into the cinema.

Suddenly I realized that I had got some sort of answer

from the afternoon. There wasn't anything at 4A The Gun Site for Egbert; whatever he was, and he wasn't much really, not to set the Gleeze on fire, he had emerged from all that we'd done to him as somebody more wholesome than his mother, more acceptable among the throng of people moving up and down the High Road. If he married that girl, I saw that he wouldn't condemn her to put up with buggy old sofas and second-hand bedsprings propped on bricks and irresponsible flitting up and down the country. He might be unfaithful to her, and he might be moody and explosive to live with, but his own children in their turn wouldn't have the bad start he'd had and would absorb a better set of standards to take with them on their way. Imperceptibly, almost miraculously, the old vicious circle of squalor begetting squalor had been broken into, and something had been saved from the wreckage of The Rat Yard.

That night I sang loudly in my Dettol bath.

I did a report on the Mimmanys for the Blique Children's Officer, and in it I said:

Mrs Mimmany was evasive on the question of adoption, but she was equally evasive on any suggestion of having the child home. If anything, I would say she has more feeling for her older children than for the most recent arrivals, and I believe that she could be persuaded, when the times comes, to give her formal consent to adoption.

Even with the most intensive casework such as is provided by Family Service Units – and there is no such Unit in this town – I do not believe that this woman's way of life can speedily be righted, if at all. If the child were to return now to these conditions, I fear that she would be dangerously neglected; and if it was planned for her to return to some problematical future date, I fear the mother's emotional resources are not deep enough to guarantee a satisfactory mutual adjustment.

I would, therefore, respectfully recommend that it is in Zsa Zsa's best interests to be placed in a good home with a view to adoption.

(Sgd) C. MAULE,
Child Care Officer

20

HARRY'S only close relative now was her father's brother, Oswald Harrison, Uncle Oz. He was a bachelor, a minor luminary at Oxford University, and he disliked Oxford; he escaped as often as he could to his cottage in a little village in the far west of Berkshire. It was in the plain, small church there that Harry and I were married.

Steve Cannon was my best man and Agnes Dashforth, wearing a gay hat, was the only guest. We walked through blazing sunshine into the cool, dark church. The ceremony was very quiet, very intimate, and intensely moving; I had tears in my eyes all through and my throat was so clenched that I could hardly speak.

At morning, when the birds were in full song, I half woke to see Harry lying smiling to herself.

'Wha' matter?' I mumbled.

She turned her head.

'I was only thinking,' she said. 'The number of times I've given Stern Warnings to my girls; and now at last I know what I'm talking about.'

Her eyes crinkled at me.

'I'll never warn them off again,' she said.

21

GOSH, I didn't want to go back to work. I didn't.

It was all right coming back to Westburn and cooking our first supper together and finding there wasn't a speck of salt in the house and searching everywhere for my clean pyjamas – that was fun. And it was all right next morning for me, going jauntily off to the office with Harry's kiss tangible on my lips and the knowledge that for the first time in my life somebody cared about when I'd be home again. It was when I came up to Seed Villas and saw the dirty old newspaper blowing round the front patch that my heart sank. I realized afterwards that, apart from the romantic excitement of the honeymoon, what I had experienced was my first break for four years totally away from Child Care. Four years had been full of listening to children, talking about children, worrying about children, straining within the whorls of my own brain to catch the elusive clue to somebody else's thought; even on those lonely leaves, in Maldon or Beaumaris, my mind had never escaped from this clamour. At last I had totally evaded it, and now I had rather painfully to realize that down I had to plunge again from the hill-station into the dusty bazaar.

I dragged myself into the office apprehensive, fearing that my first task would be to face Miss Dashforth and a lot of leering, envious remarks about my honeymoon. Rather to my surprise, however, the old Dash wasn't in, though it was well after nine; Miss Greave was rather surprised too, as she knew of no reason for her absence. So I settled myself down with the high pile of papers and files that was waiting on my table. There were reports and 'copies for information' and non-urgent letters and scribbled notes about crises that had blown up and somehow blown over and knotty decisions that had to be left to me to make, curse them, and a lot of those irritating memoranda that takes ages to answer, like from the District Auditor asking why you spent eightpence in 1923. I waded along with my spirits falling lower and lower.

Miss Dashforth came in about ten, popping her head round the door and saying: 'What ho!' and then 'Coo, isn't it rotten to be back!'

I stared at her amazed, this wasn't like her. The girl lived in a flat like a nun's cell, and a week-end for her was merely a period of impatient waiting for Monday morning and the enthusiastic dash back to The Work. Incredulously, I heard her trail into her own room and dump down her mahogany handbag.

'She must be in love again,' I thought. And then, with a sudden stab of pity for her, I thought that more likely she was deeply affected by my own radiant return from our honeymoon, and her having to face the fact that she was the only person here who did not share a precious secret experience. I sighed deeply for her.

It had been arranged that Harry would continue to work part-time, three days a week; and we were to have a new full-time officer. This was to be a huge, muscular, and intensely shy creature called Miss Chick; but Miss Chick would not start duty till 1 October, so in the meantime a fair amount of extra work was falling to Miss Dashforth and me.

I got myself sorted out a bit and heaped up the things that simply had to be done quickly and those that could wait another week, and rather creakily set out to pound the beat once more. I was out a good deal and about three days later I came into the office during the afternoon and found Miss Dashforth just replacing the telephone and looking rather shaken.

'Oh, God, Charles, more trouble!' she said, beating her hands to and fro in her hair.

'What?'

'That hostel warden.'

'What, old Christmas?' I said. 'What's the matter with him?'

'The usual,' she said.

'Oh, no! Little boys or little girls?'

'Little boys. Well, big boys – boys in the hostel; it's been going on for months.'

'Oh, hell!' I felt sickened, as I always did, though none of us was unused to this sort of revelation. You never saw it coming, and in someone you knew quite well it was always revolting.

'Is Egbert involved?' I asked.

'I don't know. I haven't heard a damned thing about this, that was County Hall, they've heard before I have.'

'I'd better go round,' I said.

I suppose it was imagination, but I thought Elysium House looked seedier than ever when I got there. The boys were hanging about aimlessly, looking guilty but excited, evidently suppressing a secret glee. The Deputy Warden was fluttering about; he was a chinless little man, a drifter, who had been successively a naval sick berth attendant, a mental nurse, and a housefather. Somebody seemed to be smashing up the Boys' Club outside and nobody was taking much notice. There was no sign of Egbert.

I wasn't much worried about him, as I thought he was healthily absorbed in the opposite sex, but you never knew, he might have submitted himself for the sake of the odd cigarette-case or lighter, so I went round to see the police inspector. He was looking very pleased with himself. The police loathe sex offenders and glow with righteous pride when they land one; then they get furious when the bloke gets off with probation.

The inspector was pretty cagey, but he said he had no evidence to suggest that Crump was involved at any time, and he had most of his evidence collated by then.

I said I was sorry to have been of no assistance, but I had really had no inkling of what was going on; and the inspector unbent a little as he perceived that I was a mere credulous do-gooder; and I said: 'I suppose this really happened,

I mean it wasn't a frame-up by the boys? That has been known to happen.'

'Judge for yourself,' said the inspector, tossing me one of the signed statements.

I skimmed through it, but it always turned me up to read the stilted police language used to describe the detailed mechanism of sexual intercourse. Yes, it was genuine, all right, no boy could fake all that. Thank goodness, Egbert seemed to be in the clear. I left the police station, feeling anger and distaste and also pity for the lonely undignfied life Mr Christmas had led, and probably would lead for evermore.

Next day the Deputy Warden rang up while I was out to say that Egbert hadn't been in all night and was still missing, though his belongings were still there. Miss Dashforth was not unduly concerned, as the lad was old enough to look after himself, but she said she would inform the police if he hadn't turned up by nightfall.

At six o'clock that evening, while the boys were having their meal, Egbert crept into the hostel, removed his clothes, and silently disappeared again.

At half past nine next morning Mrs Crump-Mimmany arrived in the office.

''Allo, dear!'

'' 'Allo, dear!'

'' 'Ere, wot you done? My dear Eg come 'ome wiv not a stitch 'o clothes on 'is pore back, it's not right, yer know, it is not right.'

My stomach went down like a lift.

'Egbert's come *home*? What, to The Gun Site?'

'Yer, course. Wiv no clothes. It's not right. I've 'arf a mind to write a letter to the Queen.'

'You'll do no such thing,' I said absently, leaning back in my chair with the papers strewn all over the table and half a hundred things to be done and a neurotic bus-conductress waiting to see me outside. What the hell could I do about all this?

'Ho, yes. A cryin' shame, that's wot. Snatch my dear boy

from me arms, and after all these years send 'im 'ome naked. That's not justice, that is not justice.'

'What do you want?' I asked.

'You do the clothing grants, don't yer? Well, then,' she said. 'An' another thing, you pay your bleedin' foster-mothers thirty shillings a week, don't yer, I know. Then why can't I 'ave it to look after me own, eh? Why? Fair's fair, mate, fair's fair.'

'I cannot pay anything to parents,' I snapped.

'Ho, no, ho, no, us pore under-privileged classes, we don't never get nuffin' for givin' up our lives to our kids, but yer pay wot yer like to a dirty ole man soddin' about in a 'ostel, don't yer? That's not right, that's not fair.'

Yes, she had me on the wrong foot, all right. I regarded her thoughtfully.

'How did Egbert find out where you live?' I asked.

'I met 'im in the 'Igh Road, night afore last. 'E was fed up an' I said come 'ome an' 'e come – wiv no clothes.'

'And he's still got no clothes?'

'Course not. We're only workin' class, mate, clean I 'ope, an' keeps ourselves respectable, but a mint o' money like some as I could mention we ain't got, not thirty bob a week to lash out in Marks on my pore dear boy we ain't got.'

I leaned forward.

'Egbert got all his stuff from the hostel last night, if he lost it on the way home that's his look-out, not mine, and I'm spending no more on Egbert, if you have him home, you take responsibility for him. You can try this lark on some-one else if you like, but don't come it on me, mate.'

'Ho!' she said in an offended way, but twinkling slightly. She knew very well it had been a slim chance, but she'd hoped to find some new young officer here. I realized with a jolt that I was a lot older than I'd thought I was.

'What about his job?' I asked.

'Oh, 'e's packed that in. Wot, three quid a bloody week? That's no good to 'im, that's sweated labour, that is.'

'He was getting a proper trade training in that shop, do you realize?'

'Huh! Training! When we needs eddicatin',' she said, lurching to her feet with great hauteur, '*when* we needs eddicatin', we'll come an' arsk yer.'

And she swept out, colliding with the frantic bus-conductress as she went.

I listened with only half my attention to the clippie's tale of woe, and promised vaguely to look into whatever it was, I forget now, and then I fumbled for a cigarette and shakily lit it.

Damnation!

My first thought was that Mrs Crump had blown into smithereens all that had been done for Egbert over the past four years. I recalled wryly my thoughts of a few weeks back, when I'd seen Egbert from the top of a bus. I may have had doubts over what we had done for the boy, it was pretty shattering to slide right back to the beginning again. I presumed that Egbert had met up with his mother just when the Christmas affair blew up. He must have felt pretty sickened about that, and about County Council dependability as a whole, and he must have felt that once more his refuge had collapsed about him like wet cardboard. I presumed that in these circumstances he had been able to see through his mother's rags and vulgarity to something unique and unchangeable, motherness, the blood tie. Fair enough, but once she'd got him home, her soggy example dragged him at once out of his job and into unemployment within twenty-four hours.

Damnation!

The Fit Person Order still had effect till his eighteenth birthday, but with Egbert well past seventeen there was no power we could invoke to force him away from his own home again, and, even if we could, how could we hold him away? There was, however, a provision that we could supervise him in his own home under the terms of the Order and do what we could on a basis of persuasion. I couldn't see that this could possibly be effective with the Mimmanies, but it was something.

I discussed it with Miss Dashforth, but she was strangely

listless these days: she shrugged, said we'd have to resign ourselves to events and suggested we revoke the Order and get shot of the whole boiling of 'em. Then I discussed things with Harry and she thought that all was not yet lost. If Egbert had absorbed anything from the experience and training he had had, he would presently, off his own bat, rebel against his mother's standards and take himself away; and if he didn't do that, he might just possibly raise his mother's standards a bit. So in the end I decided not to apply for the revocation of the Order, to keep responsibility for the boy and do what I could in the way of a last rearguard action.

Once a month, then, I dutifully trailed out to The Gun Site.

The first time I went I was pretty shaken, mostly by the leaden curtain that had fallen between Egbert and myself. As the years had gone by, we'd got on to a pleasant footing of mutual liking; it wasn't strong enough to be called a relationship, but I think he liked me as somebody who was always around without interfering too much, and if he did something daft and knew it was daft I'd call him a clot and go on being around; and I liked him as a basically decent, rather bewildered kid, who would never have been my son, but might easily have been my godson. All this casual comradeship had now gone. The eyes that watched me in the hut were muddied with suspicion, fear, and self-defence.

The hut itself was still untidy and heaped with amorphous rags, but occasionally Mrs Mimmany would smear a wet clout over the floor, and a piece of oilcloth had been nailed over the broken window. Egbert slept in the front room: the back seats from two cars had been pushed together and covered with old greatcoats. He'd got a job as a labourer on the big building site over by Dedbrough, going to work in his gumboots and his light grey suit, which was already smeared with plaster. He was earning ten pounds a week – more than I was.

Mrs Mimmany's question on my first visit was:

'Are yer goin' to let 'im stay?'

'So long as he keeps out of trouble and you look after him properly,' I said.

'Then why can't my others come 'ome, eh? If it's good enough for 'im, it's good enough for them, eh? Wot about my Cary? Where is Cary? You won't let me 'ave 'is address, will yer, is that right, is that right? You're ashamed, that's wot. Someone's soddin' about with 'im now, I know them foster-parent people. Why should a mother not even know where 'er dear child is, eh? That ain't natural, I shall write to the Queen.'

(She did, too. I heard about it weeks later, from the Home Office.)

I tried to draw her off by pointing out that she didn't have room for Cary, but she came back at me with a lot of fantastic plans, which she completely believed, about getting a caravan and a tied cottage, and in the end I sharply and rather rashly said:

'Look! If you can look after Egbert properly for six months, I'll talk to you again about Cary, but till then the subject's closed.'

After which she subsided muttering, though Egbert continued to be very aggressive about it.

The next time I went up was in the dark, and I was about to pound on the door when I heard furious voices from within:

'If you want my bloody shirt, you bloody ask proper!'

'Nyninginging uddy ummumumumun uddy shfersh.'

'It's my bloody shirt and my bloody money bought it!'

'O uddy ummun ummuneer hoho uddy shferfsh!'

'You'll bloody well do as you're told!'

'Hah-her.'

'*Wot* did you call me?'

I pounded.

'Her?'

'Oh, I'll go. Bloody insurance, I suppose, got a bob? No, you ain't, I know.'

And I got in past a scowling and ungracious Egbert.

Well, I didn't get much out of that visit, the two me
skulking and muttering and Mrs Mimmany putting on
bright hostessy air to try and divert my attention from wha
I had obviously overheard. I was, however, agreeably su
prised by the state of the hut. The floor was covered wit
new lino, thin stuff, but bright; the buggy old sofa had gon
and there were three folding chairs, Church Hall type; th
table had been inexpertly painted scarlet and on it stood a
ornament, which I presently recognized as Egbert's potter
pig he made at The Cottage by the Creek. I asked my hoste
if she had had a win on the Pools and she said no, flutterin
her eyelids, but she wouldn't tell me where the money ha
come from. I assumed it was from Egbert. Mr Mimman
was wearing Egbert's cream silk shirt.

I didn't go out there again till just a few days befor
Christmas when I was doing a whirlwind tour to deliver
present to each one of my boys. I took something to Egber
and was very upset by what I found. The hut had begun t
run to seed already; the lino was grimy and covered wit
heaps of clothing, the scarlet table was scorched black o
one side, and the ornament had disappeared, but worst of a
was Egbert himself. He was unemployed again, having bee
sacked from the building job because of bad time-keepin
I don't think that was entirely his fault, it was a long rid
from Slag End to Dedbrough and Mrs Mimmany just didn'
help her lad to get off early enough. He couldn't get anothe
job, he'd let his hair grow long down the back of his neck
his clothes were ragged and filthy, he sat pale-faced an
listless on one of the chairs, gazing sullenly at me wit
defensive muddy eyes. I was quite shocked. He seeme
to have given up. He seemed to have been overpowere
by the coils of Crumpery, pulled down to a level of squali
defeatism.

This worried me very much; I felt sure that Egbert wa
feeling helplessly miserable, and yet I couldn't get throug
to him at all to help. I promised to try and find a job for hir
after Christmas, but he only shrugged; my present to hir
was accepted with a lack-lustre grunt; I invited him to com

and spend Christmas Day with Harry and me, but he looked down contemptuously at his clothes and refused gruffly.

I departed in dejection, feeling maddeningly incompetent as I thought of the bleak and surly days Egbert was spending, at Christmas of all times. I couldn't see what I could do. Part of me was saying: 'He chose his bed, let him flipping well lie in it,' but most of me knew that he hadn't made his choice knowingly. I wanted to discuss it all with Miss Dashforth, but she was off again on one of her mysterious short leaves. Quite out of character, she was taking a lot of time off, spinning out the week-ends by anything from two hours to two days, and never breathing a word to anyone of where she'd been. My own theory was that she had had a mild nervous breakdown at the time of our marriage, and was now having rest and psychotherapy; except that just lately she had seemed very bright and lively on the few occasions when I did see her. Anyway, the fact was that she wasn't available for case consultation. It was no good discussing anything with Our Chick. Miss Chick was in an ecstasy over being allowed to take part in The Work at all, she used to blunder excitedly round the office exclaiming about the wonderful things she had seen. I had long, worried talks with Harry, and she couldn't think of anything I could do to improve the situation, but she was a bit more optimistic than I was and reckoned that Egbert might still rebel against his fate. I wondered about bringing Mrs Urmston Smith to the gun site, or even tracing and bringing along the girl in the white bell-shaped frock, thinking that to give Egbert an aim in life might jolt him out of the slough; but Harry said no, the sight of them would fill Egbert with a guilty despair he would never overcome again.

Harry and I spent a wonderfully happy Christmas together, even though I made a fearful mess of carving the chicken, and even though late in the evening of the day I found myself thinking yet again of the squalid little hut over the far side of the town. But I shrugged the thought away; they'd probably all be drunk by then.

That year we had a week-end following on Boxing Day,

so it was unwillingly that I crept back to the office next Monday, and blow me, old Dash was away again. So was Miss Greave, though I had known about this, so it was up to me to sit down and sort through the mail that had accumulated. We got quite a lot of mail, holiday period or no. We also had quite a number of foster-mothers who grew tired of the kids during the autumn, but said: 'Ow, pore little mite, let 'im stay and 'ave 'is Christmas, I'll give 'im that.' Directly after Christmas, out, 'e was tumbled. So I knew I was in for a busy time, and I got on with the mail quickly to discover the worst, and as I did so in the quiet office I heard the sound of footsteps dragging up the corridor, and in came Egbert.

' 'Lo, Mr Maule,' he said.

He looked both hangdog and defiant; or rather, he didn't look either, but a wrong word would send him one way or another. 'Hallo, son,' I said, smiling delightedly. 'Sit down. I'm just opening my letters,' and I went on with them.

There was silence.

'Fag, son?' I asked, after a while.

'Cor, thanks.' We lit them, and I finished opening envelopes, and then I said:

'Well, now son –'

'I've packed it in,' he said. 'I'm fed-up.'

'Packed your home in?'

'Yer. Walked out.'

'I see.' I smoked quietly. 'Ever going back?'

'Never,' he said, and there was a slightly tremulous lift at the end of the word.

'Uh-huh.' I didn't like to express pleasure or regret at this welcome news, fearing to make his confusion worse confounded. 'You'll need lodgings now, then.'

'Yes, sir. Please.'

'I think I can help you, son,' I said, turning back to the pile of mail and pulling out a letter that had arrived that morning. 'Have you had anything to eat today yet?'

'No.' He shrugged. 'Don't fancy nothink.'

'Oh, you've got to eat, son. Look, here's half-a-dollar; nip round to the caff on the corner and get yourself a cuppa tea and anything you fancy. I'll just clear up here and then we'll go out and fix you up. Have you got all your stuff?'

'Outside,' he said, and showed me a bulging carrier-bag with an old mac flung down on top.

'And that's the lot?' I asked, striving to keep the pity and disappointment out of my voice.

'Yes, sir,' he said humbly.

I got him fed, and then I got him washed and shaved in our cloakroom and then I found him a reasonable jacket and shoes among our emergency store of second-hand clothing, and then I took him out to the lodging that had been offered, and thank goodness he was accepted there and then and made welcome with a big dinner. When I got back to the office I set to work ringing round after jobs and got an appointment for him next morning; and by then I reckoned that the first steps had been taken to pick him up and dust him down. Not once throughout that day did Egbert refer to his mother or explain his decision to leave her; and so I never said a word about it either.

I ran lightly into the house that evening.

'Hallo-ee!' called Harry from the kitchen.

'What-ho!' I cried. 'Wonderful news, darling!'

'Yes, isn't it!' she called.

I paused, hung my mac up slowly and went out to her.

'How did you know about Egbert leaving home?' I asked.

'I didn't, what *do* you mean, how could I?'

'Well, when I said wonderful news you said yes, isn't it.'

She turned towards me with the frying-pan in one hand and a spoon in the other.

'Darling,' she said, 'has old Dash been in today?'

'No,' I said.

'No!' she said. 'They've just rung up. They're engaged: Miss Dashforth is going to marry my Uncle Oz.'

'*What!*' I cried.

She threw back her head and laughed and laughed and laughed.

'It's true, darling! The old Dash is about to become Our Auntie Agnes!'

And damn, my omelette slid out of the frying-pan slop all over my shoes.

22

EGBERT finished out his time In Care quietly and peacefully with Mrs Scatterbread.

Poor old Mrs Scatterbread was feeling a bit down in the dumps when she wrote to me after Christmas. Her Ron had married, rather young, and moved away to Tees-side in search of high wages; and her Val turned out a rather wayward little minx who didn't spend much time at home and eventually also moved away, to London as a shorthand-typist. Sidney Smee emerged from Borstal quite a reformed character and was called up; he did spend one or two leaves with her, but then he signed on as a Regular and went out to Kenya, on the Mau Mau operation. So Mrs Scatterbread was very much alone, and when it came to Christmas she wrote asking for a little girl about three, with no parents. However, she didn't mind taking Egbert and they settled down quite well together and there was never a minute's trouble.

I'd been a bit worried about finding a job for Egbert, but fortunately one of the local employers, a Mr Henderson, had just got on to our Committee and was rushing about enthusiastically. I persuaded him to give the boy a try and Egbert did quite well with him; it was only an unskilled job, packing and dispatching, but he earned decent wages and got his self-respect back. He was right down on his uppers when he left home and I was a bit chary about helping him financially, as I had spent quite a lot of the ratepayers' money on him, one way and another. However, I fiddled a bit here and there and got him a neat enough rig-out to start off with, and he was very good afterwards in spending his own clothes money wisely.

Egbert didn't tell me what had gone wrong between him

and his mother. About three weeks after he left her, Mrs
Mimmany came to the office in a sulky, aggressive mood
demanding that her son be returned to her care or she'd
have the law on me. I couldn't take a violent line with her
because I'd just had the papers from Blique requiring her
consent to Zsa Zsa's adoption, and it was mostly for the sake
of the baby that I finally agreed, to arrange a meeting between Egbert and his mother in my office and in my presence. It was with a great deal of trepidation that I held the
ring on that occasion, but fortunately Egbert was throughout icy and almost malevolent. In the end she departed,
muttering darkly that 'e'd bin got at. But I think she knew
she was licked because she didn't inquire after him again
and a few days later she signed the adoption consent without a murmur.

'Stinking old bag!' snarled Egbert after her.

'Egbert,' I said, 'I know a bit about how you feel, son,
but I don't like to hear you speak like that about your
Mum.'

'Well, wot the 'ell's she ever done for me?'

'She gave you life, son.'

'Pah!' he said bitterly, and mooched out.

It wasn't the last we saw of Mrs Mimmany, who remained
rather a menace, as though we had a nest of machine-guns
over on our left. She made a great effort to get hold of Cary,
even making the round of every school in the district in an
attempt to kidnap him, but we managed to stay one jump
ahead of her until the day she had a ghastly row with Mimmany and cracked him over the head with a bottle of Aust-
ralian Burgundy, just outside Councillor Trotter's residence.
Mimmany went to hospital and she went to gaol, and when
they came out again, their hut had a Jamaican in it. So she
went off to Cardiff with a man named Jones, and that was
the last we heard of her.

And time went on, and Egbert got his calling-up papers
and went into the Army; he wasn't looking forward to it
much, but he put on a bold front. About a year later I had a
cheery but frightfully misspelt letter from him, from Hong

Kong; I replied at once, but he did not write again. Mrs Scatterbread heard two or three times.

Meanwhile Miss Dashforth had joined the family and we'd all gone down to the little Berkshire church where her romance had started. They made a perfectly charming couple, Uncle Oz already looked ten years younger, the church was packed with their friends, and the village street lined on both sides with motor-cars. They spent their honeymoon in Italy, and then Agnes settled down to being a don's wife and made a tremendous success of it, clucking over the old boy and doing his bits for him, and neither of them had ever been so happy.

The departure of Old Dash meant that we needed a new Area Children's Officer, and I put in for the job very hopefully because I thought I was the obvious choice, but alas I wasn't even interviewed and we got a Mrs Chatterton from County Hall. We reckoned she'd made some secret deal with the Children's Officer to get the first A.C.O. post available, for she knew nothing about area work at all. She was a bulky, tweedy woman, a martinet for regulations, who produced enormous wall-charts covered with little flags showing at a glance whether our visits to foster-children were overdue. As all my visits were overdue, I came in for a lot of Petty Officer stuff, so I got fed up and applied for a transfer, but that didn't come to anything either. Poor Miss Chick couldn't take the new régime and drifted away to a job in Walsall, and we got a Miss Cudleigh, an adenoidal girl, specializing in motivation.

And time went on and one day at breakfast I opened the local rag, and there was a big headline:

CRIME WAVE STRIKES WESTBURN
'The Menace of the Dangerous Teenage Thugs'
says
Councillor Trotter

I read the story, and it seemed that the previous Tuesday the Magistrates' Courts had been absolutely bulging with the criminal classes and Their Worships had unprecedentedly been kept sitting till late afternoon. It was while peevishly dispensing justice with his stomach seething under a hasty lunch of pork-pie and ale that Councillor Trotter made thi crack about thugs. The immediate result was that severa foster-mothers decided that they were harbouring dangerou teenage thugs, and half a dozen bewildered youths in drain pipe trousers found themselves homeless at the end of the week; which was tough on me because these character hadn't a clue about finding lodgings for themselves, and ir the prevailing climate landladies gave one look at the hair styles and said No Thanks. I pushed the kids under cove somehow till the scare died down.

The next effect was the calling by Miss Wepys of a vas Conference of all those interested in combating the wave of violence and unrest. A great deal was said about how it wa all due to TV, or sex education in schools, or The Parents Of Course. The only result seemed to be that policemen found it even easier to get houses; which was fair enough, I suppose.

Mr Bland and I went to the Conference and sat at the back and said never a word, because we knew what really lay behind all this. Herbie Slythe had been discharged from the Army as medically unfit – a neurasthenic, I think they called him. A while later he was at last caught by the police actually in possession of stolen goods, and was interviewed by one of those bitter, bullying little C.I.D. men who frightened him out of his wits. The result was that Herbie began to sing and he sang so melodiously about his underworld contemporaries that the police were able to clear up a number of crimes which had baffled them over the past six months, and the underworld went quiet for a long time.

And time went on, and Harry and I moved house. Harry found that she was getting depressed by spending her married life in her parents' house. She thought it was because traditionally one leaves the parental nest on marriage and makes one's own new, purposeful nest, and there was too much hanging over her from the past to allow her to develop properly now. She had had some unhappy times in the past, I did see that, so we had a look round and were at first very attracted by the new modern houses that were being built about half-way out, on the Blethering Road. They looked slick and smart with their plate-glass and uncluttered lines, but somehow you couldn't imagine your sticky children galumphing over those bright contemporary carpets, or leaving their huge toys littered all over the Open Plan. Those weren't child-centred houses, and we wanted children, even if there wasn't a sign of one yet. So in the end we bought a tall Victorian terrace house with an enormous garden; very inconvenient in lots of ways, the house needed too much vertical movement, but it had a range of exciting little attic bedrooms and Harry used to go up there and slosh paint about, whistling merrily.

And I went on, pounding the beat and watching more and more characters form and take shape, as little boys messing about with tadpoles became big boys messing about with motor-bikes, and the garden paths I walked up went through daffodils, and then through roses, and then through chrysanthemums, and then through snow. There was a new hazard now in evening visiting, now that every roof in Westburn sprouted the dreaming spires of television aerials. If I am to see a boy actually in his foster-home, and to watch how he is actually treated by his foster-parents, I cannot begin till half past four, when the youngest boys come home from school, and the day really warms up at six, when the older ones come home from work. It was already maddening to have to knock off at six-forty-five for the Archers; I had to hang about in the rain till seven, or sit like a dummy listening to some incomprehensible dialogue, or unwittingly interrupt and have a woman switch off with ill-concealed hostility and then give you half her attention while she strained to hear what John Tregorran was saying on the set next door. All this was bad enough, but when the telly came, I just couldn't help interrupting something; if it wasn't Andy Pandy, it was Cowboys or some ghastly conjurer. Possibly because they have spent so much money on it that they can't afford to lose a minute of the damned thing, people don't turn their sets off for a visitor, at least not in the first four years of ownership. I began to find myself visiting phosphorescent hells where every inhabitant had a split mind. I attempted to discuss with small boys their innermost thoughts and feelings in rooms rocking with galloping hooves and gun-battles. I got trapped in buggy and malodorous hovels while we all watched the Flowerpot Men. Some well-intentioned hostesses obligingly turned off the sound but not the picture, which was an ordeal, because while attempting to give the lady your smiling and supportive attention, you were distracted by a number of twilit pygmies doing illogical things in dead silence behind her.

It all worked itself out in the end, when families turned off their sets with glad cries, a visitor was such a welcome change! But that was three or four years later.

And time went on, and The Rookery was closed at last, after many rumours, and Mr and Mrs Boatwright went into Old People's Welfare. We had got a lot of children established in foster-homes or in small family-group Homes, and up and down the country the big places were closing. I went up to The Rookery on some errand when it was quite empty, and found myself wandering through the rooms in a state of great nostalgia. This place had been home to a multitude of little people; it wouldn't have been home to you, and by the Grace of God it had never been home to me, but it was home to them. Here they had squabbled and screeched and raced about and grown up, had feared and loved and wandered. They might have been tortured little demons, or substandard urchins, schemers, drifters, bullies, lumps, but here they had lived, and not an inch of that rambling building was not imprinted by their physical or nervous energy. This had been the Superintendent's Office, where many a child had trembled before Authority; now it was a poky little hole under the stairs. This shadowy barn had been The Play Room: a page torn from a comic still lay by the empty grate. Pencilled on that wall where the curtains had so long concealed it was the inscription: B.R. loves J.W. That scar in the door commemorated the day when Lofty Flanagan threw his boots at the Superintendent, and even the clocks had stopped ticking in awe. I went up to the topmost windows and stood for a long time gazing down into the Memorial Field, and it was no great feat of imagination, even for me, to hear again the tumult down below and the chairs scraping back for Grace, and the pounding of feet on the stairs; and I even imagined that, just for a moment, a small hand was slipped into mine.

I went back to the office and had a furious row with Mrs Chatterton.

It was all over some beastly little form she had invented, which to my fevered imagination seemed designed to reduce children and their emotions to a sort of pre-packed dehydrated soup powder. I said things to her which really ought to have got me bounced out of the service; but to my surprise and consternation she burst into tears and gruff gulping sobs. I got her some tea and she slowly told me how she had come into this work with no other qualification than her married status, thinking that any sensible woman could deal with children. But the work had become more and more deep and elaborate until she just could not keep afloat, and her wretched little form had been a straw she had launched to clutch at. So I ended up feeling very sorry for her and became loyal, but not long after that outburst she resigned and went off to be a supervisor in a department store, where she got on much better.

And then to my surprise and delight, when I applied for her job, I got it. I hadn't really ever expected to get anywhere in what had started off as essentially a woman's world; indeed, when I started, men like me were regarded as rather sissy, suspect creatures. But it had gradually dawned on the people I moved among that in a normal family there is a Dad as well as a Mum, and the more we thought about mums without dads, the more did Dad emerge from the shadowy corner to which he had been relegated for so long. It was such a simple thing to discover that it staggered everybody, but the result was that more men began to be recruited into our Departments to deal with the dads, and the potential dads, and even with the deserted mums.

Well, I wasn't a dad yet, though I hadn't got long to wait now, I used to think exultantly; but I was an Area Children's Officer. More than that, I had a bigger staff. Harry had retired now, of course, but I had Miss Cudleigh, and now I got two more new girls, Miss Tew and Miss Goring; and the reason for this increase of staff was because we had slowly and painfully made another elemental discovery.

When I first came galloping out of the University, in shining armour and with all pennons flying, it was To the Rescue of the Deprived Child. Light and air were going to be flooded into the dark places, all those miserable public waifs were going to have a new square deal. And indeed over the years this had happened, we had brought a measure of increased happiness to the children In Care. What we hadn't stopped to consider was how they managed to get there in the first place.

Well, of course, when we did finally get around to considering it, and when we began to read the academic studies on the subject, we began to see that there were circumstances where the sweetest-smelling Children's Home, the most loving foster-parents, were no damned good. Every child leaving his parents suffers an enormous blow, the younger the child, the bigger the impact, and in its shadow we began to see how feeble were our efforts to create a substitute. Of course, lots and lots of times you can't avoid this rupture, but we began to try harder and harder to prevent it if there was a way.

But we'd only taken a few cautious steps in this direction when Whitehall seized upon the development with glee: here was an even better and even *cheaper* way of caring for children, so cheap it didn't cost *anything*! Don't care for them at all! So we had a mad stampede and slogans like: 'The dirtiest home is better than the cleanest Home' and 'Prevention is Better than Care', and we got a lot more staff charged with the duty of keeping families together and not hacking bits off them. Well, we had some more painful discoveries ahead of us even along the new path, had we but known; but for the time being there we were, getting enthusiastic all over again and hoping that in due course our Department would become so efficient that it would wither away because no more children would need to be In Care.

And there I was in my little office, beginning to do a little less direct work with the customers and spending more time on supervising the work of the team. I was sitting there one morning mulling over the mail and waiting for coffee to come up, when the faithful Miss Greave came in and said: 'There's a man to see you.'

'Can't one of the girls see him?'

'Well, he asked for you specially,' said Miss Greave. 'In the waiting-room.'

'All right, I'll wander down,' I said.

I finished and initialled the report I was reading and wandered down. I found a shortish, broad-shouldered, deeply-tanned young man who came to greet me with a beaming grin.

23

'Egbert!' I cried, delightedly. 'Well, this is jolly nice to see you again, cock!'

' 'Lo, sir!' he said, pumping my hand.

'How are you after all this time?'

'All right, sir. 'Ow's yerself?'

'Oh, struggling on, son, still struggling on. Are you back for good now?'

'Yer. Demob leave. Thought I'd just look in.'

'I'm jolly glad you have. Look here, Egbert, we can't talk properly here, come round the corner for a cupper tea.'

I told Miss Greave where I was, in case anything urgent came up, and led Egbert round to a new caff which hadn't been open long, it had small tables and benches with high backs so that you got a bit of privacy. It was quite clean.

Egbert told me a bit about the Army. He'd been in Hong Kong and then in Malaya, and had flown home a fortnight before.

'What are you going to do now, Egbert?' I asked.

'I'm goin' back in garridge work. Bloke I used to work with in High Road Motors, 'e's startin' up on 'is own, see, and I'm going in with 'im. I know a bit about it now, see, did a bit in the Army.'

'Where are you going to live, son?'

'With Mrs Scatterbread, for the time being. She's been very good to me, and I don't like leavin' 'er alone, now the ole man's gorn. Course, it's a bit far from the garridge, but still. 'Ere, Mr Maule, you'll laugh – I got a car of me own now!'

'Have you, Egbert, so have I. What have you got?'

'Morris Minor '33,' he grinned.

'I've got a Morris Eight, '37,' I said. 'I shall have to bring it in to you for servicing.'

'Yeah, do that. I 'ear you're a family man now, Mr Maule, eh?'

'Well, not quite a family yet,' I said. 'The baby's due next month.'

'Oh, yer. What you goin' to call it?'

'Martin, if it's a boy; Caroline for a girl.'

'Very nice.' He evidently didn't think they were attractive names.

'How about yourself, Egbert? You engaged or anything?' He looked confused.

'Well, er – sort of – well, goin' steady, like.' He pulled out an obviously much-loved, rather dog-eared, snap of a girl standing in Trafalgar Square; not a flashy girl, but a plump pleasant-faced little thing.

'Very nice. What's her name?'

'Peggy. Peggy Jeffs. You don't know her, I expect?'

'No, I don't, but I hope I will one day. You'll have to invite us to the wedding.'

He looked pretty taken aback at that, but when the idea sank in he grinned over it, and said: 'Yer, yer, awright.'

'This is my wife,' I said, proudly bringing out the portrait of Harry I always carry around.

'Oh, yer,' he said, scrutinizing it carefully. 'I seem to know her, Mr Maule?'

'Yes, you've probably seen her in the office, she used to work there. She was Myrna's welfare officer.'

'Oh, yer.' A shadow seemed to flit acros his face, there was a pause, and he drank some tea.

'I'm sorry to see the old Rookery isn't a 'Ome any more, Mr Maule.'

'Yes, it is a shame, isn't it? It closed last year, you know; Mr and Mrs Boatwright went down to Broadstairs.'

'And Matron and Sir?'

'Oh, they're still very much alive and kicking down in Haverfordwest.'

We talked for a bit about the children he used to live

239

with, young men and young women now, and I said:

'That seems the hell of a long time ago, Egbert.'

'Yer. Yer, well, a lot's 'appened since then, 'asn't it, sir?'

'It has. Tell me, Egbert, when you look back, what do you feel about those days in The Rookery?'

He scowled and fidgeted with the effort of recall and editorship.

'Well, sort of all right, well – course you only remember the good bits, don't you? I dint like it at first, cor! I 'member when you took me from the court that day, I was dead scared and then I dint like it at first. I nearly run away. But then after, well, yer get used to anything reely, don't yer. I reckon it done me a bit o' good, well, it did when it came to the Army, you know, bein' with a crowd of blokes, well, I'd 'ad that before, see, sort of knowing wot it was like.'

'You were in a lot of places in your time, Egbert; tell me, what was the best place really, do you think? The place you enjoyed most?'

He frowned down into his mug.

'Oh, well, see, it's sort of – well, I never did like goin' to a new place, see, it was awful goin' to a new place, and then when you got there after a bit it sort of got better an' you 'ad some good times. I mean I 'ad some 'appy times in all them places I was in, but somehow, well, I never thought it would last long. See, like them Mr and Mrs Urmston Smith, they was good people and I was ever so sorry about the old chap, and she was, well, she was a nice lady, but somehow I knew it'd never last long. I mean somehow, I dunno, it dint seem natural.'

'H'm. Why I'm asking is this, Egbert; supposing you had my job, and you had to do the best you could for the kids, what would you wish for them?'

'Cor, that's a question, Mr Maule. I'd rather you than me. I s'pose we're all different, aren't we? I mean, take my brother Cary; well, he's been there all the time, 'asn't 'e, ever so 'appy, an' it just suits 'im down to the ground, I mean they're mum and dad to 'im now. Well, good luck to

240

im, but I don't reckon I'd have settled. I'd 'ave kicked up in he end, I spect.'

'Even though you didn't like going to a new place?'

'Yer, well, see, put it like this: when you're my age now, t sometimes seems rotten you 'aven't got a 'ome at all, but then o' course I know I'm goin' to 'ave a 'ome of me own quite soon. Bought the table and chairs, I 'ave.'

'Good.'

'But when you're a nipper, see, well, you don't always want to belong to a 'ome at all, see, you don't reelly ever think of being twenty and feeling this way. I dunno 'ow it is, but some'ow you think, well, if you muck in an' sort of belong to foster-parents, some'ow you've, well, sort of lost.'

'H'm.' I gazed thoughtfully at him for some time, but he didn't seem able to add to this, and presently he said:

'I saw Cary.'

'Did you, good. All right?'

'Oh yer. 'E's a bit frightened about 'is call up. Still 'e'll be all right. Funny, 'im goin' in the Army jus' as I'm comin' out. Still, 'e's got a place to come back to, 'asn't 'e?'

'Oh, yes. Have you seen Clark? He's married now.'

'So I 'eard. No, I ain't seen 'im. I seen Gloria.'

'Good. She getting on all right?'

'Oh, yer. Now she's got the Council 'ouse she's all right. I was wondering if I could go an' see Winston before I start work.'

'Yes, do go, Egbert, he'll be delighted to see you,' I said.

'He's leaving Melcombe this term, but I've got a place lined up for him, people he's spent holidays with, he'll be all right. I'm not so sure about Clement, he's a bit of a tinker at the moment, but I reckon he'll probably join up with Winston in the end.'

'That'd be nice.'

'Now, who else is there: Celia, I don't think you know her very well, do you?'

'No, I don't remember 'er.'

'Well, she's in a foster-home and doing very nicely. And touch wood, Sabrina seems to be settling in hers too, though she's a proper little madam, she is. Yes. You're doing quite well really, all of you.'

He said in a small voice: 'There's Myrna.'

'Oh, yes,' I said, in an equally small voice, and sighed 'Yes, I'm afraid we failed with Myrna, I don't know where she is or what she's doing now.'

He looked serious but didn't seem so upset as I'm sure I would have been if I'd had a sister like that.

'But you never know with these things,' I said. 'I remember a girl we had years ago, Rosemary Something, Miss Dashforth dealt with her. She was an absolute shocker, never settled anywhere, went on the streets in the end. And then years later, out of the blue, we got a letter from this girl, and she said she was very happily married and had a little girl of her own. She wanted to thank Miss Dashforth very much for all she'd tried to teach her, because now she realized what it all meant and she wanted to see that her daughter grew up the right way.'

'Yer?'

'So maybe Myrna will settle down in the end. You never know. We lose a good many battles, but I don't think we often lose a war.'

We both brooded reflectively for a moment and then I said quietly:

'How about your Mum, Egbert?'

He sucked his lips in and said: ''Ave another cupper tea, Mr Maule.'

When he came back with the mugs, he put something else down on the table and said:

'You 'member that, sir?'

I prodded it cautiously; it was a queer lump of what looked like a pottery, rather fist-like and smeared with red.

'What the hell is this, Egbert? Something you got in China?'

'No!' he laughed. 'Don't you 'member? Comin' back from that Creek place?'

Something tickled the back of my memory, but I said:

'No, I'm sorry, Egbert; I don't get this.'

242

He took a rather noisy gulp of his tea.

'Well, see, one day in that place old Potty give us a lump f clay each and says now come on, he says, make what you eally *hate*. So, well, I made my mother.'

There was a pause. He was looking far past me.

'Funny, really, 'ow I kept it. I found it the other day, up t 'ome. Reckon I did 'ate her then, too. I started off hatin', well, you, sir, takin' me away like that. Then I reckoned you was only doin' yer job after all, an' it was 'er who'd let me lown reelly, must 'ave done. That's when I made that. Then I got to thinkin': well, there must 'ave been a reason. I eckoned p'raps it was Dad, whoever Dad was. I called that thing Dad for a bit, but it dint fit properly. I chucked it away when I was at Urmston Smith's; then, next morning, I went and fished it out the dust-bin. I dunno what I thought. I dint *reely* think my mother was like that. Reckon that's why I went 'ome in the end, to find out.'

'What happened there, Egbert?' I murmured.

'Well, see: it was all right at first; I mean, uncomfortable, but Mum seemed glad to see me. So I reckoned I'd do something for 'er, she was in a bad way, see, poor an' that. I got some stuff in, brightened the place up, she seemed pleased. Seemed like bleedin' cupboard-love, only the other way round, you know?'

'I know,' I said.

'Then came Christmas. Well, I dunno, Mr Maule, I don't believe in Church an' that, God an' that, but Christmas is a family time, int it, Mr Maule? It always is. Family. An' that very Christmas Day she 'ad a bloke in. With me there: but she'd rather 'ave some bloke. She dint care, yer see; she dint care.'

'You still hate her?' I murmured.

'No. Not now. I did then, got that thing out again. But you know, Mr Maule, I don't s'pose you 'member sayin' this to me, but once you said to me, son, you said, never forget she gave you life. I never 'ave forgot that, neither. It's a lot, ain't it?'

'It is a lot, Egbert.'

'It's all she ever gave me, o' course. An' I reckon yer Mum 'as to give yer more than that, a lot more'n that. But I s'pos my Mum just 'adn't got any more. No, I don't 'ate 'er n more, cos I reckon I can do something with wot she did giv me. She can go 'er own way now; I'll go mine.'

And when presently we parted, I had the little head, an he marched off down the street whistling.

I spent a quietish day in the office and went home at six I didn't like staying out late. I had a good staff, Harry wa in her ninth month, and as far as she was concerned it wa one month too many.

'Hallo, darling,' she said, moving carefully to meet me, a grave and serene as ever, but with a secret radiance in he face.

'How are we, sweetheart?'

'Fine,' she said. 'Lovely to have you home early, you tea's all ready.'

She came and sat with her feet up while I ate, and said:

'I heard from Agnes today.'

'Oh, yes? How is she?'

'Flourishing. Very happy. She's just got on to some com mittee for Korean Relief. And she sent this for Twiggle.'

Martin-or-Caroline, whose presence was visible in a serie of violent galumphing movements under Harry's smock had obviously recognized our pet name.

'I say, how handsome,' I said, looking at the book Auntie Agnes had sent. It was bound in crimson leather and had gil lettering on it: 'Our Baby's Progress Book.'

I said: 'When you're writing back to her, tell her I had an old friend in today – Egbert Crump.'

'No, really? How is he?'

'Seems fine.' I told her how the conversation had gone and finished my tea and lit a cigarette, and then sighed and said: 'Oh, dear. I hope he'll be all right.'

'Well, why ever shouldn't he be?'

'I don't know, but when he marched off down the street looking so debonair, I thought that somehow he looked rather pathetic too.'

'I expect he did. After all, you were watching the end of an epoch, that's always rather sad-making.'

'No, I don't think I was sad,' I said. 'Well, perhaps I was, but he looked not quite finished off in some way. Perhaps I was regretting all that I had left undone which I ought to have done.'

'Oh, nonsense,' said Harry. 'I think you did very well with Egbert.'

'Good Lord, I'm sure I didn't. All I seemed to do was to come pounding along on my great flat feet about a mile behind him. I never seemed to have any plan for him, ever.'

'You steered him through all right.'

' What, from a mile behind ?'

'In a storm,' said Harry, concentrating on a difficult knitting stitch, 'sailors throw out a kind of anchor which floats astern and keeps the ship's head to the wind. They'd be wrecked without.'

'What a marvellous simile, Harry, I must remember it next time the Committee ask awkward questions about Herbie Slythe. I say, I think we ought to do more for these kids than just float astern of them.'

'Well, so we do for the little uns, and a jolly good job, too; but the teenagers, I don't think any parent can be more than a sort of jury-anchor, that was the word I wanted. Now, I'll tell you what you did for Egbert, as you don't seem to know yourself.'

'What ?'

'You cared about him,' she said. 'You cared all the time. You never stopped caring, did you ?'

'Well, I don't think that's much.'

'Isn't it ? What happened when his mother stopped caring ?'

'Well, I got paid to do it.'

'Oh, good lord, we'll be back to the plastic toast-racks in a minute,' said Harry, fidgeting her legs about. 'You know jolly well you'd care even if you weren't paid. You know jolly well most people don't care tuppence for these kids,

245

call them layabouts and Teddy boys and generally give up hope.'

'But just caring about them isn't enough.'

'It is if you care enough. No, I know, you've got to understand and act, too, but tell me: what was Egbert wearing today?'

'Gosh – er – a blue suit, I think, a bit bright but – well reasonable.'

'Conventionally cut?'

'Yes.'

'Getting more like you every day, Charles! You see, he had to have somebody to model himself on, somebody he reckoned he wanted to be like when he grew up; somebody steady and loyal and friendly and always there.'

'What, *me*?'

'Yes: someone who stood for order and hope and unbeatdownableness.'

'Well, damn me, Harry, that's not me: I always thought I was a terrific rebel.'

Harry threw back her head and roared with laughter which must have made Twiggle fear for his security.

'Oh, Charles, you're terribly conservative! Why, even your pullover is navy blue!'

'Oh, wrap up!' I said, offended.

'I wouldn't have you a mite different, darling. Thank goodness Twiggle is going to have a nice, steady Dad to hang on to; he may turn out as well as Egbert.'

'Gosh, not by the same route, I hope,' I said. I picked up Our Baby's Progress Book. 'Still, there's room for an elaborate case-history in this: all his foster-homes and special schools and residential establishments.'

'Oh, don't Charles, poor Twiggle.'

'I say, this has got a lot in it, hasn't it? My Friends are: My Favourite Toys are: My First Word was: good gracious, you're going to spend all your time writing reports on the kid.'

'Well, I've had plenty of practice.'

'Hallo, there's a lot of blank pages at the end, we shall

ave to fill them up with something. I know, jot down all
his deviations and inversions, and all his traumas and subli-
mations and emotional blocks and defence mechanisms and
build up a word-diagram of his dysfunctions and oedipus
displacements and characterological syndromes. Eh?'

'Oh, really, I thought you'd grown out of all that!' said
Harry. 'That psychological stuff is all very clever – but who
cares?'

*Some recent Penguin books
are described on the
following pages*

WEEKEND IN DINLOCK

Clancy Sigal

1836

The road to Wigan Pier has changed since Orwell walked down it in the thirties. Clancy Sigal has suited his exploration of a Yorkshire mining village to the conditions of today: he went without condescension but equally without reverence. The result was amazing – somehow or other this young American penetrated the suspicious reserve of the most defiantly enclosed community left in Britain. How he did it and what he found out comes to life again in the sharp-edged prose of this book, in which all his experiences in Yorkshire pit villages are compressed into the semi-fictional *Weekend in Dinlock*. The central thread is an account of a miner-artist called Davie, trying to break with the pit. But there is much more besides: the miners' attempts to knock Sigal out with Scotch, the sentimental songs on Saturday night, and above all the physical reality of the pit itself.

'He has dug deep into a section of English life, and turned up with a rich and wonderful book' – Alan Sillitoe in the *Evening Standard*

'Incredibly sensitive to the mood and atmosphere of this community' – Keith Waterhouse in the *New Statesman*

STEPHEN POTTER

'It is astonishing that Stephen Potter should have been able to sustain this joke so long. ... What is so good in these books of Potter's is the brevity and compactness of the presentation. As in any practical manual, the principles are stated and concisely illustrated. Nothing goes on too long' – Edmund Wilson in the *Nation*

'A man less witty than Mr Potter might have worked his devices to death; it is far otherwise with the Master of Station Road, Yeovil. On he goes, continually scintillating and rarely probing into his victim without a preliminary anaesthetic of good humour' – C. E. Vulliamy in the *Spectator*

The following titles are available in Penguins:

GAMESMANSHIP · 1826
'The Art of Winning Games Without Actually Cheating'

LIFEMANSHIP · 1828
The sequel to *Gamesmanship* which covers the whole art of life

ONE-UPMANSHIP · 1827
'Being some Account of the Activities and Teaching of the Lifemanship Correspondence College of One-Upness and Gameslifemastery'

SUPERMANSHIP · 1829
'How to continue to stay top without actually falling apart'

THE BIG CITY

Alex Atkinson and Ronald Searle

1856

Henry Mayhew's famous survey, *London Labour and the London Poor*, painted a glaring picture of the poverty and degradation of the last century. *The Big City* – or *The New Mayhew* – stages the dim, pastel tragedies that are daily being enacted, in this century, between Holloway and Streatham.

For the metropolis has no lack of poverty and degradation today, although much of it hides in the dark corners of tawdry souls. With their forlorn ambitions or dull resignation the Moving Picture Girl, the Encyclopaedia Seller, the Vicar, the Decayed Nobleman, the Literary Man, and the Lady of the Streets pluck at the heart-strings like the echoes of a Victorian ballad. To this social round-up Alex Atkinson lends a unique flavour with the rotund and sentimental prose of the last century, and his portraits are exactly complemented by Ronald Searle's ludicrous-pathetic character-sketches. *The New Mayhew*, with its melancholy and satirical comment on our affluent society, first appeared in *Punch*.

THE LIGHT AND THE DARK

C. P. Snow

1824

The Light and the Dark is one of the Cambridge novels in C. P. Snow's *Strangers and Brothers* sequence – although the action of the story moves at times to Monte Carlo, Berlin, and Switzerland. In it Lewis Eliot narrates the brief career of a brilliant but controversial linguist, Roy Calvert, whom he has known since childhood. The account opens in 1935, when the Master of their college is campaigning to get Roy elected to a fellowship, and closes with his death in action in 1943. Calvert's charm, his bouts of melancholia, his outbursts against elders who are not betters, and his flirtation with Nazism are intimately and sympathetically studied in his relations with all kinds of personalities.

'A novel written with the intuition of a woman and the grasp of broad essentials generally reserved for men … As full of life as life itself' – John Betjeman

HOMECOMINGS

C. P. Snow

1734

Homecomings is the sequel to *Time of Hope* and continues the direct experience of Lewis Eliot, the central figure and narrator in C. P. Snow's large sequence of novels, known as *Strangers and Brothers*. A complete story on its own, the novel follows Eliot's life during his thirties and early forties, predominantly during the war. After the personal tragedy of his first wife's death, he is closely involved at the Ministry in the wartime conduct of industry. It is only afterwards that, with the help of his second wife, he learns to commit himself emotionally in a true relationship. And here, as along the corridors of power, C. P. Snow's insight into character is masterly.

'As good as anything Mr Snow has written. The power of this solid, slow-moving, reflective narrative over the reader is quite remarkable. Again the reminder is of Trollope, and at times Mr Snow seems to be the exponent of a new literary movement, which can only be called neo-victorianism' – *The Times*

All the novels so far published in the *Strangers and Brothers* sequence are now available in Penguins.

MALONE DIES

Samuel Beckett

1691

Originally written in French by the author of *Waiting for Godot* and here translated by him, *Malone Dies* is a prose-poem rather than a novel. It is the death-bed soliloquy of an old and helpless man who is tired of life. Up to the moment of crossing the bar he amuses himself with the shreds of a few stories. Memory flickers uneasily in the ashes of a dying intellect which is concerned to tell nothing but the truth.

As in Willian Golding's *Pincher Martin*, the reader is shown consciousness at several levels: but the power of Beckett's writing lies in the free play of an unanchored imagination and in a mating of words and ideas which is at times Shakespearean in suggestiveness.